He led her through the brush to the place where the three killers had waited. With the muzzle of the Savage, he parted the brush and showed her the site. "See? Just like I said, three of them. They sat here, smoking and waiting for their little trap to spring. Now let's see where they went from here."

They paralleled the road, with MacGonigal occasionally turning into it to check the tracks. The three men had kept to the road, never moving off it except to hide and wait—and all that was necessary was an occasional confirmation.

When they got to the country road, MacGonigal left Susan well back in the woods while he scouted the road. The three men were still on foot. Their tracks were a little more difficult to follow on this road, which had had a little traffic that day, but MacGonigal soon confirmed that they had headed down toward the low-water bridge. He went back to where he had left Susan.

"Come on. I know where they are."

Soldier of Fortune books from Tor

SOLDIER of FORTUNE
MAGAZINE PRESENTS:

MACGONIGAL'S WAY

VERNON HUMPHREY

TOR

A TOM DOHERTY ASSOCIATES BOOK

MACGONIGAL'S WAY

Copyright © 1987 by Omega Group, Ltd.

First Printing: November 1987

A TOR Book

Published by Tom Doherty Associates, Inc.
49 West 24 Street
New York, N.Y. 10010

ISBN: 0-812-51223-5
CAN. ED.: 0-812-51224-3

Printed in the United States of America

0 9 8 7 6 5 4 3 2 1

to
**Major R. B. "Rifle Bullet" Anderson,
5th Special Forces Group**

I.

She was cold. It hurt. She explored her body, moving as best she could in the narrow, confined space. She realized that she was naked. Her hands were tied, but her feet were free. She drew her knees up a little higher, trying to compact herself into a ball to conserve body heat as best she could.

It was terribly dark. For a long while, she couldn't understand why, but at last she realized that her eyes were swollen shut. She tried to open them, tried to see. It was horrible to be confined so closely, to be tied so tightly, and to be unable to see as well.

Her recollections were hazy, and they came to her in swatches. She vaguely remembered them holding her, stripping her, while she kicked and fought to gain her freedom. But her struggle had gained her only a blow to the side of her head and a shocking burst of light that erupted in her brain. She could remember that.

He had hit her again and again, backhand and forehand, hitting her long after she could no longer bring herself to resist. And then they had torn the rest of her clothes off and done all the other things.

Where was she now? She tried to think. She

remembered being carried down the stairs—what she really remembered was the painful jolting of each step. She remembered seeing the car. They had opened the trunk and dumped her in.

The bumping that had slowly intruded itself into her consciousness stopped. She tried to think. *That means the car has stopped.* Suddenly there was light. She could see. Someone had opened the trunk of the car. Hands reached in for her, pulling her out. She tried to tell them.

No more, please, no more. Do what you want and kill me, but don't do that anymore.

Francis X. MacGonigal was, in the opinion of Francis X. MacGonigal, a bum. Never one to form opinions without mature reflection, MacGonigal considered again. He stroked his unshaven chin, feeling the five days' growth of whiskers, and looked down at his stained jeans. It might not be accurate to think of myself as a bum, he mused. A bum, he had always heard, was someone who wouldn't work, while a hobo was someone who would work but didn't happen to have any prospects at the moment. Of course, MacGonigal had no job and wasn't looking for one, but he wasn't exactly shiftless. He was gainfully employed at the moment—although not under salary.

He emerged from the woods, high up on the ridge, and looked down at his cabin. He stood a moment, admiring his handiwork, then cradled the rifle in his arms and started down to the cabin. He hung the squirrels outside, then went in and laid the rifle on the table, taking the bolt out as a reminder to himself to clean it, then gathered up a basin, a piece of clean cloth, the salt shaker, and a large platter. Outside, he expertly slit the squirrels along their backbones with the little Jimmy Lyle knife and shucked them out of their hides. As he cleaned each one, he dropped it into the basin, and when he finished the last he filled the basin with cold water from the creek, added salt to counteract the taste of bloodshot meat, and thoroughly washed the little carcasses. When they were clean, he placed them on the folded cloth in the platter and carried them in.

He had begun to prepare the batter when he heard the motor. Aside from his pickup, only one other vehicle ever traveled the road that he had built, and he knew that Jeff Siler was up in Missouri on business. His curiosity aroused, he put the bowl aside and climbed the rough stairs to the loft. From a window in the front gable of the cabin he could see a long way down Bear Pen valley.

He saw the plume of dust before he saw the vehicle, and that angered him. Although it hadn't yet crossed his property line, it was on his road, and it was not treating that road with proper respect. He watched until the vehicle at the head of the dust cloud became visible. It was a jeep, a CJ-5. Hunters, he muttered to himself, damn city hunters! As if the national forest weren't enough room for 'em! A hunter himself, MacGonigal had a natural reaction to any other predator encroaching on his territory.

He shambled down the stairs and took up the Winchester .22 Hornet still lying on the table, slipping the bolt back into place and thumbing fresh cartridges into the magazine before shoving it home.

The top cartridge fed out of the magazine into the chamber. Rifle in hand, he went out the door.

MacGonigal had deliberately built the cabin where it was difficult to see from the road. Here and there an alert visitor might see the roof through the trees as he approached, but from the foot of the falls, where the road ended, the cabin was completely hidden, set high above and well back.

MacGonigal took up a position at the head of the foot trail leading to the top of the falls and waited. The sound of the motor was loud now, and he could hear the jolting of the CJ-5. Soon it came into view, still traveling too fast for the road. The driver, suddenly realizing that the road ended at the falls, slammed on the brakes, skidding sideways and near-ly hitting the shed where the pickup was housed. The dust cloud almost obscured the vehicle as it caught up to it and swirled around it, but MacGonigal had gotten a good look at it. It was almost new, with Arkansas plates, and a window sticker that indicated that it was rented.

MacGonigal watched as the driver got out. He was alone—a tall, fair man dressed in a checkered shirt and khaki trousers. His feet were encased in light hiking boots, and on his belt he wore a folding knife in a black sheath. So far as MacGonigal could see, the man had no weapons. The almost mandatory window rack full of guns was missing. As MacGonigal watched, the man reached back into the jeep and pulled out a map case. There was a compass mounted on the dash, but he ignored it and fished a small plastic orienteering compass out of his shirt pocket.

He puzzled over the map and compass for a few moments, while MacGonigal squatted on his heels far above. After a while, the stranger folded up the map case and stuffed both map and compass into his shirt. He cast around a bit before he found the trail leading up the falls and started up it without hesitation.

MacGonigal silently moved back, keeping low, and scuttled to one side, off the trail. From his new position, he couldn't see the stranger anymore, but he could hear him. He waited patiently as the man made his way up the trail. When the man's head suddenly appeared above the rim of the caprock, MacGonigal kept silent, waiting until the man had come up all the way. He let the man walk past him while he crouched in the bushes, not five yards away, then rose. "Something I can help you with, stranger?"

The man whirled, surprised, but made no move for a weapon—that was a point for him. The Winchester was casually pointed at his belly, and MacGonigal had his finger on the trigger, his thumb on the safety.

The man quickly overcame his initial surprise, his face smoothing into a relaxed grin. "I didn't see you standing there, Francis. You gave me a start." MacGonigal said nothing, but kept the Winchester pointed at the stranger. To an observer, it might have looked as if he were simply careless about where the weapon was pointed, but both he and the stranger knew different.

The man didn't seem disconcerted by MacGonigal's action, or by his lack of reply. He smiled easily. "Don't you remember me, Francis? 'Nam, '69 and '70?" MacGonigal ignored the question. The man was familiar, though, and his mind raced, seeking to place him. The man stood perfectly still, while the muzzle of the Winchester was trained on him. At last he broke the silence: "I thought we parted friends, Mac. You remember me, don't you? George Harris? We were in III Corps together."

"Yeah, I remember you, ya fuckin' spook. What are you doin' here?"

Harris smiled, the sort of smile a patient adult might give somebody else's brat while its mother was watching. "I was just in the area, and I thought I'd drop by and see my old buddy, Francis." MacGonigal sighed and lowered the rifle.

"I'm touched." he said sarcastically. "To think that after all these years, you'd go out of your way to look up your old buddy."

Harris maintained his smile. "Look, Francis, I came to see you. Doesn't that entitle me to at least an invitation to step into the house?"

MacGonigal shrugged. "Yeah, come on in. I was just fixing breakfast. How do you like your fried squirrel?" Without waiting for an answer, he led the way up the path to the cabin, and Harris fell in behind him.

As they went up the steps, Harris said, "This is quite a place, Francis. Did you build it yourself?"

"Yeah. I hired a couple of guys to help out, but most of it I did myself. Planned it for years, and finally built it."

They went through the door. MacGonigal jerked the bolt out of the Winchester, ejecting a .22 Hornet cartridge onto the table, and then hung the rifle on pegs that stuck out of the bare wooden wall. Harris ran his eyes over the room, taking in the guns that hung above and below the Hornet: the muzzle loaders above the big stone fireplace, the holstered Colt Woodsman that hung from a solitary peg next to the rifles. Along the opposite wall was a bookcase. Harris wandered over and inspected some of the titles. There was a little fiction. There were also books on history, economics, mathematics, agriculture, psychology, anthropology, and computer programming. There were several English-Irish dictionaries and some books in Irish Gaelic, as well as Spanish, Arabic, and Vietnamese. A folding screen stood at one end of the bookshelves, and Harris saw that it was covered with 1-to-24,000 topographic maps of the surrounding area. They had been neatly matched edge to edge and glued onto the screen, then covered with acetate. Harris estimated that the maps would cover an area about fifty by sixty miles, with MacGonigal's place located in the center.

"I repeat, this is quite a place you've got here, Francis. It reflects your personality."

MacGonigal, busy with the pitcher pump at the sink, grunted noncommittally. Harris went on. "What's that thing on your belt? Did you lose that big Randall you used to carry?"

"No," said MacGonigal, "it's over there." He flipped his thumb toward the bookcase. Harris followed the gesture with his eyes and saw the big bowie knife lying sheathed on one of the shelves in front of the books.

"I'm surprised that you're not wearing it. That little dinky thing just doesn't fit your personality." He mused a moment. "I don't think that I've ever seen you without that Randall."

MacGonigal shrugged. "That's for war. It's peacetime now, in case you hadn't noticed."

Harris's eyes went up in mock amazement. "Really? The way you kept that thing trained on my stomach, I wasn't sure."

He stepped over to the table and picked up the .22 Hornet cartridge lying there. "A handload. Cast bullet, too." He held up the cartridge between his thumb and forefinger. "If things are so tight that you can't afford to buy ammunition, I have a proposition you might find interesting. There's a nice chunk of change in it for you."

MacGonigal turned around, his smile broad and genuine. "I was wondering when you'd get around to it, you bastard. It must really hurt your conniving soul to come to the point. But you can forget it. I ain't doing any jobs for the Company."

Harris assumed an expression of bland innocence. "I'm not with the Company, Francis. Never have been. This is just a private offer."

"Yeah, I'll bet. Just like it was private business when you were running around in 'Nam with 'DAC embroidered over the pocket of your jungle fatigues instead of US Army." He snorted. "Department of the Army Civilian. You were as much a DAC as you were a duck."

Harris pulled one of the chairs away from the table and turned it around, sitting on it backward with his arms crossed over the chair back. He kept turning the little cartridge over in his fingers. "Look, Mac, I've got a deal for you. It won't hurt you to listen to it. You might find it interesting."

"So go ahead and get it over with. That's the only way I'll get rid of you. Get on with your pitch."

Harris smiled. "It'll keep awhile. Let's have breakfast first and renew old acquaintances, sort of take up where we left off. Which brings me to a question that's been nagging me for a long time: How'd you get away at Nui Chua Chan?"

"How do you think? I played dead and crawled off in the weeds when they passed by. Then I hid out for a week. Crawled down to the road and waited for the 11th ACR. They picked me up."

"Must have been rough . . ."

"You could say that. My leg was broken and half my guts were hanging out. I tied up my belly with a cravat bandage and lived off of what water I could find in dead Dinks' canteens. Most of 'em were full of rice wine, though. Never will be able to get the stink of that stuff out of my nostrils."

Harris grimaced. "Jesus, Francis, I'm sorry. I passed the word when I got back, even though I thought you were dead. There was just too much going on for anybody to come back and look for you. Things were too hot. You know they were."

"Yeah, I know, George, things were hot all right . . ." He took the smoking frying pan off the stove and began to fork pieces of squirrel into a platter, which he placed in the center of the table. He took a pot of home-canned string beans off the back of the stove and dished them up in a china bowl.

They ate for a while in silence. At last Harris spoke. "Do you live this way because you like it, or because you can't afford any better? Christ, you don't even have electricity here! Or a phone, either."

"Don't need 'em," said MacGonigal. "Telephone's the most uncivilized thing in the world. Why pay money for a machine, just so some asshole can ring a bell in your house and bother you? But I do have electricity. Got a generator. Don't use it for anything but the computer, though, and the power tools."

Harris looked around. "You've got a computer? What the hell do you use it for?"

"It's upstairs in the loft," said MacGonigal. "I keep records with it, do a little writing now and then. I've got a word-processing program. Makes things easier."

"Write? I didn't know you wrote. You're an amazing man, Francis. Know how I found you? Nobody had your address. I traced you to a post-office box through your bank. Then I asked around about bagpipes." He pointed to the set of Irish warpipes that lay on top of the cupboard. "No point in hiding out if you're going to play those things. Just as soon as I mentioned the pipes, people knew who I was talking about. Know something? Your neighbors think you're crazy."

"Who gives a shit what they think? I don't bother anybody, and nobody bothers me. And I like it just fine that way."

Harris shook his head. "Yeah, you're a strange guy. You always were. What the hell are you doing way up here in the woods, for chrissake? You could get a pretty good job if you tried."

"I like it here, George. And I don't need a job. That's why I'm going to hear your offer and then kick your ass out."

Harris permitted himself a superior smile. "No you won't, Francis. If you wanted to kick me out, you'd have done it back there by the waterfall. You're interested in what I've got to say. This is all a big act with you. You can't wait to hear my proposition. And you need the money."

"If you think that, George, you're dumber than I thought, and that's saying a lot. If you've been to my bank and checked, you know that I don't need your money. I don't spend all my pension now, and I've got a little bit tucked away. And if you think I'm dying to hear what you've got to say, just get up and walk out. See if I chase you down."

Harris made a deprecating gesture. "Sit down, Mac. I didn't come here to waste your time. I came to make a straightforward business proposition. Now, do you want to hear it, or not?"

"So get on with it," said MacGonigal, slumping back into his seat.

Harris rubbed his hand over his face. "Look, Francis, I've got a little business going, and I've got a client that needs a vacation somewhere private, where no one can bother him. I'm willing to pay a hundred dollars a day. Plus expenses. Now I've made you an offer. What's your answer?"

MacGonigal gathered up the plates and took them to the sink. He scraped them into a bucket, then primed the pump and filled a tub with water. He put it on the stove and poked up the fire. Harris sat silent while MacGonigal puttered around. At last MacGonigal turned. "Don't bullshit me, George. That 'vacation' line is the most transparent crap you've ever come up with. For a hundred bucks a day, you can buy all the privacy this 'client' of yours can use, and get maid service in the bargain. What is it you really want?"

"It's fairly simple, Francis, but if you've got to know, then here it is. This business of mine is a sort of security service. We protect clients. Sometimes the best way to protect them is to put them where people can't find them."

"That's what I thought. Now answer me two questions. Why'd you pick me, and what's the real story? Because I don't believe a word of what you just said."

Harris sighed. "That's always been your trouble, Francis. You see plots and schemes where there aren't any. I picked your place because it's isolated, and that's the simple truth."

"Like hell it is!" growled MacGonigal. "You're still with the Company. Or if you aren't, you're with some other outfit. And you're looking for a safe house. What I can't figure out is why. The Company doesn't contract safe houses, it buys them. Unless . . ." MacGonigal paused a moment, then smiled a grim smile. "You almost had me there, George. You pulled the one trick that I would never have suspected: You told me the truth. You're not with the Company anymore, but you do need a safe house. The only question is, why pick on me?"

"Because you're reliable and resourceful, Francis. And because you've dug yourself into one of the

most isolated spots east of the Rockies." He waved
his pipe. "I could search for a hundred years and not
find a place like this. And on top of that, you're
established. You're part of the local scene. You've
got cover and protective coloration. I could park my
client here, and no one would ever find him."

"Sure, George. Except that whoever you're protecting your client from is probably a lot smarter
than you are. They don't have to find this place. All
they have to do is put a tail on you and follow you
right to my doorstep. Doesn't matter how well
something is hidden, if you keep visiting it you'll lead
someone right to it, sooner or later. I don't want any
part of it. You'll fuck up and I'll have to pay the
consequences."

"Hell, man. You've got yourself a fuckin' fortress
here. The walls are a foot thick, all the approaches
are covered, and you've got a bloody arsenal."

"Is that your deal, George? For a lousy hundred
bucks a day, you want me to feed, diaper, and burp
your client, mix drinks for him, keep him entertained, and fight an occasional firefight? Is that all?
Hell, and I thought you were trying to pull another
of your slickies!"

Harris changed his tack. "Look, Francis, there
won't be any trouble. You don't think that I'd leave
you alone to handle a really hot situation, do you?
After all, I'd lose the client, too."

MacGonigal laughed. "Hell, yes, you'd leave me
alone. You've done it before. And you'll make damn
sure you've got the client's money first, so what do
you care about what happens next?"

"Honest to God, Mac," said Harris, "I'd never do

that. And you're wrong when you say I'll short-end the client. In the business I'm in, word travels fast. If I lose even one client, I'm done." He could see that MacGonigal was taking his argument in, and he continued. "As far as babysitting, this client will take care of himself. You won't even know he's here. He'll do his own cooking and cleaning, or I'll have someone do it. All you have to do is to provide a place, and keep intruders away. And you do that already. People around here say that nobody goes on your land, you're death on trespassers. And you know every square inch of the country for miles around. You're just like you were in 'Nam: Three days in a new area, and you know more about it than people who've been there all their lives."

MacGonigal looked scornful. "George, you're so anxious to sell me this bill of goods, you're stepping all over yourself. If you bring someone in to take care of your client, that's a potential leak. Besides which, people will get suspicious. There'll be talk, and talk gets around."

"Look, Mac, we can work it out. I'll get someone reliable, somebody that can be depended on to stay put. When I bring in the client, the hired help will come in at the same time. And they'll stay right here. That means that you'll have to do the shopping, but you can spread it around. People won't even know that you've got guests."

"I don't do much shopping, anyway, go to town maybe once a month or so. But that's for me. What will your client think about this kind of life? He may be tough to keep under control."

Harris brightened. MacGonigal was talking as if

he would go for the deal. He slipped into the manager role, leaving the negotiator role behind. "I'll guarantee that he'll stay put. In fact, I'll tell him that if he leaves the property, he's not your responsibility any more. He'll sit tight. Do we have a deal?"

A big smile slowly spread across MacGonigal's face. "No, George, we don't have a deal. We're a long way from a deal."

Harris put on a pained expression. "Well, if it's the money, I guess that I can sweeten the pot a little. How about a hundred and a quarter a day? And fifty for whoever takes care of the client? I can't go any higher."

"It isn't money, and you know it, Harris. It's the reason behind this charade. I want to know the details, buddy. Just who is your client, and who is he hiding from, and why?"

"I can't tell you that, Francis. It would be a violation of professional ethics. The client's business is private."

"Ethics, bullshit!" MacGonigal exploded. "Listen to me, you fuckin' weasel! You've probably got Hitler and Bormann for clients, and you want me to hide 'em out for you. Well, I'll tell you one thing: Nobody crosses my property line until I know exactly who they are, and why they're here. Understand?"

"Come on, Francis, be reasonable. I'll make it a hundred and a half. And a full seventy-five for the hired help. And all expenses. You can't ask for more than that," he said, spreading his hands wide.

"Wrong! I'm asking for the straight skinny. Now, put up or shut up. Who's the client, who's after him, and why?"

"Mac, I really can't tell you. But maybe I can give you some details. It isn't a he, it's a she, a lady who used to work for a rather shady figure. She kept his books, and now he's after her. She's got enough evidence to cook him."

"Sure, George. I really believe that some little old lady in tennis shoes who's spent her life keeping books has enough bread to lay out two hundred and twenty-five a day—and that's without your cut, which is at least twice that—until the heat's off. I really believe that. Don't bust your ass on the way down."

"No, look, it's the truth. There are some details that I can't tell you, but everything I have said is true."

"Right. Every last word. Beat it, George."

Harris flushed, the angry red creeping up his jawline. "Mac, what you want is to worm enough info out of me so that you can slip in and grab the whole show." He stopped, as if unable to go on. His jaws were clenched so tight that the muscles bulged like walnuts. He kicked the ground with his light hiking boots. "OK, buddy. I'll give you the dope. But if you try anything funny, I'll kill you. So help me God, I'll kill you."

MacGonigal laughed aloud. "Take it easy, George. You play it square with me, and I'll play it square with you. Lay the whole thing out for me, and then we'll see if we've got a deal."

MacGonigal sat sprawled on the sofa, the tanned deer hide scrunched up under him. Harris sat across from him in the one easy chair, MacGonigal's reading chair. Sipping the Irish Mist that MacGonigal had poured, he began his story.

"I got out after that last time in 'Nam. Started up a security business in New Jersey, mostly small stuff, providing night watchmen and that sort of thing. Now and then I'd get a nibble at something a little bigger—bodyguard, security checks, sweeping for bugs, checking out credit applications—the usual thing.

"Anyhow, I got a contract with a guy named Teddy DeLisle. Teddy had some bookstores and a few other ventures, and he wanted me to provide him with watchmen."

MacGonigal cut in. "Why the hell would a bookstore need a watchman?"

"I'm getting to that. This DeLisle distributed films, ran a string of coin machines—he had a lot of businesses. He also had some stiff competition, and they weren't above obstructing his operations with a little harassment."

"You mean he ran a porno operation," said MacGonigal, "and his competitors were trashing his outlets."

"That's pretty much the way it was. Anyhow, I put some bodies on his outlets and the trouble stopped. DeLisle was pretty pleased with the way things went, and he hired me for a few other jobs."

"What kind of jobs? Acting in his sleazy movies? That's right up your alley, George."

"You don't have to get sarcastic about it, Mac. All this guy was doing was selling a few skin flicks. What's the harm? Don't try to tell me you've never watched one."

"Yeah," said MacGonigal, "I've seen some pretty

raunchy things in my time. But lately things have gotten too much for even me to stomach. I don't mind some guy and gal screwing on the screen, but when you make a movie of some eight- or ten-year-old kid giving a grown man a blowjob, that's too much. And that's what the porno business is all about these days, George."

"Well, I didn't make the flicks, or do any of that stuff. I just worked under contract. Checked the stores, saw to it that none of the employees got their hands in the till, collected debts. One time I got the goods on Teddy's wife. She was shacking up with some young stud from one of his flicks.

"Well, Teddy had this girl working for him, named Susan Ennis. She was smart, a real genius, and she kept those books like nobody's business. I had to deal with her quite a bit, since I was into the financial end of the thing, and she pretty much ran that part.

"Like I say, she was a genius, a real one—and organized? She ran things like a clock. She kept three sets of books for Teddy: one for tax purposes, one for his partners—he had some big-time guys as partners—and one for Teddy. And she kept them so straight nobody could have broken them. I mean, that girl juggled invoices and bank accounts like you wouldn't believe. When she put an entry in the books, she could prove it—in front of a jury, in front of Congress, in front of God, for all I know. She had it all down pat. And of course, the next set of books had the same kind of backup, but painted a different picture.

"She was indespensable to Teddy. I mean, she could not only have got him sent up the river, she could have got him sunk to the bottom. His partners play rough!

"But she could handle it. She was something else. And Teddy had the hots for her. Hell, everybody had the hots for her, including me. I don't know if Teddy ever got next to her or not, but I tried. Didn't score, though.

"Anyhow, what was bound to happen finally happened. What with her juggling those books for Teddy, she got the idea that she should do a little juggling on her own. I don't know how she did it, or how much she got, or how Teddy caught her, but one day he calls me up and tells me he's got a special job for me. He offers ten grand, straight up, and when I asked him what the job is, he tells me that Sue's been dipping in the till, and he wants me to find out where she's stashed the money.

"I figured that it would be an investigative job, but when I got there, he's got Sue. Her face is all black and blue, and he's slapped her around quite a bit. He tells me that his wife's coming home, and he's got to get her out of there. I'm supposed to take her to one of the film warehouses and get the info out of her. See, I'd told him that I'd been in intelligence in 'Nam. You know, just a little bullshit to impress the client, but he got the idea that I could get anything out of anybody.

"Well, Teddy's got this black guy named Larry working for him. Larry—Blue Larry, they call him —mostly breaks in whores. He's about six-six, weighs about two-fifty, and he likes his work. I've heard him bragging about killing a chick—beat her to death. Another time, he killed this little blonde chick, she was a runaway from Minnesota, about fifteen. He choked her to death. With his cock!

"Anyhow, Larry's there, and Sue's tied up. Teddy had shot her up with something, and she was out of it. Larry and I are supposed to take her downstairs and into my car. Then we take her to the warehouse and get the info out of her.

"So Teddy's telling me all this, and there's Sue there—they had her buck-ass naked and hog-tied, with her head lolling around and bruises all over her. Teddy says that he was afraid that Larry would kill her before he got the info out of her, that's why he called me.

"Anyhow, when Teddy finishes with his spiel, I asked him the obvious: 'What next?' I mean, they've really got her roughed up, she looks bad. What am I supposed to do with her? Take her to a hospital and say this lady fell down the stairs? And Teddy laughs. He says 'You know what to do with her, George.' Can you beat that? I mean, I liked her, and he wants me to grease her.

"So I tell him no dice. I ain't killing Sue. And you know what he says then? 'Give her to Larry.' Just like that! 'Give her to Larry.'

"Well, that wasn't the time or place to argue. I said fine, I'd get the info out of her, and I got a spread off of the bed and we wrapped Sue in it. She was limp, just barely squirming now and then and groaning a little, so I told Teddy that it would take quite a while to get anything out of her. She'd have to be conscious. So Teddy says he doesn't care how long it takes, just so long as I get the info, and then he doesn't care what happens to her afterwards. And

Larry licks his lips when he hears that.

"I took the head and Larry took the feet, and we carried her down and put her in the trunk of my car. Larry's sort of humming all the time. You can tell what he's thinking. I'm telling you, Mac, it made me sick.

"Anyway, we got to the warehouse, and I tell Larry that he better check inside, to be sure there's no one there to see us carry her in. I'll stay outside, to deal with anything that comes up. So he goes inside, and I've got a .22 with a silencer under the dash. I get it out and slip in after him. He's checking the place out, and I let him have it.

At first, he thinks that it's bugs or something. I shot him in the back, and he reached back over his shoulder and slapped at it, like it was a mosquito bite. I went through a whole magazine, and he keeps slapping his back. I was lucky I had a spare mag, because this guy was huge, and the way he was absorbing those .22s was giving me the shits.

"At last, he turns around and sees me. Even then, he don't realize what's happening. He thinks there's something wrong outside, and he comes toward me. He's like a bull, and my hand is shaking, but I let him get close and pump the rest of the second magazine into him. Then he realizes what's happening.

"It was funny. When he thought it was bugs, it didn't faze him, but as soon as he got the message that he had been shot, he crumpled up. Didn't die, though. Just lay there, looking up at me, like a sick dog. I stood there and reloaded one magazine while he watched me, then I put the muzzle behind his ear and let him have it. I wasn't sorry, either. I knew what he'd have done with Sue. What a sick bastard!"

MacGonigal reached across and helped himself to Harris's tobacco pouch. "So then what did you do, George?"

"Well, there I was with this bastard bleeding all over the warehouse floor. It was a porno warehouse, lots of books and films and TV cassettes—all that stuff is palletized, with plastic wrapping, big sheets of polyethelene. They wrap up the whole pallet and run it through a heat tunnel and shrink it, so that it makes a nice, neat package. I took my pocket knife and cut the plastic off one of the pallets—I was careful not to leave fingerprints—and wrapped the bastard up in it. Then I got him up on the forks of a forklift and put him back behind some pallets. I polished up my brass—twenty-one times. I shot that bastard, and I had to get down on my hands and knees looking for the empty cases. And I hosed down the floor—there was a lot of blood."

"You mean you just left the body in the warehouse? They'll find it."

"Yeah, they'll find it sooner or later. But what are they going to do about it? Tell the police 'I found a dead body in my porno warehouse'? That's Teddy's problem. He'll have to cover it up, just to protect his own skin.

"Anyhow, I cleaned up and pulled out. Sue was still in the trunk of my car, so I just drove off. I made a quick swing by my office to pick up all the cash I had—I kept a few thousand in a safe there—and then I stopped and got some clothes and stuff for her before I got out of town, and I just kept going. I guess I was in the middle of Pennsylvania before she really came to. I kept off the main roads, and I'd stop and check on her every now and then. When she finally came around, I pulled off down a country road and got her dressed.

"Man, she was really a mess! I got a lot of pancake makeup, and we kind of covered up the marks on her face, but she looked bad. I stashed her in a motel in West Virginia and traded cars—I switched cars several times, because I knew that Teddy or his partners would be after me as soon as he figured out what happened.

"It's Teddy's partners that worry me. Teddy hasn't got the balls to really be dangerous, but those partners of his are real mobsters, with connections all over. There's one—name's Nazario—who's supposed to specialize in contracts. All the other hoods call him in when they want somebody snuffed."

"But if this Teddy was fiddling the books on his partners, he wouldn't want to bring them into the picture, would he?" MacGonigal asked. "I'd think he'd just cut his losses and keep his mouth shut."

"He can't do that. Sue always used to attend the monthly meetings, and they'd want to know where she was. She knew too much about the business for them to let her walk. Besides, with the cash she siphoned off, Teddy's in big trouble. Those partners of his expect the business to make a profit, or else. Teddy's got to have some excuse, and Sue is it. He'll have to make up some kind of story, but a broad outline of what happened will have to come out."

"So Teddy's partners will be looking for Sue? Who are they?"

"You probably never heard of them. Nazario, for example—he's got connections in Vegas, L.A., all over. He'll put a contract out on her. Teddy will try to fix it so it's a straight kill, he won't want them finding her and bringing her in where she might talk."

"So how long do you think it will take before there's a contract out?"

"Man, it's out already. I risked a call from a pay phone to a guy I know—I gave him a story about being out of town on a job, and just wanting to check on things at home. He didn't even want to talk to me. Treated me like I was poison! I've been on the run with Sue for three weeks now, and I've about run out of places to hide."

"So you figured you'd look up your old buddy, F.X., did you? How'd you find me?"

"I've still got a few connections around. I knew that you were retired, and from the way you'd always talked, I knew that it would be somewhere remote. I got in touch with a buddy at the Army Finance Center at Fort Ben Harrison. He tracked down your bank account number, and I conned the address out of the bank. Then I came down here and asked around for a bagpiper."

"And you figured that I'd just open my arms to you like you were my long-lost brother, did you?"

"Yeah, something like that. I really didn't have any choice. I had to get out fast, with no time to make any plans. Hell, I didn't ever figure that I'd ever need an E & E plan. Anyhow, I've come to the end of my rope. I've got to stash Sue somewhere—I can find my own place to hide, but together, we're too obvious. We've got to split up for a while."

"For a while? How long is a while? A week? Six months? A year?"

"I don't know. I guess until I can establish a cover somewhere. I don't think that it will ever be safe for either one of us to go under our own names again. These boys have long memories."

"So I'm supposed to put this dame up until you can think of something else. It looks to me like you haven't been doing too well in the thinking-of-something-else department lately, George."

"Look, Francis, I've been on the run. If I can unload Sue, it'll take the pressure off me, and I'll be able to come up with something."

"What you mean is, you've got the money, and you want me to sit on the girl while you put some distance between you and her. I'm not stupid, George. You're not going to leave me holding the bag on this one."

"I swear to God, Francis, it ain't like that at all. I don't know where the money is. She stashed it somewhere—probably invested it, if I know Sue, where it's making big-time bucks. But she won't say."

"How much is it, did she say that?"

"She didn't, but Teddy was ranting and raving about how she did him out of three million."

MacGonigal whistled. "That's big bucks, George. And here all along I thought you were just helping a lady in distress."

"It's big bucks, all right, Francis. Big enough so that they'll hunt for a long time. But I really don't know how much she got. She won't say a word about it, except to say that she's got enough, and that it's where it won't be found until she's ready to find it."

"Are you sure that she isn't just stringing you

along, George? After all, she's in a tight spot. She needs you, and the money is the only hold she's got."

"No, she's got it. Like I said, Sue's a genius. I bet she's been planning this thing for years. I don't know how she got caught, but I'll bet that it was just bad luck. Teddy just stumbled onto her. But I know that he didn't have a clue where the money was, that's why he called me in."

"And what has she promised you for helping her? Are you her partner?"

"I'll level with you, Francis. She hasn't promised me anything, except that she'll make good all my expenses. She's one tough lady, Mac. Even half dead, she hangs in there. But sooner or later, she's got to do something with that money, and she can't do anything without me. I'm all the protection she has. And until she gets her hands on the money, she hasn't got a cent."

"So what's your game plan?"

"I've got her in a motel about thirty miles from here. I'll go back and get her and bring her here. Then I'll take off and keep in touch by mail. When I've got a cover established, I'll come back for her."

"And you're going to pay me two twenty-five a day? How are you going to do that, George?"

"Francis, by now you've figured out that I haven't got that kind of money. You'll have to wait until she can make arrangements to get the money. Then we'll pay you, I swear."

"Looks to me that she's the one with the money. Has she agreed to all this?"

"Well, that's a little problem, Francis. I've been telling her all about you, talking you up to her. But she's stubborn, or maybe suspicious. It's no deal until she meets you and talks to you. She wants to check out the setup. If you and I have a deal, I'll go get her and bring her here."

"No, George. If your friends are as hot as you say, even one visit here was too many. Let me see that map you have."

Harris blinked with surprise, then pulled the map and orienteering compass out of his shirt. "I should have known that you were watching me, Francis." He passed the map, in its clear plastic case, over to MacGonigal. MacGonigal unfolded it. It was a standard U.S. Geological Survey seven-and-a-half-minute quadrangle, a twin to one of those glued to the folding screen behind his chair. He saw with distaste that the location of his cabin had been marked on it. He showed the mark to Harris. "You're not big on security, are you, George?"

Harris made no reply, and MacGonigal spread the map on the table. "Here's how we'll do it, and this is the only way we'll do it." He pointed at a spot on the map. "You come up this road, from north to south, tomorrow at one P.M. Make sure you're not followed. When you get to this place, you'll see a cut. Let her out at the south end of the cut and keep going. Make sure nobody sees you. If there's another car in sight, keep going for a couple of miles, turn around and try the drop again. Tell her to walk west, uphill. I'll meet her and talk to her. You drive back past the drop in twenty minutes. If she's not there, the deal's on. Keep going. I don't want to hear from you for at least six months. And burn this damn map!"

II.

Harris stuffed the map back into his shirt. MacGonigal was looking directly at him. "I mean it, Harris. Burn that damn map. And if you've got my name or address written down anywhere, burn that, too. I don't want any link between us, none at all. You can let me know what's happening once a month or so, but like I said, don't try to contact me for at least six months. I'll write you a report on how things are here and mail it when I hear from you."

"Okay, Francis. You don't have to give me any security lectures. I'll get back and tell Sue what we've agreed to. Let me warn you that she might not go along with it; she can be pretty stubborn."

"She can be anything she likes. When one o'clock comes tomorrow, I'll be waiting. When one-twenty comes, I'll be on my way back here, Sue or no Sue. But if she doesn't like the terms, tell her not to bother. And don't come back and try to renegotiate the deal, George. They look unfavorably on trespassers around here."

Harris let himself out and started down the path. He had reached the falls and was about to start down when he heard MacGonigal strike in his drones. He shook his head. Crazy fucking Irishman, he said to himself, as the first notes of "O'Donnel Abu" began to swirl around him. He shook his head again. MacGonigal was one crazy bastard.

Ain't this a hell of a note, said MacGonigal to himself. Here I am back in business with George Fucking Harris, the sleaziest son of a bitch that ever walked the earth. He gathered the drones and chanter together under his arm and then he turned back into the house and climbed the stairs to the loft. There he waited patiently until he heard Harris's jeep start up. Taking a pair of 10×50 binoculars from a peg, he uncased them and focused them on the first spot in the road where Harris's jeep would appear. In a minute or so, he saw the vehicle. With the powerful glasses, he could tell that Harris was alone in the vehicle. He watched it until it was out of sight, and there was no slowing or stopping. So far as he could tell, Harris was alone.

That doesn't mean he'll be alone tomorrow, thought MacGonigal. If I know George, he's probably left a trail a blind man could follow. He thought it over carefully. The isolated pickup site would be the logical place for an ambush.

Well, he thought, It's the first man on the ground who sets the ambush. He slung the binoculars over his shoulder and made his way around the loft, picking up items here and there.

In a short time, he had assembled a small pile of equipment, a nine-by-ten-foot tarp, a light down sleeping bag, a Svea stove and Sigg fuel bottle, a tiny cook kit, a few odds and ends of woods equipment, a closed-cell foam pad, and a ground sheet.

He packed his gear in a small rucksack, strapping the binoculars, sleeping bag, and pad to the outside, then clattered down the stairs. For a long moment, he paused in front of the racked weapons. At last he selected a Savage model 99 in .308 caliber.

He opened the ammunition drawer in the built-in set of drawers that ran along the wall below the guns and took out a twenty-round box of .308 reloads. He turned back to the rucksack, then stopped in midstride, reconsidered, and went back to the drawer. He took out five more twenty-round boxes and two extra magazines for the Savage.

He scooped a holstered revolver, an old Colt .357 with a six-inch barrel and an action like glass, off one of the bookshelves and dumped the weapon and boxes of cartridges beside the rucksack. He unhooked the canteen from the rucksack and filled it at the pitcher pump.

For a moment, MacGonigal paused to examine his motives. He had told the truth when he said that he didn't need the money. He had enough to get by on, more really than he needed. Besides, the odds of actually profiting from this deal were fifty-fifty, at best. He had enough experience with George Harris to realize that. He wondered, too, how his mysterious lady guest would feel about the deal once she saw the accommodations. Looking around the cabin, he had to admit that, however much it satisfied Francis Xavier MacGonigal, it was not likely to be the sort of place a lady would want to live in for an indefinite period.

He shrugged. It didn't really matter. He rose and gathered up his gear, threading the revolver on his belt. At the door, he paused to take his parka off the rack. It might get chilly out there. For a moment he debated going up to the loft to get the liner, but decided against it. With the rucksack slung on his back, the parka under one arm, and the Savage under the other, he manuevered himself through the door, closed it carefully behind him, and went out to the tack room.

He sorted through the varied collection of riding gear and selected a saddle scabbard for the Savage, one with a somewhat ungainly outline, a hump to fit the rifle's scope sight, and strapped it to his favorite saddle, adjusting the straps until it hung as he wanted it.

In a small room off the main tack room was the feed room. A neatly carpentered bin held horse and mule feed. With an old coffee can he dipped out several feeds and dumped them into a sack, which he secured to the lashing strings on the back of his saddle.

The horses were in plain sight. Usually they sought refuge in the trees that bordered the paddock, but MacGonigal supposed that they were feeling the effects of the fall weather and staying out in the sunshine as long as they could these days.

He poured a little feed in their trough and as the horses began to eat, slipped binder twine nooses around Harry and Smoke. When the horses finished, he passed loops through the nooses and around their noses, forming impromptu halters. With the big rangy bay and the smokey-gray roan in tow, he opened the gate, led them through, and shut it behind him again.

When he had the horses saddled, he put the rucksack on Harry's saddle, and carefully stowed the Savage in the scabbard that was strapped to Smoke's. He lashed his parka behind the saddle, and gathering up the reins and the end of Harry's longe line, he put his foot in the stirrup and swung himself aboard.

The horses reacted almost immediately, waltz-stepping sideways, half-rearing, crow-hopping. He firmly jerked Harry's longing line to establish control, and clamped his thighs around Smoke's barrel. He neck-reined the big roan around and touched him gently with the spurs, guiding him up out of the valley onto the ridgeline.

It was about eleven o'clock when MacGonigal started out, and he had a long way to go. He didn't want to be seen, not going or coming. That meant that he had to cut straight across country, avoiding roads and trails.

Up on the high ridgeline there was little likelihood that he would encounter anyone until he reached the Mozart Road. Before then, however, he planned to turn off and make his way down to Meadow Creek. He knew that this creek was shallow enough to allow him to use it as a highway, but too wide and too powerful when in flood to be fenced. He would simply follow the creek for most of the way.

He made his way down the ridge without incident and was soon riding along the creek, the horses slipping occasionally on the loose, flat stones that made up the bottom. Whenever they came to places where the horses had to wade belly-deep MacGonigal would check his equipment, draw his

Savage from the saddle boot and hold it across one shoulder so it would not get wet.

By midafternoon, MacGonigal had reached a high ridge overlooking the road on which he intended to make the pickup. The ridge was about a mile from the pickup point. He crossed over it and headed for a spot on the far side, where he remembered seeing an old corral. He soon found it, a double strand of barbed wire tacked from tree to tree, probably put there years before by loggers to pen their mules. He off-saddled the horses and put them into the corral, the marks of the saddle blankets pressing down their fluffy coats. He spread the two blankets and poured a measure of feed onto each one, then set to work while the horses ate.

He dug into the rucksack and pulled out the spare magazines for the Savage and loaded them, putting one in each pocket and inserting the third in the weapon. He threw the lever, chambering a cartridge, and checked to make sure the safety was on. That done, he shouldered the rucksack, picked up the Savage, and started up over the brow of the ridge, headed for the road. He climbed slowly, not so much from the physical effort of the climb as from caution. He held the Savage ready, as if expecting to need it with every step. He reached the crest and slid out of the straps of the rucksack, cacheing it behind a tree while he took the binoculars and rifle and moved slowly and cautiously forward.

For a long time he scanned the road, the shoulders, and the opposite ridge. He concentrated on the area immediately around the designated drop point, but did not ignore more distant spots that might serve as a hiding place for a man or a vehicle. Only when he was satisfied that no one was around did he go back for the rucksack.

He made his way down to the road, not to the drop site, but to a point nearly a quarter of a mile north of it. He approached the gravel surface with extreme care and concealed himself in a fringe of bushes on the verge. For a long time he simply sat, doing nothing but listening, watching, and waiting. Then he suddenly burst out of the woods, sprinted across the road, and plunged into the bushes on the other side. His performance was followed by absolute silence.

He waited a full ten minutes, never moving. Then slowly and almost noiselessly, he slipped out of his hiding place and drifted deeper into the woods. He spent an hour making a circuit of the drop point, keeping fifty yards back in the woods, out of sight of the road—but scanning every deer trail that led to the road for signs of recent human activity.

It took him nearly an hour, for he moved carefully, not snapping a twig, not allowing a branch to swish back after he passed. He moved as if he were stalking deer, and he was an expert stalker. He covered the distance between the point where he had crossed the road and the drop point and went on to search an equal distance to the south of the drop point. Occasionally he moved closer to the road and searched visually with the binoculars. Once he had completed the search, he repeated the process of waiting carefully near the road then dashing across.

On the other side, he made the same careful scout. Several times he chided himself on his play-acting, but he reminded himself that there really was a threat. If there were contracts out on Harris and the woman, then the drop point would be the primary danger point. He could do nothing if they had already been located and were hit before they showed up, but he could take precautions against an ambush here. He also wanted to make sure that the drop was unobserved, and that they had no evidence of where the woman was hiding. His isolation would be no protection if the woman was located.

Once he had completed his search, he started back uphill, climbing faster now that he knew that the entire area was safe. He climbed to a point where the crowning sandstone and lime cap of the ridge rose in a jumble of boulders and low bluffs. He searched through the tumbled rock until he found what he was looking for, an overhanging ledge with shelter from the weather and a flat space where he could pitch his tarp. From there a good mile of the road was in view, as well as the foot approaches to the drop point.

He placed his rifle against the bluff, then took off the rucksack and spread the groundsheet. That done, he laid out the things he would need for the night, then secured the corners of the tarp to two small bent saplings that had managed to find enough soil for a tenuous foothold in the rocks, then tied the other corners into fist-sized rocks that he wedged in cracks in the bluff. In a short time he had a comfortable camp.

He stepped back in satisfaction to survey his work. The green tarp blended in well with the foliage and the moss-covered rock wall. He cut a few cedar branches and placed them here and there to add to the concealment of his camp.

That done, he spread out his sleeping bag, fluffing it to get full loft, and took out his Svea stove, priming it with a few drops of white gas from the fuel bottle. In a short time he had a pot of water boiling. He opened a package of Mountain House freeze-dried beef-and-rice stew, divided the contents in half, and added boiling water to one portion.

It was nearly dark when he finished his meal. He stripped down to his shorts and slid into his sleeping bag. For a moment he hesitated, then reached out and extracted the .357 Magnum from the holster and brought it into the bag with him. It would ruin one hell of a good sleeping bag if he had to use it, he thought. But if he needed it, it wouldn't matter about the bag.

He was awake before the alarm on his watch went off. It was still an hour before dawn, and cold. He worked one arm out of the bag and dragged his clean clothes into the warm cocoon. The cold cloth made his skin break out in goose bumps. When the clothes warmed up, he pulled on his wool shirt and, still undressed from the waist down, pulled the bag down far enough to free both arms and primed the stove. Once it was going, he put on a quart pot of water. While he waited for it to boil, he pulled on his pants and finally forced himself out of the sleeping bag.

It was cold, cold enough to make his hands clumsy and to make camp work painful. He pulled on the olive green parka and the ski gloves and set about stuffing the sleeping bag in its stuff bag. By the time the water boiled, he was nearly packed up. He poured oatmeal from a plastic container into the plastic plate and mixed in powdered milk and boiling water. He used the rest of the water to shave.

The hot water on his face felt good, and the hot oatmeal laced with brown sugar and the inevitable hot chocolate assured his feeling of well being. He was ready for the day, even though it was only breaking dawn.

He had a long wait ahead of him, and settled down with the binoculars to watch while the light slowly grew. Through the powerful lenses, with their light-gathering properties, he could see well enough to make a visual search of the terrain around the road worthwhile. He sat in the lee of a large deadfall and began a slow scan. A flicker of movement caught his eye, and he gave it his attention. It was a doe, moving slowly along the verge of the road. He watched her with interest, then began to search the woods around her. After a moment he found the buck, standing motionless while the doe tested the crossing. Pleased with himself, he watched the two deer cross the road, first the doe, then, when he was sure there was no danger, the buck. He's a nice one, thought MacGonigal. I'll have to remember this spot, come deer season.

For a long time, he found nothing else of interest. About eight, a pickup truck came down the road, raising a plume of dust long before the vehicle came into sight. That's good, thought MacGonigal, I'll know well ahead of time if anyone's coming along the road. He watched the pickup as it passed the drop point and continued on. It didn't slow, and he could follow the dust trail long after it passed out of sight.

He continued his vigil until almost noon, then primed and fired up his little stove again and finished the rest of the stew. He packed the stove and utensils away and resumed his vigil. Now was the critical period. If there was a leak somewhere in Harris's scheme, if he was being followed, whatever was going to happen would happen pretty soon.

He scanned the far ridge, but nothing was moving. He scrutinized the road, but drew a blank there, too. He leaned back against the deadfall and rested a moment, then took up the binoculars and went through the same routine. As he lowered the glasses, he saw a haze of dust in the distance. His pulse quickened. He glanced down at his watch. Twelve fifty-five. There had only been one vehicle on the road all morning, the pickup truck. This must be Harris. He did another slow scan of the road and surrounding terrain, then turned the glasses to the point where the vehicle would first appear. He waited with growing impatience until it came into view. It was the same red CJ-5, and from the dust cloud, he could tell that there was no other vehicle following it. He looked quickly up the road. No dust from that direction, either. He returned the glasses to their case, picked up his rifle, and started down toward the road.

He hadn't moved far at all when the jeep reached the drop point. It halted, and he pulled the binoculars out again. He saw her climb out, a slim figure in jeans and a checkered shirt with a scarf around her head. She seemed a little uncertain as the jeep drove off, but in a moment or two began to climb up the ridge toward MacGonigal. He knew that she couldn't see him, and he moved down to intercept her.

He soon lost sight of her, but he could hear her thrashing through the brush. A city girl, he thought. Doesn't know how to move in the woods. That was somehow encouraging. Nazario and DeLisle, or anyone they sent, would likely be city types as well. If they came down here, they'd have to deal with MacGonigal on his home turf. And MacGonigal was pretty good on his home turf.

He kept moving until he could see flashes of her checkered shirt and bright scarf through the trees. He took up a position near a large boulder and waited. She was following a deer trail, and it led right past this spot. Looking down at the ground, MacGonigal saw fresh tracks. The doe and buck he had observed earlier had passed that way. This spot would make a good stand, he thought.

He let her come on until she was only twenty feet away, then stood up. "Over here, Miss Ennis."

She jumped nearly a foot at the sound of his words, then flushed angrily. "Do you enjoy playing these games and scaring people?"

"No, ma'am. Or maybe yes. It doesn't make much difference, I suppose, if what George Harris said is true. If you hadn't played a little game of your own, you wouldn't be here."

She made no reply, but looked him over carefully. MacGonigal felt as if he were a specimen under a microscope, or a used and rather shabby piece of furniture at a flea market. She's a cool lady, all right, he thought, as he returned her inspection. She was about thirty, slim, with small, high breasts, long waist and gently swelling hips and long legs. Her light brown hair was confined under the scarf, but he could tell that it was long and straight. It probably reached her waist when unconfined.

She had a self-possessed attitude, almost regal, and MacGonigal could see why Harris had been impressed by her. Aside from her obvious attractiveness, she had an air of unattainability, with a hint of an explosively passionate nature kept in check. MacGonigal grinned. "Will I do?"

"Not for a hundred and fifty a day. George has told me about you, but I've learned that George isn't very good at judging people."

MacGonigal smiled again. "I agree. But if you're hooked up with George, you can't have any claims in that direction either."

She looked directly at him. "I don't have a lot of choice. But I'm not going to pay you a hundred and fifty a day. I'll pay a hundred. Take it or leave it."

"You'd better think over what you just said about not having any choice. But I'll take it. The hundred and fifty figure was for George. Since you're paying, I'll take less." He paused. "I suppose all that jazz about him finding someone reliable to do the chores for you was some of his usual bullshit?"

"There won't be anyone else." She stopped a moment, as if making a decision. "If a hundred a day is all right with you, then I guess we have a deal."

"I guess we do," said MacGonigal, picking up the rucksack and slipping his arms through the straps. "I hear George coming back. Let's get out of here, just in case someone's following him." He turned and started back up the ridge. He could hear her thrashing along behind him. In the background he could hear the sound of Harris's jeep. It slowed as it approached the drop point. Damn him for a fool, thought MacGonigal. It was a perfect drop, but he's got to give a tail another chance at figuring out what he did with her.

They climbed steadily, and when they reached a point where the road could be seen again, MacGonigal stopped and pulled out the binoculars again. The jeep was out of sight, but MacGonigal swept the road. The dust pattern indicated that there had been no tail. He lowered the glasses.

"What are you looking for?"

"Just making sure that no one followed Harris. Come on." He slung the binoculars around his neck and strode off, pushing the pace. She was in good condition, he thought, but she wasn't used to climbing. He could hear her breath coming in gasps as they made their way up the ridge. She's too proud to call a halt or ask me to slow down, he thought. George was right. She's one tough lady. He was surprised to find that the same word Harris had used to describe her came to mind.

At the top of the ridge, he ducked behind a leaning slab of rock and waited for her to catch up. "How're you doing?" She put one hand against the rock and paused a moment to catch her breath. "Okay, I guess. Are we going to keep this up all day?"

MacGonigal grinned. "No. Just until we get out of the danger area. I've got horses waiting a couple of hundred yards ahead. Can you ride?"

"I don't know. I've never tried. But I can learn."

She took a few deep breaths. "I'm ready to go on now."

He led the way at a slower pace, and since it was all downhill, she was able to keep up with him. "George tells me that you live in a log cabin, just like a pioneer."

"George exaggerates. I live in a log cabin, all right, and it'll seem pretty primitive to you at first. But you'll get used to it."

"I'll have to. But how did you come to live here?"

"It's a long story. I've lived all over the world. When I was a boy, my father was in the oil business. When I was about fourteen, he retired and we moved to a place in Independence County. That's about fifty miles away from here. Dad sold the place after Mom died, but I always wanted to come back. I guess that I just like living in the woods."

"But you must get pretty lonely? George says that you don't have a television or a phone, or anything."

"If I get lonely, I go somewhere where there's people. When I get tired of them, I come home. That's the advantage of living in a place like this. I don't need TV or a phone; I get along without them and never miss them."

"Aren't you interested in what goes on in the world?"

"Sure. I subscribe to about fifty magazines and book clubs. I keep up with things."

"Isn't your news kind of stale that way?"

"I suppose," MacGonigal said patiently. "But nothing earth-shattering ever happened because I found out what was going on a few days later than the rest of the world. And usually I know more about what's happening than anyone else, because I take the time to read and digest."

"George says that you don't have any plumbing, either."

"Well, that's not quite true. I have a cistern for rainwater, and a pump and a sink. That's all I need, anyway. I live pretty close to the creek, and a septic tank and tile field would leach into the water. I won't do that."

She seemed a little put off. "What do you do about . . . other facilities?"

He laughed. "I have a Clivus Multrum." She looked puzzled. "That's a composting toilet. It turns human waste into sterile matter. It's odorless, or pretty much so, and it's clean. It doesn't foul the creek, and the results make good fertilizer."

She gave him a startled look. "I thought human waste caused disease if you used it for fertilizer."

"It does, if you use it fresh, like they do in the Orient. But what comes out of a Clivus Multrum is sterile, like I said."

One of the horses stamped and blew, and startled Susan. They had come to the corral without her noticing the animals. She looked at them with suspicion. "They're awfully big. I hadn't realized that horses were so big."

MacGonigal laughed. "Haven't you ever seen one before?"

"Yes, but not from up close. . . . They look different when you're close to them."

"They look bigger than they are because you know that you have to ride one. Don't worry, though. He holds you in as much awe as you hold him. And his awe won't wear off unless you let it."

He hauled the saddles and gear down and stepped into the pen with a halter and longe line. Harry was a little reluctant to be caught, but there was nowhere he could run in the little pen. MacGonigal slipped an arm around his neck, pulled the halter up over his nose, and led him out.

"This is Harry. He's yours. You'll have to watch him and make him behave, but there's nothing to worry about. He hasn't got a malicious bone in his body."

Sue watched in silence as MacGonigal brushed Harry down, placed the blanket, then heaved the saddle up. As he tightened the girth she asked, "Do horses really blow themselves up when you do that?"

MacGonigal turned. "Some of them do. Usually because someone cinches them too tight. Where'd you learn that?"

"I read it in a book somewhere. I also read that you're supposed to wait awhile and come back and tighten the what-do-you-call-it again."

"That's right." MacGonigal was enjoying her curiosity. "Always tighten the cinch the first time you stop. Of course, if you're going any distance, when you stop you should loosen it. Makes the horse more comfortable. Then you have to tighten it before you get on."

He brought Smoke out of the pen and saddled him while Susan watched. "OK, it's time to mount up." She looked apprehensively at the big bay. MacGonigal had noted earlier that she was a tall girl, about five-nine, but the top of her head barely reached Harry's withers. She walked gingerly toward the big horse and reached out timidly to touch him. "Don't worry about him. Whack him on the neck and give him a shove, just to let him know who's boss." He strode over and pushed the big bay's nose aside, then followed his own advice by striking the side of his arched neck with the flat of his hand. "See? They like it. It's affectionate. Horses are used to a sort of rough camaraderie with men, and they expect a firm hand." He gathered up the reins and looped them around the saddle horn. "Always make sure that you've got the reins. That's how you control him. Now," he said, taking her small hands in one big paw, "put both hands on the saddle horn, with the reins under them. The left foot goes in the stirrup." He picked her left foot up and placed it in the stirrup. "Now give a heave, and you're aboard."

She tensed her muscles and swung smoothly into the saddle, giving MacGonigal a view of a trim, arched butt as she did. He regretted that she had mounted so easily. He would like to have grabbed that butt and pushed. Well, he thought philosophically, you can't have everything, me boyo. He picked up her big shoulder bag and looped it over the saddle horn, then lashed the small duffle she had carried behind the cantle.

He wrapped Smoke's reins around the saddle horn and vaulted into the saddle, settling with a thump onto the polished leather, then pulling the horse's head around and squeezing him with his knees, all in one motion. MacGonigal, me boyo, he thought, you're letting this woman get to you. First you pretty yourself up, and now you're showing off. He kept his eyes off her, though, and concentrated on guiding

Smoke out of the thick saplings that grew near the pen. Behind him, Harry took the hint and began to move. "Bring him up here, alongside. Don't let him lag back."

"I'd rather do it this way," she called.

"Well, I wouldn't. It's a bad habit for a horse to get into, going single file, and I don't want my horses picking up bad habits. Bring him up here."

She sawed at the reins, obviously not too sure how to get Harry to do what she wanted. "Pull his head around. Use both reins. That bit is only there for show, or to stop him. Neck rein him. Now touch his belly with your heels."

MacGonigal could see that the situation was deteriorating. He reined Smoke around and siezed Harry's longe line and pulled him into position. "There. That's the way. Just pay attention to him and don't let him drift back on you."

They rode a good way in silence, ducking branches and going around obstacles that they couldn't ride over or through. After an hour, MacGonigal called a halt, ostensibly to rest the horses, but really to see how Susan was doing. She dismounted rather stiffly, and MacGonigal had to hide a grin. She would feel this ride the next day.

He loosened the girths and pulled the bits from the horses' mouths to allow them to graze a little, clipping the longe lines to the bits and tying them high to an overhanging branch to keep them from wandering. Then he rummaged through the rucksack for his stove. She watched, absorbed, as he primed and lit it, then put water on to boil. "Want some hot chocolate?" he said.

She grinned, a conspiratorial grin. "I love it. You must be psychic."

He returned the grin. "No, but I've spent enough time in the cold to know what goes good."

They rested about half an hour and then he saddled the horses again. Susan seemed a little stiff as she mounted, and he noticed that she lowered herself gingerly into the saddle. "It's not all that much farther, another couple of hours. We'll be there well before nightfall." He paused a moment. "You'll be more comfortable if you stand in the stirrups. That's what they're for, and it saves wear and tear on your jeans."

They rode in silence for half an hour, silence broken only by an occasional warning on his part when they came to tricky terrain. Susan seemed to take steep hills and thick brush in stride, but when they came to the creek, she seemed a little reluctant to enter the water. "Can horses swim?"

"Better than you can. But they don't have to. The water isn't that deep. We'll just wade, and mostly just knee-deep."

She was doubtful. "It looks awfully deep. I'm sure that it's more than knee-deep."

He reassured her. "I came this way yesterday. Believe me, you're not going to have to swim. Just give Harry his head, and he'll get you through. But don't let him wander on you."

He could tell that she only half believed him, but she followed anyway. When they came to the first spot where the water was belly-deep, he looked back to see how she took it, but she just drew her feet up like a veteran.

When they came to the first fence, he gave her Smoke's reins to hold and set to work to pull the staples. "Won't the owner be mad if he finds you pulling staples out of his fence?"

"Maybe. But he won't find me. And I'm going to restaple it so that he won't even notice. Take the horses through now."

He felt a thrill of pride when they finally reached Bear Pen valley. He brought her down Bear Pen Creek without a word and let her find the cabin. He was curious as to what her reaction would be.

"It's perfect! It's just beautiful!" She rose up in the stirrups and looked around her. "You must have planned it for a long time."

"I had a lot of time, in a lot of strange places."

They rode up to the tack room. MacGonigal helped her down. She stretched her stiff legs while MacGonigal unsaddled the horses. Out of the corner of his eye, he watched her, admiring the clean lines of her long limbs. They led the horses to the paddock together.

"George told me that you've completely isolated yourself. Why?"

"I'm not isolated," he said gruffly. "I live alone. There's a difference."

"But you don't even have electricity?"

"I have electricity. One of the first things I did was put in an impulse turbine. It's fed by a pipe from the falls. I'll show it to you later."

"But George said that you didn't have lights."

"I have kerosene lights. I prefer them. If I need something brighter, I use a Coleman lantern."

"But why, if you generate your own electricity?"

"Because that's the way I like it. I do things my way, and fuck the rest of the world."

She didn't flinch at the word, as MacGonigal half expected she would. "So you're self-sufficient? What are you, a what-do-you-call-it, a survivalist?" She pronounced the word as if it were capitalized and slightly distasteful.

"No, I'm not anything. I'm MacGonigal, and I do the things I like, the way I like. This is the way I live, and if you like it, fine. If not, I suppose you're in for a miserable time of it."

They went up the steps to the porch and MacGonigal held the door for her. Inside, she stopped just beyond the door and looked around. Standing behind her, MacGonigal saw the cabin as she must be seeing it, clean, with a certain neatness about it, but full; full of things, things that were intimately linked to MacGonigal. Her eyes swept over the rows of guns on the walls.

"You're certainly well-armed." There was a hint of sarcasm in her voice.

"I like guns. I like to hunt, and I like to shoot. As I said, if you like it, fine. If not, tough."

She wandered over to the bookshelves and began to scan the titles. "You like to read, too."

"Yeah, I read quite a bit. You can pick and choose what you read. It's not like some other things, where you have to take what they give you."

She picked a slim volume off one of the shelves. "Poetry? I didn't think you'd read poetry."

"I like some, and there's some I don't like," MacGonigal responded.

She continued to look over the shelves. "There

must be something here on everything in the world."
She stood on tiptoe and looked at a set of tall, slim,
dark blue volumes. *"Tables of Calculated Azimuths
and Altitudes.* What's that about?"

"Sight reduction tables. For celestial navigation. I
once sailed a boat across the Pacific. I used them
then."

"A ship? George said that you were in the Army."

"It was a sailboat. A thirty-eight-foot Atkins yawl,
named *Adventure*. I took her from San Francisco to
Australia. I sold her there."

She moved over to the kitchen area. "I like the
way you've built this place, all one big room, I mean.
Everything happens all in the same place." She
stopped by the wood stove. "Even when you're in
the kitchen, you can still enjoy that big fireplace."

"That's what I had in mind when I built it."

She looked at the big, shaggy bear rug in front of
the fireplace. "I suppose you killed that yourself.
That's something I don't understand. How can you
be so in tune with nature, and kill things?"

He sighed. Another bleeding heart. "I don't just
kill things. I hunt. That's part of nature. And I don't
hunt things that can't stand being hunted. I took that
bear in Alaska. There are lots of them there, and
there always will be, if somebody doesn't fuck things
up and pave the place."

She touched the stove—it was cold. "I'm hungry.
If you'll show me where things are, and if you'll show
me how to operate this thing, I'll fix us something to
eat."

MacGonigal smiled. "Through that door. There's
a pantry in there, and a refrigerator and freezer

—I'm not completely primitive. But I'll get the stove going. Using a wood stove's an art." MacGonigal heard himself bragging.

She went into the pantry, and he could hear her rummaging among the canned goods on the shelves, opening and closing the refrigerator door. He gathered a handful of kindling from the brass bucket beside the stove and opened the firebox door. He was down on his knees, laying the fire, when she came back out.

She fixed a light meal, a sort of omelette, and MacGonigal watched her, admiring the unconscious grace of her movements. She looked at home in the cabin, he thought, as if she belonged there.

When the meal was over, he put the tub of water on the stove, and did the dishes. She neither protested nor acted as if it were condescension on his part. As he brought the soapy dishes out of the hot water, however, she rinsed and dried them.

"Is that how it's going to be, a cooperative effort?"

"I suppose so," she said. "We're both in this together. George told me that he had to promise you that I'd take care of myself, but at a hundred dollars a day, I don't think that I should have to do all the housework. Does that make sense to you?"

"Of course it does. I'd be doing it for myself, anyway. This way we split the work. Just don't be surprised if there are some things that I prefer to do myself."

He put the dishes away and emptied the dishwater into the sink, rinsing out the tub, then refilling it and putting it back on the woodstove. "It's cool enough

to justify a fire. Suppose I light one in the fireplace."
She agreed, and he went on, "Would you like a
drink?"

She hesitated. "I don't think that would be a good
idea."

He didn't press it. "Well, the water will be hot
enough for a bath soon. There's a big tub in the
pantry that you can use—I usually just bathe out of
the little tub, myself. I don't have a bathroom, but I
can string a line across the room that you can hang a
couple of blankets across, if you want a bath."

She looked at him gratefully. "I'd like that." She
paused a moment. "I think that we'd better get
something straight. I know that we're alone together, and I know that George told you a little about the
kind of business I was in. But my job was to keep the
books, just that. I just want to make sure that we
understand each other."

For the next week, they lived warily. MacGonigal
went about his usual chores, caring for the animals,
checking fences and other details, while Susan grad-
ually took over the housework. He did not resist, but
shared that work with her, and in turn she sometimes
accompanied him in his work out of doors. She
quickly learned to care for the horses, and adopted
Harry as her own, cleaning his hooves, grooming
him, and caring for his tack.

In the fall weather, MacGonigal loved to slip out
of the house and ride along the deserted back roads
and trails, breathing the clean, cold air of the new
day. He exulted in the feel of the horse between his
legs as they cantered along, making swirls in the mist

that hung in the low places. The first time he slipped out to ride, he returned to find Sue still asleep. He took down his pipes and went outside. She found him standing on a stone overlooking the falls, oblivious to everything, the drones thrust back over his shoulder, the chanter wailing. She stood and watched him as he played.

"What's that tune?"

" 'The Dawning of the Day,' Irish reveille. It's to wake sleepyheads like you."

"I'd have been awake if you had called me. Why didn't you wake me up when you went for a ride?"

He was a little taken aback at the intensity of her tone. "I didn't think you'd want to be disturbed so early."

Nothing more was said, but the next morning, when he planned to go hunting, he made it a point to wake her, creeping up the stairs to where she slept in the loft with a candle in his hand. He found her snuggled under the covers, the fire in the potbellied stove long since gone out. Her long brown hair strayed across the pillow and her features were clear and relaxed. He gently shook her shoulder.

"Sue? Sue? I'm going out. Want to go with me?"

She awoke totally, with no transition between sleeping and waking. "What time is it?"

"Just six o'clock. I thought I'd go hunting. Do you want to come?"

She sat up in bed, holding the covers to her slim body. They didn't quite conceal her small, delicate breasts. "I've never been hunting," she said. "When are you leaving?"

"In about half an hour. I've got the stove going downstairs, and there's hot water for you if you want it."

"Go on back down. I'll be down in a few minutes."

MacGonigal put the candle on the table beside her bed and went down the stairs, guided by the yellow glow of the kerosene lantern in the living area. He had already heaped his coat and a few odds and ends, along with the .22 Hornet, on the couch, and a pot of coffee was brewing on the stove. He poured himself a cup and sat back with his feet up, waiting for her.

In a short time she came down, her slender form encased in jeans and a bulky sweater. Over one arm she carried a heavy coat, one of his. "I thought I'd better have something warm to wear," she said, by way of explanation.

"It's going to get a lot colder. I'll order you some things from a catalog. It'll create suspicion if I go shopping locally for women's clothes." He waved toward the stove. "The coffee's hot. Have a cup."

She put the coat down on the couch with his hunting gear and took a cup from the cupboard. "What about breakfast? Want me to fix some?"

"Nope, unless you want some, that is. I usually wait until I get back. I hunt better on an empty stomach."

She looked across at him, her features almost unreadable in the soft yellow light. "You really are strange, MacGonigal. I think deep down you're a wild animal. You regret having been born human."

He chuckled. "You're right. I haven't seen anything about the human race to be especially proud of."

They went out the cabin door, bundled up against the cold. "You know," she said, "if someone had told me two months ago that I'd be going out like this, I'd have said that they were crazy." She fell silent as they walked through the blackness. "I really don't understand it. I can't reconcile killing animals with living like you do. I can't explain it, but there seems to be a contradiction there."

MacGonigal let out his breath, forming a steamy, faintly luminous cloud in front of his face. "Is that you talking as you used to be, or as you are now?"

She didn't answer immediately, but walked on as if puzzled. "I'm not sure. If I had thought about it awhile ago, I would have said that I'd never go out to kill some harmless little beast. But now it seems different. I'm not sure how."

He shifted his Winchester from hand to hand. "It's because you never saw it like this. I think that the essense of the problem is to define what's good. In spite of my cynicism, I subscribe to the proposition that 'Man is the measure.' What's good for Man is good, and what's bad for Man is bad. I live here, and it's good for me, and therefore it is good. I walk in the woods, and that is good. I pick the berries and the muscadines, and that's good. I harvest what the woods offers, including the squirrels, the deer, the rabbits, the quail, and the turkey, and that's all good. On the other hand, if I were to poison the hardwood trees, like the Forest Service does up in the National Forest, that would be wrong. That's senseless killing, and growing all those damn pine trees to make newsprint doesn't make it better."

They walked on in silence. Finally they came to a grove of hickory trees. MacGonigal showed her an old stump, brushing her hand over it so that she could feel the hulls of the nuts that littered its surface. "That's what they feed on. About dawn, they'll be out in force. We'll just get comfortable and wait for them." He took up a stand where he could see the tops of the trees against the dawn sky and motioned her to sit beside him.

They waited as the light slowly increased. Suddenly there was a crash in the foliage just above them. Sue flinched, not knowing what it was, but MacGonigal silently put a finger to his lips. In a moment a big fox squirrel jumped to a tree a little distance away. They watched as it swirled around the limb, then paused a moment, sitting on its haunches as it cracked a nut. MacGonigal had the Winchester to his shoulder, and Sue jumped at the sound of the shot. She whirled at him. "How could you do that?" He shushed her, pointing overhead. She sat still, not moving in the absolute silence that followed the shot. MacGonigal slowly brought the rifle to his shoulder again, and she followed the pointing barrel with her eyes. She could see nothing, but the scope showed MacGonigal the clear outline of a pointed ear projecting from what seemed to be a knot on a limb high above. The rifle spat again, and a furry dark shape plummeted from the tree.

"I didn't even see that one. Where was he?" MacGonigal pointed silently. She looked up doubtfully into the maze of branches and colored leaves above, then sat back and began to scan the branches, anxious to see the next squirrel.

They waited for fifteen minutes, and at last MacGonigal said, "I think we've made a little too much noise here." He strode over and picked up the two carcasses and attached them to his belt. "Two's enough, anyway. Now you'll see what it's like to have a breakfast that you've hunted for yourself."

They started back through the woods, climbing slowly up the ridge. It was full dawn, but under the trees it was almost as dark as it had been when they had come out. MacGonigal led the way again. "How can you find your way in the dark?"

"I suppose that it's all just a matter of getting used to it. I've been finding my way around at night all my life. And I know this ground pretty well. I guess I could find my way blindfolded."

The light slowly grew, and he watched her as she walked alongside him. She was a big girl, but she looked appealingly small enveloped in the big coat, like a waif. She saw him watching her and smiled at him. They walked together in silence. He had an almost ungovernable urge to put his arm around her waist, but he controlled it.

At the cabin, she watched fascinated and repelled as he skinned their quarry. "I don't see how you can touch them," she said. "It's all I can do just to look at them."

He smiled grimly. "There wouldn't be much point in it all, would there, if we didn't eat them?" He saw her wrinkle her nose. "You know, I think there's something in this. Most people wouldn't eat meat if they had to prepare it themselves—I mean do the slaughtering and dressing out. But they get others to do it for them. That's not very honest, is it?"

She bridled a little at his words. "It isn't that I don't have what it takes to do for myself, it's just that I've never done this before. Give me a chance, will you?"

He nodded his apology. "I didn't mean you. I guess I was thinking out loud. I'm sorry."

"Don't be. You're right. I really never thought about all the things that insulate me from the world. It's like when I worked with DeLisle; I knew what he was doing, but I didn't *see* it, and so I wasn't part of it, if you understand what I mean. I felt that I was clean—it was the ones who made the movies, the pimps and pushers, they were the dirty ones. I was fooling myself."

They had finished cleaning the squirrels, and she took the platter out of his hand. "I'll fix these, if you'll tell me how. You just get those things of yours and make some music for me."

He explained the simple recipe, then took the pipes down and checked the valve. She was humming as he stepped out the door and blew up the bag. As the air began to hiss through the drones, he set them with a blow of his hand and listened critically. Satisfied that they were in tune, he swung into "The Risin' o' th' Moon" and went swaggering out to the projecting rock as the strains of the old Irish war tune filled the valley.

He played for half an hour, lost to everything but the pipes, and finally turned to find her sitting on a rock near him, wrapped in his coat, hugging her knees to her breast. "That's beautiful. You play well." He bundled the pipes under his arm. "Not all that well. Most people can't tell good piping from bad."

They went back into the cabin again for breakfast. As Sue put the crisp squirrel on the table, she looked at him. He was unshaven, with his thick black hair tousled, one wavy lock straying across his forehead. "You're a strange one, Francis. I'd like to learn everything about you. You don't mind if I ask you questions?"

He looked up at her. "No, not if you don't mind if I don't answer them now and then."

"You can ask me questions, if you like. With the same stipulation, of course."

"That's not my way. I don't ask, I just observe and learn."

She began to eat, using the meal to cover her silence. At last she said, "Aren't you interested in the money? George Harris wouldn't let me alone about it."

He looked directly into her eyes. "No, I'm not. I don't care about it, and I get the impression that you don't want to talk about it. Let it stand like that."

They passed the day self-consciously, not talking directly to each other about the money or about the agreement they had. Sue asked him a few questions, where was he born, what had he done, had he ever been married. He answered directly, but asked no questions of her in return. She, however, found herself compelled to talk about herself, how her first marriage had ended, how she had remarried quickly, and how that marriage had ended. She told him about the jobs she had held, how she found herself in one low-paying secretarial job after another, and

how she had finally worked herself into an accounting job with a large corporation. She had examined
the books one night, and in a flash of intuition, had
found the solution to a major cash-flow problem the
company had. She had taken it to her boss, and in six
weeks of intensive work, they both transformed the
company's accounting practices. She had been making six hundred dollars a month, but received only a
fifty dollar raise for her inspiration. She quit in
disgust, and drifted awhile from job to job, finally
finding work with DeLisle.

When night came, he put on the tub and they
bathed, separately. Afterwards, they sat before the
fire and read in the light of the hissing Coleman
lantern, but she was unable to concentrate and soon
went up to the loft to bed.

For a long time, she lay there in the darkness,
troubled by some undefined problem. At last she
rose and wrapped the coat around her and came
down. The living area was empty, but the light shone
from under the door to the bedroom. She knocked
shyly, and he answered as if expecting her. She
entered to find him in bed, a huge volume lying open
on the covers.

They talked aimlessly for a while, but suddenly
there were no more words between them.
MacGonigal put his lips against hers, feeling the
yielding firmness of them. His hand grasped her
buttocks, squeezing them together. "No," she said,
"don't do that. Please don't do that."

He ignored her, and began to explore her neck
and shoulders with his lips, working his way slowly
down. He pulled the coat away and began to kiss her

nipples. She pulled his head down, holding him closely.

When they were finished, they lay in each other's arms. He held her closely, tenderly. At last she spoke. "You did that just right. You know just what to do. You never touched me, never made a move until I was ready."

He reached out and stroked her face. "I didn't need to." He gently kissed her on the lips. "I wasn't out to score with you. I learned to like you and respect you, and I knew that if anything like this were to happen between us, it would happen at its own time." He pulled her to him and ran his hands gently over her hips and buttocks. She put her head against his chest. "Rub my back," she said.

She lay silently, enjoying the feel of his hands on her, moving slightly as he squeezed her buttocks, massaged her legs. For a long time, he worked over her body, and when he finished, she was asleep. He lay down beside her and pulled the covers over the two of them and took her in his arms.

III.

The light streaming through the gable window woke her the next morning. She lay breathing quietly in his arms, and suddenly she was awake, nuzzling gently against his chest. She looked up into his face, her eyes wide and tender, her voice tinged with concern. "Have you been like this all night? Didn't you sleep at all?"

He held her to him, feeling the length of her body against his, and smoothed away the strands of fair brown hair that strayed over her face. "No. I stayed awake. I was on guard. I wanted to watch over you."

She pushed her face into his chest. "I'm glad," she murmured. "You make me feel so safe. But you need sleep too. You can't stay awake every night."

He made no answer, but put his lips to the top of her head, kissing her gently. After a while she stirred in his arms and turned her face up to his. Her hands began to steal over his body, and soon he could stand it no longer. He bore her backward and positioned himself over her, his lips still pressed to hers.

She was strong, lithe, and she used her strength. He could feel her straining against him, her hips moving under him, her long legs wrapped around him. There was a clumsy, tender reluctance about him, as if he were afraid that he might hurt her, but she drew him on. Her lips were against his ear, murmuring, urging him on, driving him beyond the point of control. He lost himself completely in her, and still she urged him on, clung to him and whispered fiercely to him.

When at last they drew apart, nearly exhausted, she smiled at him. "I'm not made of glass, you know. You treat me as if you're afraid I might break."

He smiled, a little guiltily. "I suppose I am. I was worried that I might hurt you."

She put her arms tightly around him. "Hold me tight."

He wrapped his arms around her and pulled her to his chest. "Tighter. Can't you do better than that?" He tensed his muscles until he feared that her ribs would crack. She mocked him, "Is that as strong as you are? You'll have to do better." He squeezed as tightly as he dared, and still she mocked him. At last, afraid that he really would hurt her, he released her. He could see the sharp imprint of the hairs of his chest etched in the tender skin between her breasts. "That's enough," he said. "You're scaring me."

They lay together for a while longer, as the sunshine streamed through the gable window and motes of dust danced in the light. At last she raised herself up on her elbow and looked down at him, her long hair trailing down his chest. "I was afraid of you, you know. You're so big. I've always stayed away from big men. But you're a pussycat. You won't hurt me."

He stroked her hair. "No," he said, "I won't hurt

you. Not ever. It's not in me to hurt you."

They lay together a while longer, and at last she said "Shall we have a bath?"

He got up and walked naked into the living area and built up the fire in the stove. He put water on to heat, then climbed back into the still-warm bed. They pulled the covers over them and talked and played gentle lover's games while they waited for their bath to heat.

After a while, they got up again and stood in the tin bathtub, pouring water over each other and soaping each other down. He marveled at the direct, frank way she sought out the private places of his body and washed them. There was no false modesty to her, no coyness, but an open enjoyment that they shared.

They stepped out of the tub and dried each other. MacGonigal enveloped her in the towel and gently caressed her until she was dry. When it was her turn, she scrubbed his body with the towel until the skin glowed. He laughed at the intensity of her attack. As she climbed the stairs to the loft to get her clothes, he stood and marveled at the grace of her movements. He was enthralled by the lines of her body, by the cat-like movements she made.

He was standing in front of the mirror, still naked, shaving, when she came down the stairs. "What are you waiting for, lazybones? Let's go for a ride. Don't shave. You'll look a lot better with a beard than you do with stubble."

He wiped the lather off his face and pulled on the jeans she had thrown at him. Grinning, he finished dressing, unbuttoning his jeans to tuck in his shirt. She gaped at him in mock horror. "My God, the man's insatiable!" She gave him a lascivious leer. "Control yourself for a while, big boy, and I'll take care of you tonight."

She was already at the door. He swept the Colt .357 off the shelf and threaded the holster on his belt. She watched him. "You're going to have to teach me how to use that thing one of these days."

He didn't answer, but slipped his arm around her waist. She twisted out of his grasp and ran across to the tack room. In a moment she was back outside with a coffee can in each hand. "I'll race you to the paddock!"

He ran alongside of her, his mind more on the way her legs flew over the ground than on the race. They pulled up at the gate, panting a little. The horses had seen them coming, and were cantering across the paddock, tails flying erect like plumes. They crowded around her as she poured the feed in the trough. She wrapped her arms around Harry's neck. "Don't think that you're my only lover around here," she said, sticking her tongue out at him.

When the horses finished eating, they led them to the tack room. Sue rummaged in the big tack box for the comb and brushes and began to groom Harry while MacGonigal carried out saddles, blankets, and bridles. She stood back and watched critically as he placed the blanket on Harry, then heaved the saddle up and slid it back. "Why do you do it that way? Put it on too far forward, then slide it back like that?"

"Makes sure that the hair isn't knotted up under

the saddle. If you put it on too far back and then push it forward, it rucks the hair up and makes his back sore," he said, as he reached under Harry's belly for the girth. She took the brushes and comb over to Smoke and began to groom him as MacGonigal finished with Harry. He backed the big bay away from the shed and slipped one arm around his neck, then began working the bridle up his head. "Let me do that," she said. MacGonigal, wordless, passed the bridle to her and went to work on Smoke.

As he worked, he could hear her dancing around with Harry. He put the saddle on and settled it, then tightened and knotted the girth, then turned to see what was going on. Harry was being obstreperous, holding his head up and refusing the bit. Sue hung with one arm around his neck, her feet off the ground. MacGonigal laughed, then grabbed the re-calcitrant's forelock and pulled his head down. "Give me the bridle," he said. She passed it to him, and he slipped it up over Harry's ears. With his weight on its neck, the big bay was much quieter. He held the head down and forced the lips apart. "See that gap between the front and back teeth? Put your fingers in there. He'll open his mouth, and you can slip the bit in."

She grasped the horse's lower jaw while MacGonigal held its head and slowly forced the bit between its teeth. MacGonigal straightened out the curb and buckled the throat latch, then handed her the reins. She gathered them up and, wrapping her hands around the saddle horn, swung into the saddle, barely touching the stirrups. From the saddle high above she grinned down at him. "How was that?" she asked.

"Not bad," he replied as he heaved himself off the ground and dropped into Smoke's saddle. "In a little while, you'll be riding like an Indian."

They cantered up the trail, going over the ridge and down the other side until they struck Mozart Road. MacGonigal reined up and they hung back in the woods for a moment before he led her out onto the verge of the gravel road. There was no traffic, and they cantered along for a quarter of a mile before he began to get nervous and plunged into the brush again. "Where are we going now?" she called out to him.

He drew rein and waited for her to catch up. "I thought we'd cut across country and I'd show you why I love these hills. We'll only go a few miles."

"All right, but let's not stay out too late. For one thing, I'm hungry. We haven't had any breakfast, you know."

They rode a half mile or more, then turned out of the dim trail they were following and rode across country until they reached the highway. MacGonigal put his horse to the bar ditch and jumped it. Sue looked dubious, but Harry made up her mind for her. Having seen Smoke jump the ditch, he simply gathered his haunches and sprung across, with Sue holding to the saddle horn.

"Whoops!" she said, as Harry left the ground and then gave an explosive "Whoof!" as he landed on the other side. It took her a moment to regain her composure.

"I didn't know he was going to do that! I don't think I'm quite ready for that sort of thing yet."

MacGonigal grinned. "Stick with me, m'lass, and I'll have you sailing over fences and ditches like a deer in no time."

She gave him a dirty look. "Well, next time, tell me so I can be ready."

He laughed again. "If I'd told you, you probably wouldn't have done it. This way, you know you can do it. Next time, it'll be a snap."

"I just hope the snap isn't my neck breaking!"

They rode a long way in silence. At last Susan said, "Mac, why did you take this job? I mean, you don't need to take me in, and, well . . ."

"Beats the hell out of me. I usually would have more sense than to let George Harris talk me into anything."

She was quiet for a long time. "It couldn't be the money, could it?"

He grinned. "A few hundred bucks a week will come in right handy. Of course, I'm not denying that the pleasure of your company also has some effect on me."

She turned in the saddle and looked directly at him. "Mac, did George tell you how much money is involved?"

"George said that you took this guy you worked for, what's his name, for a bundle."

"DeLisle," she said. "That's his name. DeLisle. Did George tell you how much it was?"

"No," he said, shortly, and rode on.

"Aren't you even curious, Mac?"

"Hell, yes, I'm curious. But I don't want to

know." He paused a moment. "Look, I know that what's happened between us gives you the right to find out just exactly what kind of guy I am, so I'll answer you straight out. I don't want your money —except for what we've agreed you'll pay for staying with me."

"And that's it?"

"That's it." He shook Smoke's reins and rode on. "Sue, I'm not all that callous. It's just my way of telling you to keep quiet about the money. I'm not interested in it, and I don't want to hear about it."

"Did George give you any idea of how much there is?"

"George said that he didn't really know, but he thought that it was about three million."

She reined her horse to a stop and sat there looking at him. "And what about you, Mac," she said flatly. "What do you think?"

He backed the roan and returned her stare. "I don't think anything. I just live here. I agreed to keep you with me, and that's all that concerns me. But if anyone's after you, I have to know why so I can guess how much danger there is. Beyond that, I don't care."

"Are you sure about that? I like you, Mac, maybe more than any man I ever met, but I can't help wondering about what you're really thinking."

He rode forward until he was knee to knee with her and looked down into her eyes. "Sue, I have everything I want, except one thing. And money can't buy that. I don't give a big rat's ass about how much you've got. You can believe that or not, it's your choice. If you don't trust me, if you want me to take you somewhere and put you on a plane, fine."

"Look, Mac, I don't want to leave here and I don't want to have a fight with you. I really trust you, or I think that I do, but most people would do anything to get their hands on the amount of money I've got hidden."

"Yeah, I heard all about Blue Larry, or whatever his name was. And if you want my opinion, to get George Harris to stick his neck out for you, you must really have a bundle." He unstrapped the revolver and handed it to her. "From now on, you carry this thing. Any time you think I'm dealing from the bottom of the deck, you can let the hammer down on me."

She kept her hands on the reins. "Is this some kind of grandstand play, Mac? Are you trying to bluff me, to prove that I can trust you?"

He thrust the end of his belt back through the holster loop and rebuckled his belt. "Come on." He wrenched the roan's neck around and started up the trail. "We won't settle anything this way. I'll tell you what," he said over his shoulder, "you get the money, and I'll jam it up that cute little ass of yours."

They rode down the valley and dismounted at the cabin. "Go on inside. I'll take care of the horses."

"No, I'll help you. I didn't mean to make you mad, Mac. I'm sorry."

"There's not a goddamned thing to be sorry about. You're worried about your money, and I would be, too, if I was in your shoes. Forget it."

He was silent as they unsaddled the horses and put them away. She tried subtly to break through his reserve. They headed back to the cabin and he stoked the stove. Without a word, she went to the pantry and busied herself rearranging the shelves. MacGonigal laid and lit the fire in the fireplace and then went up the stairs to the loft and busied himself with an article he had been working on sporadically for several weeks. He sat in front of the keyboard for several minutes, but couldn't get started. He heard her step on the stairs.

"Mac?" she called softly. "Mac? I'm a little stiff from that ride. Would you rub the kinks out for me?"

He turned and saw her standing at the head of the stairs. She was naked, with her soft brown hair falling in a fan to her waist. MacGonigal caught his breath and rose, knocking over the chair. He reached for her, then drew back. "I smell like a horse," he said.

"So do I," she replied, "but don't get any ideas, I just want a back rub."

He put his hands on her upper arms and pulled her gently toward the bed. "No," she said, "not here. Downstairs, on the rug in front of the fire."

He lifted her off her feet and cradled her in his arms. She languidly put her arms around his neck as he started downstairs. He crossed the living area with her and put her down gently on the bearskin. He began to unbutton his shirt. "Oh, no," she said, as she rolled over. "None of that. I just want a massage."

He looked down at her, at the long, clean sweep of her back, her softly rising buttocks, her long, tapered legs, and the cloud of light brown hair that spread around her. He pulled off his shirt and tossed it aside, then sank to his knees, straddling her, and put his hands on her shoulders.

He lost track of time, completely absorbed in his task, lost in her silken nearness. "You'd better take those jeans off," she murmured, "they're rubbing me raw."

He rose, kicked off his boots, and pulled his jeans and shorts off. Naked, he straddled her again, and began to work his way slowly down her body. The yielding firmness of her back muscles under his hands fascinated him. He sunk into an almost trancelike state, but he could feel himself erect and pressing against her buttocks. He was in a state of almost disembodied euphoria, one part of him slowly and blissfully working over her body, another part wild with excitement and barely under control.

He slid back, his hands now on her buttocks. She lay with her head to the side, pillowed on her hands, her eyes closed, her face reposed, as if asleep. He gently kneaded and rubbed her buttocks, then continued his journey down her long legs, massaging her thighs and calves. Her muscles, tense at first, were loose and relaxed. He worked his way back up her legs and slid his hand between her thighs. She raised her hips for him, and slowly, agonizingly slowly, he entered her.

As they moved together, she drew up first one knee, then the other under herself, so that she lay crouched beneath him. At last she raised herself up on her hands and knees. MacGonigal knelt behind her, marveling at the long, delicate expanse of her back, the cascade of her hair as she hung her head down. He put his hands on her flared hips and pulled her to him, controlling her movements and his. He ran his hand under her, along her stomach to her breasts where they hung free. Her breathing was rasping now, and he could feel her climax build. He himself was completely beyond control, wrapped in intensity. He felt her shudder and slowly slide forward onto the rug, and he went forward with her, spent, released. He cradled her gently, protectively, in his arms and put his lips against her hair.

They lay close together for a long time on the bearskin, with the fire throwing flickering golden and ruddy tones across their bodies. Sue ran her hands over the rough fur, smoothing then ruffling it. "Mac, did you kill this bear?"

"Mm-hmm. I told you I did. Are you still mad at me for doing it?"

She pressed herself against him. "No. I'm beginning to understand why you did it." She turned over in his arms and pulled a little away from him, still in his encircling arms. "Tell me about it. Tell me how you killed him."

He looked at her, running his hand along her side and thigh. "It was about six or seven years ago. I was in Alaska—great hunting there, lots of bears, both black and grizzly."

"Is this a black or a grizzly?"

"Well, he's a grizzly, although they say that grizzlies taken near the coast are officially called brownie bears. Brownies are the same kind of bear as grizzlies, but for the most part brownies are bigger. I guess it's all the fish they eat."

She pouted a little. "Well, what kind of bear is he? You won't even tell me."

"He's a brownie, and a big one. I hunted him for about a week. There were four of us, we took two canoes into the area, paddled for three days, then walked about fifteen miles and set up camp. There was bear sign all over, and the other guys got theirs in the first couple of days. I had a chance at a smaller bear, but by then we'd seen this fellow, so I passed on the other bears."

"You wanted the biggest one." There was something about her tone and her expression that made something stir inside him.

"Yeah, that's right. The first time I saw him, I wanted him. He was wary as hell, though. Kept to real thick alders. That's tough going, especially when you know there's a bear in there. Tends to make a fellow a little cautious."

"Why is that?"

"Well, you can't see more than a few feet. You're liable to walk right up on him, and that could be bad."

"But you had a gun. You had all the advantages."

"Yeah. I had that .30-06 over there." He pointed to the racked rifles on the wall. "But a brownie's tough. There are lots of cases of a brownie absorbing a half a dozen .30-06 rounds and still outliving the fellow that shot him by an hour or more."

She got up and walked naked to the wall of racked

guns. She put her hand on one. "Is this the one you used?"

"No. The one above it. 'Old Bill,' I call it, after Old Bill Ruger. He's the fellow that makes them. Or rather his company makes them."

She took the weapon down from the wall and examined it. The polished walnut stock contrasted with her honey-colored skin, and MacGonigal felt strange things stirring inside himself as he watched her. She brought it to her shoulder and pretended to aim at a spot over the fireplace. "It's big. I'm not sure I could handle it. Would you teach me to shoot it?"

"Sure," he said. She walked back to the rug and sat cross-legged, the rifle in her lap. "Go on. Tell me how you killed the bear."

He put his hand on her bare thigh and stroked it gently. "We tracked him into a patch of alders. I could hear him in there, and went in after him. One of the other guys went with me, as a backup. The others stayed out. You don't want too many people in a tight spot like that. If things get exciting, they get in each other's way.

"Anyhow, we followed him a little ways. He'd move whenever we got too close. We never did see him, but I guess we got to within about ten yards of him a time or two.

"We started getting on his nerves. Brownies have a terrible temper, and he didn't like being crowded. All of a sudden, he came crashing through the brush at us. I got off one shot—all I could see was a patch of hair—and he was right in the middle of us.

"Brownies can outrun a horse, and they're as

quick as a cat, but somehow we managed to get out of his way. He knocked Frank, my backup, spinning, and whirled on a dime. I shot him in the boiler room at about fifteen feet. I guess that slowed him down, because I had time to chamber another round. He was right on top of me then, and I just shoved the muzzle in his jaws and fired. That put him down for good.

"After that, we had a hell of a time. Frank had a broken arm, and his scalp was cut. We boiled some water and I sewed up his scalp. Then we had to skin the bear and pack out the hide and skull. With all the gear we had, and the other hides and skulls we had to pack, it took about four trips to reach the canoes. And Frank couldn't pack anything, of course, or handle a paddle. It was pretty rough on old Frank —took five days to get him to a doctor. And there was a hell of a lot of paperwork."

She put her hand over his. "And that's how you killed him, put the gun in his mouth and shot him?"

"Yeah. If you look, you can see where the taxidermist repaired some of the teeth that were shot off."

She put the rifle aside and crawled over to the head of the monster and peered in his mouth. MacGonigal watched her, savoring the graceful, flowing lines of her body. "Poor bear," she said. "I guess that's somebody else that's learned not to fuck with MacGonigal."

MacGonigal laughed and grabbed her ankle, dragging her backwards. He put his head between her breasts and said, "That doesn't hold true in every case."

She looked down at him in surprise. "My God, MacGonigal, you're insatiable!" MacGonigal, his mouth otherwise occupied, did not answer.

Later she gathered herself and rose from the rug. "It's already dark outside," she said. "Do you realize that we haven't eaten anything all day?"

MacGonigal stretched. "Do you care?"

"Yes, I care! You may be able to go days without eating, but this girl needs regular meals."

He surrendered. "OK. I'll go take care of the horses, and you fix us something to eat."

He got up and pulled on his jeans and shirt, then sat on the rug to pull on his boots. He grabbed the horsey sweater hanging beside the door and went out to check on the animals.

He threw down a bale of hay for the horses and brought them an extra ration of feed, fed the chickens, remembering that he had not looked for eggs for two days, then closed up the barn and tack room. When he got back, she had supper on the table. He sat down to a meal of steak and potatoes, surprised to find that he was suddenly hungry. They ate in silence for a while, and finally Sue said, "Do you think we should make some kind of decision about what we should do now?"

He chewed it over. "I don't think we need to decide anything right now. I'm not one of those who believe that you should do something, even if it's wrong. Let's wait a while and see what develops."

She nodded, "I'll sleep with you tonight. I'll probably sleep with you tomorrow night. But one of these nights I'll want to sleep alone. Sometimes I have to be alone, that's just the way I am. I don't want you to misunderstand."

"I won't. I found out a long time ago that being with a woman, liking her, being interested in the same things, being able to talk to her, is probably the most important thing. And sex is better with some-one you respect; it gives you a different perspec-tive."

She reached across the table and squeezed his hand. "Come on, love, let's do the dishes." He got up and helped her clear the table, then put on the water to heat. While they waited, they sat together on the sofa, quietly enjoying each other's company. At last she said, "Don't you want to know about the money?"

"Let's stay away from that subject; it starts fights. I think I could handle a fight, but I'm not sure I'm quite up to the making up that follows."

She pinched his side. "Don't get smart, Mac." He winced. "Seriously," she said, "I want to tell you about the money. Do you want to listen or not?"

"Not. I'm willing to listen to anything you have to say, but the money is none of my business. I told you that. Talk about something else."

"What I want to talk about now is the money. Really, Mac, I need to talk about it. I won't, if you really don't want to listen, but I feel like I have to tell you."

He sighed. "Okay, tell me. But remember, I told you that I didn't want to hear. Don't come around later, accusing me of worming it out of you."

"I won't. I promise. But I need your mind. I have

things figured out pretty well, but maybe you can look over what I've done and find some flaws in it."

He settled himself on the sofa. "Okay, I'll listen. But I want you to remember that I tried not to. The deal we have is a straight salary, not a piece of the action, and I don't want you accusing me later of trying to cut myself in."

"I understand," she said. "I'll remember that I asked you to listen. But I may need your help for a long time, and I think you really need to know what went down.

"When I first went to work for DeLisle," she went on, "it was a legitimate job. I don't mean that I was led into the shady side of the business, but at first all I did was handle the legitimate books—the magazine sales and that sort of thing.

"They were pretty raunchy magazines," she continued, "but legal. Of course, I knew that DeLisle was into some crooked business as soon as I went to work for him. You only had to look at him and you could tell that he'd never made an honest dollar in his life, except by accident, or as a cover for something else.

"Anyhow, little by little, I began taking over other accounts. DeLisle was a real paranoid, and he didn't trust anyone. But he couldn't keep the books himself —he was too lazy and disorganized. And he was paranoid about the IRS, afraid they would find holes in his system and bust him. And they could have, too. I showed him lots of places where they could really put him away.

"I think that's when he started to trust me a little,

when I showed him how vulnerable he was. He seemed surprised that I didn't use it for blackmail, or turn him in for a reward.

"Anyway, I already knew enough by then to be dangerous to him. He gave me a few more things to do, mostly with the porno accounts, at first.

"Now don't get me wrong. When I said that I wasn't led or lured into anything, I meant it. But I didn't really have any idea of just how bad it was. I mean, DeLisle didn't just buy and sell pornography, he made it. He had a whole system, pimps and chicken hawks cruising the bus stops and other places to pick up kids. Runaway kids were kind of the basis of the thing; the pimps and chicken hawks would pick them up, take care of them, break them in, and DeLisle would use them in his films and things. And if a kid wouldn't cooperate, well, there was always Larry. I didn't learn about him until later, though.

"DeLisle wanted me in with him. I mean, he wanted me to act in his flicks, go to bed with him, and run his business for him. He was always after me. I'm no prude, you know that by now, but he made me sick, really physically sick. But if I hadn't been so valuable to him, I think he might have got his way. He had methods of getting people to do what he wanted, if you see what I mean." She shuddered, and for an instant MacGonigal saw red. He was momentarily consumed with hatred for a man he had never seen before.

"Anyway, I was in pretty deep already. I mean, I hadn't broken too many laws. I don't think I'd have been convicted, except for maybe helping him evade his taxes, and they couldn't prove that. But I knew a lot about his operations. I was dangerous to him. I think if I'd tried to walk out on him . . . well, I didn't know then about Larry, but I knew enough to know that DeLisle wouldn't let me go.

"I kept getting in deeper and deeper. All the money, from the prostitution, the porno, the drugs, and a lot of other rackets, was flowing through me. DeLisle introduced me to Nazario, and he tried to put the make on me, and he would have done it, too. DeLisle I could handle, but Nazario was different.

"I guess he had other irons in the fire, because he didn't push too hard. But every time we had a meeting, the way he looked at me . . . I knew that sooner or later . . . well, I had to figure some way out.

"That was the problem. There wasn't a way out. They had connections all over the country, and there was no place to run. All I could do was stall and hope to stretch it out as long as I could. But I knew that one day Nazario would have me, and when he got tired of me, he'd start passing me around to his friends. I couldn't take that.

"I finally figured out that money was the key. If I had enough money, I could buy all the protection I needed. And lots of money went through my hands. All I had to do was see that some of it stuck.

"It took some time to set up. To be honest, I was thinking about it before I met Nazario. But he really gave me the motivation to go ahead.

"DeLisle had about twenty-seven companies, and

he used them to launder his money. Some of them were fairly legitimate—contracting companies and so on. Some of them were part of his actual operations—printing shops, film processors, and things like that.

"Anyhow, I set up a few more companies for him. By the time I left, he had sixty-eight corporations, some of them real, and some of them just paper. And they did business with each other—the flow was really complex—and I had to stay on top of it every minute.

"While I was setting up his corporations, I set up a few for myself. I started selling to DeLisle. At first, I'd buy films from him, stash them, and let them cool off, then change the titles and sell them back through another company—with a markup.

"I got the money for the first buys from DeLisle and Nazario themselves. What I'd do is make a payment from one of their companies to another—I was always doing that, and they didn't have the capability to follow all the transactions. But when I drew the money out of one corporation, I'd circulate it through my corporation. I'd just hold it there for a day or so, then pay it into one of DeLisle's other concerns. But when I did, I'd pull the same stunt with another pair of their companies. So I always had money in my company's account."

MacGonigal shook his head. "That must have kept you hopping."

"It did. At one time, I had over thirty transactions going, involving seven of my companies and about twenty-five of DeLisle's. And I couldn't afford to make a mistake. Of course, I had a backup system. As soon as I got enough ahead, I put a little cash aside, so that I could make a spot deposit if anything went wrong.

"After a while, I began to branch out. I bought into a few legitimate businesses—I learned how working for DeLisle. I even used some of his muscle once or twice, when a laundry I owned was being vandalized. The muscle thought the orders came from DeLisle.

"I also opened a legitimate film processing business. I bought the equipment through one of DeLisle's corporations and sold it to several others, cutting the price each time. He thought it was a tax dodge. The last company that bought it was a paper dummy I had set up. As soon as I got the stuff, I liquidated the company so it couldn't be traced.

"Invoices were really tough to handle, but some of DeLisle's people were ripping him off. I knew about it, but kept quiet. They were clumsy about it, and I let him stumble on them, with a hint or two from me. Then I 'adjusted' the books to account for the thefts. Of course, I chalked up a lot that wasn't stolen.

"The funny thing about it all was that DeLisle would never let me handle cash. He would brag to Nazario, 'She's straight. I don't ever let her get her hands on real money.' And the damn fools would laugh about it. They figured that with just the books, I couldn't touch the money.

"After a while, I got quite a bit of reserve capital, and I started siphoning it off. I had a few little businesses that I put money into—I suppose that's all gone now, because I'll probably never be able to surface and claim it, unless George can fix me up with a new identity that they can't crack."

MacGonigal got his pipe and began to charge it. He struck a light and held the flame over the bowl, drawing it downward into the tobacco. He took a few puffs, then tamped the pipe and relit it. "I wouldn't pin too much hope on George, honey. I don't think he can pull it off. And if he does, he's liable to take you for everything."

"No, he won't. I'm a lot smarter than George Harris. I can handle him."

"Maybe so. But he'll try, I can guarantee that. But you may never get to test that guarantee—I think that if you hang in with George, you're committing suicide, if these guys are really after you. But you do what you think best, don't let me influence you."

She looked at him. "Do you have any better ideas?"

He puffed on the pipe. "If you mean, am I angling to replace George, the answer is no. You stay here until you think it's safe to leave. Then you go, or do whatever you want. F. X. MacGonigal wants no part of your money."

"Not even if I told you that it's a lot more than even DeLisle thinks? Not even if most of it is stashed where I can get my hands on it in perfect safety?"

MacGonigal took the pipe out of his mouth and regarded it closely. "Is this some kind of test? If it is, I'm not taking the bait. I don't want the money, I wouldn't take it if you stacked it on the table in front of me. But if you can get it safely, what the hell are you on the run for? Why don't you just get it and skip the country?"

She smiled. "There is one little problem. I can get most of it, but it will take a while. I have to establish an identity somewhere, an identity that will allow me to make large transactions without attracting attention. I couldn't just wire for four or five million dollars from the nearest telegraph office without a lot of comment. And that's what they'll be looking for, somebody who doesn't have any business having a lot of money suddenly making sizable transactions."

"How the hell will they know about it?"

"Simple. The drug trade owns banks. They can get information through normal channels. As soon as I pop up, they'll check me out. That's why I've got to have a plausible identity, to keep anyone in the financial world from remarking on it when I get the money."

"And how in the hell are you going to accomplish that trick? No, on second thought, don't answer. I don't want to know."

"Oh, come on, Mac," she teased, "don't you want to know where the money is? Don't you have any curiosity at all?"

"Yeah, I've got my share. But I can restrain it in this case."

"Well, I'll tell you anyway. It's in banks, banks that are controlled by the drug trade. A lot of it's in the Bahamas."

He sat up. "Why in the hell would you want to put it there? That's really sticking your head in the lion's mouth."

"You're right. But there were two reasons; one was that those banks can be manipulated, that's why the drug traders own them. The other reason is that I didn't expect to be caught.

"You see, I set up a second string of companies, completely separate from the ones I used to milk DeLisle and Nazario. I channeled the money through them into the banks. I made sure that nobody questioned those companies, but when I start draining their assets, somebody's going to notice it, and I've got to have a good, solid cover."

"But won't the fact that they're inactive right now draw attention?"

"No, because they're not inactive. I've set things up so that deposits and withdrawals are made regularly. It's done automatically, just a matter of shuffling assets around to give the appearance of normal business."

"So you've got the money right under their noses. A great scheme. Except that you can't touch it," he said, with a trace of sarcasm.

"Oh, I'll get it, sooner or later. Don't worry about that. If George doesn't come through for me, I'll find some other way."

MacGonigal blew a cloud of smoke. "So with all this fancy footwork, how'd you get caught?"

She grimaced, as if the memory were painful. "I got greedy. The cash flow went down, and Nazario began to lean on DeLisle, really hard, too. The skimming that I put him onto explained a part of it, but when it continued, he really started to get desperate.

"I really didn't care. I thought I had covered my tracks, but I didn't count on him being as paranoid as he was. He started to check out suppliers and outlets, and he found one place that I had used, and that's when the roof fell in.

"He was like a wild man. He called me over to his place—I didn't think anything of it, because we did a lot of business right in his apartment—and started screaming at me. I played innocent and just screamed right back, and that's where I made my mistake. He had Blue Larry in the next room, and when Larry heard the screaming, he came busting out and knocked me flat. When I came to, I was naked and tied up.

"I knew that they were going to kill me then, so I didn't care what I said. I admitted that I'd taken the money. They tried to get me to tell them where it was, but I wouldn't tell."

"That must have taken guts, to hold out like that."

"No, it was just a matter of knowing that whether I told or not, I'd get the same thing. Why give them the money, when they're going to torture you anyway. I mean, once I came to and saw Blue Larry, I knew how it was going to end."

"But George got you out."

"Yes, George got me out. And don't think I'm not grateful to him for it. But at the same time, I'm not a fool. I'll see to it that he gets a reward, but I'm not about to turn the whole thing over to him."

"Well, that's what he's got planned, if I know George."

"I've got plans of my own," she said, rising.

"Right now, my plans call for you dragging out that tub and filling it with hot water. I'm going to give you a good scrub before we go to bed. I lied to you—men who smell like horses really don't turn me on."

IV.

"You must have a ladyfriend, Francis. This is the first time I've been able to cut your hair without running a curry comb through it first."

MacGonigal, swathed in barber's cloth, relaxed in the chair. "Hell, Clarence, can't a man try to look halfway decent without you starting all kinds of gossip? It so happens that I do have a ladyfriend —maybe more than one—but I don't care for the whole town to know it."

Clarence chuckled. He'd been cutting Mac-Gonigal's hair for a long time. In fact, he had just started his shop when the elder MacGonigal had retired to his dream farm in the Ozarks from years of rattling around the globe as an oilfield worker. MacGonigal, a teenager at the time, had come in for a haircut every two weeks until he joined the Army, and had ever after made it a point to stop by Clarence's shop for a trim whenever he came home on leave. When John Francis MacGonigal died, and his little farm was sold to pay the inheritance taxes, a couple of years passed when MacGonigal didn't see Clarence. But after he bought his own place, he

dropped by whenever he came to look over his
property. Since he had retired and moved onto the
place, he stopped by whenever he was in town
—which was seldom enough.

"Well, it's about time you started looking over the
fillies. You ain't getting any younger, you know.
How old are you now, Francis?"

"I'm twelve years younger than you are, you
butchering old coot. But I've got a lot more miles on
me than you have."

Clarence chuckled. "That's what I mean, boy.
You're all full of piss and vinegar now, but wait until
you get to my age."

MacGonigal had to grin at that. Clarence had
been telling him that since the first time he came
home on leave, a buck-assed private. But Clarence
was an old man, and had been for more than twenty
years. His hollow chest, wide hips, and pot belly
gave him the appearance of a bowling pin. His face
was covered with tiny, ruptured veins, and ever since
he could remember, MacGonigal had been fascinated by Clarence's arms. They were flabby, with a
rope of fat on the underside. MacGonigal wondered
how a man could work all day with his arms at chest
level, and not have some sort of muscles in his arms.

"Clarence, your problem is that you're lazy. If
you'd do some real work, that pot would disappear,
and you'd feel twenty years younger."

The barber snorted, his scissors clipping away.
"Yeah, Francis, you been saying that, and it's all
right for you young ones. But us older fellows got to
be careful.

"Now, you take yourself. You're hard as a rock,

don't look near your age. But you got to watch it. Don't get tied in with a young woman. She'll kill you sure."

He swept the cloth off with a flourish. "And if you're messin' around with two of 'em, like you're lettin' on, well, I reckon the next time I cut your hair, I'll have to come to you."

MacGonigal looked quizzically at him. "What's that supposed to mean, Clarence?"

The barber's saggy jowls spread in a grin. "It'll be to the undertaker's. That's the only time the customer doesn't come to me."

MacGonigal dug out his wallet and tendered a five dollar bill. Clarence, who either didn't realize how much he could make if he called himself a hair stylist and charged what barbers charged in more sophisticated places, or else knew, but dared not try it for fear of being called a faggot, rang up the transaction on his old cash register and gave him a handful of change.

"Just you mind what I tell you, boy. Them women will screw you into an early grave."

MacGonigal went out the door, then leaned back in. "Yeah, but what a way to go!"

Letting the door close behind him, he swaggered down the street, whistling as he went. People turned to stare at the bearded Irishman whistling "Garry Owen," and MacGonigal waved gaily to them, gathering smiles in return. "Where's your bagpipes, Francis? Play us a tune." MacGonigal broke off his whistling. "Left them home, Charles. I'll bring them next time I come."

He walked along the main street of the small town,

greeting friends here and there and making his purchases in various stores, dropping them off in the cab of his pickup truck whenever they became inconvenient to carry. He didn't bother to lock the truck. Nobody would steal in such a small town, and nobody in his right mind would steal from MacGonigal.

At Lancaster's Hardware he bought several cannisters of 3031 rifle powder, plus an assortment of bullets, mostly in .30 and .22 caliber. He stacked his purchases beside the cash register. "Looks like you're planning on doing some shooting, Mac."

"Yeah, Henry, I am. I've been thinking about going back to Alaska for a hunt. Which reminds me, you got any .338s? Two-twenty-five grain, Nosler partition jackets, if you've got 'em."

"That sounds like bear medicine, Mac. Wish I was going with you."

"Wish you were, too, Henry, but I think maybe I've already got me a hunting partner."

Henry grinned at him. "Yeah, I'd heard that. Who's the lucky girl? Does she know what she's getting into?"

MacGonigal returned the grin. "Damn, news travels fast around here. Who'd you hear it from?"

"Here and about. 'Course I didn't believe it until I saw you just now. You don't look like the same man. I mean, you got your hair combed, and you got clean clothes on."

"It's the beard, Henry, that's what it is."

"Hell it's the beard! You've been taken in hand by some sweet thing. Good thing, too. You were getting to the point where I was beginning to worry about you."

"Well it's good to know that somebody worries about me."

Henry gave him a crooked grin. "Everybody worries about you, MacGonigal. Some folks worry that you'll fall off the cliff some night when you're drunk, and some folks worry that you won't." He paused. "Now what was it you wanted? Oh, yeah, .338s. I think I got some." He searched through a few drawers behind the counter and produced a small, heavy box. "Just one box. That do you? You plan to shoot more than a hundred bears?"

MacGonigal snorted. "You're funny, Henry. No, I only plan to shoot one, if I even go. But I want to work up a good load, accurate, and with a full charge. Commercial loads don't reach the full potential of the cartridge."

"Well, if I was going after a bear, I wouldn't carry any ammo that I loaded myself. I'd want the best stuff the factory makes," Henry said, as he rang up the sale.

MacGonigal tendered a bill. "I made that mistake once. I had to feed the bear my rifle. I'm getting too old for that kind of nonsense, as Clarence just reminded me."

"Clarence, that crazy old coot! I swear, Mac, he's as crazy as you are."

MacGonigal hefted his purchases. "Yeah, probably so. Take care." He sauntered out and put the bag with the others in the cab of the pickup. He climbed in and started the motor and pulled out into the brick-paved main street. In a few minutes, he was climbing out of town, motoring up the twisting road that led up into the mountains. At the last curve before the top, he turned, as he always did, for a last look back at the town. It was a sort of symbolic taking leave of civilization for him, for although the town only numbered some six thousand people, to him it represented a way of life to be avoided as much as if it had been New York City.

As he headed out of town, he saw two teen-age girls on horses riding along the shoulder of the road. He slowed to pass them, when he heard an engine behind him. In his mirror, MacGonigal saw a green pickup coming fast. The truck roared around him, honking and swerving. As the truck approached the two kids, it swerved again and the passenger leaned out of the window and thumped the door, yelling. The horses shied, almost throwing their two young riders. As the truck went on down the road, MacGonigal got a glimpse of a pimply face with long, tangled blonde hair.

He pulled his pickup off the road. "Are you kids all right?"

The older of the two had her horse under control. MacGonigal grabbed the bridle of the other, holding the animal still and stroking its neck. He looked after the departing green pickup. "I guess some people can't resist the temptation to show what assholes they are," he said.

The pickup continued down the road for some distance, then slowed and began to turn around. "Here they come again. I'm getting off until they get tired of this game," said the older girl.

"No need for that," said MacGonigal. "They'll be tired damn soon, I'm thinking." He picked up a rock and walked out onto the pavement. He stood in front of the two girls, tossing the rock from hand to hand. The driver saw him standing there and slowed down, as if uncertain what to do. Fifty feet away, the truck stopped. MacGonigal stared at him a moment.

He walked up to the left-hand window and looked down at the thin-faced youth with long, greasy black hair who was driving. "You boys having a little fun, are you?"

The driver said nothing for a moment, then answered sullenly. "What's it to you, asshole?"

MacGonigal ripped open the door, thrusting a big hand in, and dragged him out. He shoved him up against the side of the truck, twisting the boy's collar until his face purpled. "I don't like people scaring horses—that's what it is to me. Understand?"

He heard a door open on the other side of the truck, and one of the girls gave a little squeak of alarm. He pushed the driver aside and turned to see the passenger approaching him with a folding knife held low in a menacing manner.

"You want to put that down, sonny, before somebody jams it up your ass."

The driver suddenly grabbed his arm. "Get him, Jerry!"

The passenger moved rapidly, coming around the hood of the truck as MacGonigal struggled with the driver. Keeping his eyes on the knife, MacGonigal pivoted, hauling the driver around and shoving him at the one with the knife. The man staggered and lost his grip on MacGonigal's arm. MacGonigal followed up with a powerful kick that doubled him up and brought both of them down in a tangle.

He didn't give them time to get up. The knife had fallen from the driver's grasp, and he scooped it up. He put one booted foot on the passenger's arm and looked down at him.

"How about it, sonny? You really want this up your ass?"

Neither of them answered. He stood aside and let them get up. He threw the knife into the bushes.

"Now, you boys better get your asses out of here, and keep 'em out of this county, because next time I see you, I'll kick your asses right up between your shoulder blades."

They sullenly got back into the truck, nursing their bruises. The driver started the engine, then leaned out the window.

"We'll get you for this, you motherfucker! We know where you live!"

He let the clutch out and the pickup leaped forward, burning rubber and accelerating rapidly. MacGonigal watched them drive out of sight around a curve, then climbed back into his own truck.

He drove away slowly, watching the road ahead of him to see if the green pickup had pulled off anywhere. After a while, he settled his attention on the road ahead of him. The highway was an old road, built nearly forty years ago, the first paved road, in fact, in the county. It was narrower than it should be for safety, and it had several dangerous curves. MacGonigal liked it that way. He had once turned out in kilts and pipes to protest a proposal to modernize the road. Since most of his neighbors

stood to lose farm land in the project, the proposal
had been scrapped. As a by-product of that venture,
MacGonigal had become mildly famous locally, and
was considered something of a natural resource, the
craziest Irishman in captivity.

He whistled to himself as he negotiated the muddy
road leading to his turnoff. Suddenly he threw on the
brakes, sliding dangerously. There in front of him
were his own tracks, made when he was coming out
that morning, and on top of them was another set.

He struck the steering wheel with his fist. Damn
George, anyway! The son of a bitch couldn't follow a
plan to pour piss out of a boot if it were written on
the heel. It had been a bare three weeks since
George had left Susan off at the drop point, and they
had agreed that there would be no communication
between them for six months, and then only by mail.
And now George shows up, big as life, probably with
a tail.

When he came to his own property line,
MacGonigal swore even harder. The gate was open,
dragged back barely far enough for a vehicle to
scrape through, and left that way. To MacGonigal, it
was a personal insult, and he began to imagine with
pleasure the things he was going to do to George
Harris.

Suddenly he stopped the truck with a jerk. What
the hell would Harris be doing back so soon? He
pondered a minute, trying to think of a plausible
answer. Nothing fit. From what Susan had told him,
the essential thing was to establish a solid cover so
that she could drain the assets of her phony companies without arousing suspicion. Harris couldn't have

done that in so short a time.

So maybe it wasn't Harris. In that case, who was it? MacGonigal ran through several possibilities: First, it might really be Harris, with some scheme to get the money out of Susan. Second, Harris might have sold her out. That didn't seem too likely, since he had saved her, but MacGonigal regarded it as at least theoretically possible, given his general assessment of George Harris. Third, it might be some of DeLisle's or Nazario's people. They could have found Susan's hiding place. Again, MacGonigal's assessment of Harris made that a likely possibility.

At that point, he stopped. There were several likely explanations for the tracks in the road that had no sinister implications at all, but there were equally likely ones that did, and that was enough for MacGonigal.

The problem now was what to do about it. Right away, MacGonigal ruled out simply driving up and seeing what was up. He would leave the truck where it was, blocking the road, and see who was on his property. He killed the engine and put the key in his pocket.

Then he thought about a weapon. He didn't have a gun in the truck. He sat a moment, cursing himself for an addle-brained Irishman, then slid out of the pickup, closing the door behind him and locking it to delay anyone who might try to flee down this road.

Squelching through the wet, cold brush, he paralleled the road for several hundred yards, then swung away, fearing that whoever the mysterious visitors were, they might have left a guard on their vehicle. He cut through the woods and climbed the side of the valley, aiming to strike a point above the cabin, where he could see what was going on.

He worked his way slowly uphill, avoiding loose rocks and thick brush as much as possible, until he reached a place where he could see the end of the road. He had to crawl out on a rock spur to do it, and from that point, both the cabin and the end of the road were visible. MacGonigal crept out and surveyed the scene.

Parked at the end of the road was a green pickup. MacGonigal swore softly under his breath. So the greasy little bastards wanted to try something! He should have known!

He turned his attention to the cabin. There was no sign of any activity at all there, except for the plume of smoke that rose from the chimney. MacGonigal lay flat on the rock and watched carefully, hoping to catch a flicker of movement behind a window, some sign of what was going on. There was nothing.

He backed away from his perch and took to the woods again, slabbing along the ridgeside, working his way behind the cabin. He covered a couple of hundred yards or so, and then turned down, coming to the valley floor at a point behind the paddock, out of sight of the cabin or the outbuildings.

As he made his way through the fringe of trees along the edge of the paddock, he saw something that made his bowels freeze inside of him. A dark mound lay near the paddock gate. It was familiar, but it's lines were just a little wrong. MacGonigal knew what it was. *The bastards shot my horses!* A cold resolve began to grow inside him. He dared not think what they had done to Susan, but he had already decided what he would do to them.

He forced his eyes away from the carcass of the horse, lest it distract him too much. He squatted and carefully scanned the area sweeping first the nearground, then the middleground, then the background, moving his eyes slowly and methodically over each area before moving on to the next. He picked up another dead horse, lying in the edge of the trees on the other side of the paddock. He couldn't be sure, but he thought it was Harry. The one by the paddock gate was definitely Smoke.

He moved forward until he had just a strip of open ground between himself and the tack room. He glanced at the still form of Smoke by the gate, and then watched the cabin. Nothing moved behind the windows. He looked the tack room over carefully. No sign of anything there, either.

Crossing the open ground was a risk, but he would have to take it. Once in the tack room, he could fashion some kind of weapon and try to sneak into the house. He gathered himself up and suddenly sprinted for the door, his shoulders hunched in anticipation of a shot from the cabin.

There was nothing. He eased the door open and let himself in. For a long moment, he stood there, half expecting to find one of them waiting for him. Then he crossed to the window, crouching so as to be able to look out at the cabin without being seen himself. Suddenly he heard a noise overhead. He sprang back to the wall.

"Mac? Thank God you're here!"

He looked up at the loft. "Sue? Is that you?"

She peeked down. Her hair was awry, and her face

was streaked with dirt and pinched with cold. "Help me down. I'm almost frozen."

He took her hands and steadied them while she put one small foot on his shoulders, then slid down into his arms. He held her tight for a moment. "God! I thought they had you! I was afraid to think about it!"

She buried her head in his chest for a moment. "No, I heard them coming. I had just fed the horses—Mac, did you see what they did to your beautiful horses!"

He squeezed her tightly. "Yeah, I saw," he said through clenched teeth. "Wait until you see what I'm going to do to them."

She pulled back gently from his embrace. "They're in the house, Mac. They've got all your guns, and the guns they brought with them. What are you going to do?"

"I haven't quite figured it out yet. But there's one thing sure; they can't stay in there forever. And they don't know we're out here. Sooner or later they're going to get tired of waiting and make a mistake." He snorted. "They've already made several. One was coming here, and another was killing my horses."

She looked up at him. "You don't have a gun, do you?"

He grimaced. "No, like a damn fool, I don't. I own a few dozen, and now that I need one, I don't have even a .22 pistol."

Her face was almost expressionless. "You'd better let them go, Mac. They'll kill you."

He looked down at her, his face hard. "They'll

play hell, too. I'm damned if I let the bastards go after what they've done."

"Mac, don't. They'll kill you. Really they will. I know that you make a big thing out of taking care of yourself, but not this time. Let them go."

He pulled her hands away. "Damn me if I do." He went to the door and slipped out as she watched. He slipped along the wall and reached the corner of the tack room, where the roof hung over to form a wood shed. He worked a wrist-thick length of firewood out of the piled logs and then slipped back into the tack room. "You'd better get back up in the loft. If I don't make it, I don't want them to find you."

"No, I'm not going back up there. I'll wait for you here, if you're determined."

"Determined isn't the word for it, honey." He kissed her gently on the lips and slipped out the door, going around the other side of the tack room.

At the corner, he halted and lay flat on the ground. Then he peered around the corner at the cabin. If they were watching in that direction, they wouldn't expect to see a man at ground level, and he'd have a better chance of escaping detection.

The wet cold seeped in through his parka as he lay there, but he watched for a full five minutes, just one eye exposed. There were three windows on that side of the cabin, two from his bedroom, and one from the loft. He scanned them carefully. There was no sign of motion. He drew back and got to his feet. Without a further look at the cabin, he crossed the yard and gained the little back porch just outside the pantry. He stepped cautiously up on the porch, careful not to let a board creak under him or let himself be seen from the windows.

Once on the porch, he crouched down and sidled along the wall, looking in the windows. They were in the living area. His bookshelves had been stripped, and the books lay in a pile in the middle of the floor. Several things had been broken, and the guns had been taken down. Obviously they intended to cart those down to their truck and make off with them.

MacGonigal studied the two carefully. The pimply-faced one was lolling on the sofa, a bottle in his hand, the last of MacGonigal's Irish Mist. As MacGonigal watched, he tilted the bottle back and took a swallow. Drunken slob, thought MacGonigal, pimply little bastard. The other had dragged up a chair and was seated in front of the front window, where he could see the approach from the trail up the falls. He had a shotgun cradled in his lap.

MacGonigal slipped back and tried the pantry door. It opened noiselessly, and he cracked it slightly and peered in. The door leading into the living area was open about a foot. From where they sat, the two intruders wouldn't be able to see him come in. He eased himself inside and shut the door gently behind him. He could smell a strong odor of burning grass. Well, he said to himself, they've really set themselves up, the fucking punks. Between the alcohol and the grass, and anything else they might have taken, they weren't likely to be at the top of their form.

He edged forward until he stood just behind the pantry door, his shillelagh held across his body. By squatting and leaning out a little, he could look into the room. The pair hadn't moved. Now all that remained was to wait. Sooner or later they would get tired of sitting.

It seemed like an hour that he waited. His legs grew stiff, and he constantly squatted and stood to relieve them. He could hear occasional small sounds and muttered conversation from the living area. Once he heard a crash. He guessed it was the bottle of Irish Mist being thrown into the fireplace. He grinned to himself, a humorless grin. They were getting restless.

At last he heard one of them stand. He took a stance by the door, with a fresh grip on his club. He held his breath as he heard a slurred voice say, "I'm gonna see if there's some beer in that icebox." He could hear unsteady footsteps crossing the floor. He raised the club and poised himself to strike.

It was ridiculously easy. The pimply youth simply staggered into the pantry and MacGonigal brought the club down on his head with a crunch. He fell in a heap, making a clatter as he did so. MacGonigal heard his companion's chair scrape. "Jimmy? Jimmy? What's wrong?"

MacGonigal could hear footsteps crossing the floor. "Hey, man, can't you handle it? We both got to be ready when that fucker comes home."

The greasy-haired one stepped into the pantry and MacGonigal brought the club down on his wrist. He heard the bone snap, and the shotgun went flying to the floor. The intruder jumped back and stood bent over, holding his broken wrist and moaning. MacGonigal stepped out and confronted him. The youth looked up at him, his eyes filled with pain and fear.

"Hey, man, you broke my arm!" He saw MacGonigal raise the club. "Hey, man, we were only going to give you a little pay back. We weren't going to do anything else." He backed away. MacGonigal followed implacably, the club raised. "Hey, man, you could kill a guy with that thing."

MacGonigal thought about his horses, looked the man straight in the eye, and brought the club down with all the strength he could muster. He felt the skull crunch under the blow, and the intruder dropped as if he had been struck by lightning. MacGonigal looked down at him. He lay huddled. He turned him over with his foot. The eyes were wide open and stared unnaturally from their sockets. Blood ran in a thin stream from his nose and ears. He stepped back into the pantry and turned the other one over. He was dead, too.

He prodded the corpse with his foot. No reaction. He went back into the living area and threw the club into the fireplace. It was littered with shards of glass. He could feel broken glass crunch under his boots as he walked on the bear rug. He went back and looked at the bodies again. "Well, I've done for you, you little bastards," he said quietly. He felt strangely calm, as if he had passed through a great ordeal and come out unscathed. There was no emotion left in him. He stepped over the bodies and went out the door, walking stolidly across the yard. As he turned the corner of the tack room, he saw Susan standing against the wall, her eyes wide. "What happened?"

"It's over."

"Did you . . . kill them?"

He didn't answer, but she could see it in his eyes. "Mac, I've never been so scared. But . . . was it necessary?"

Anger boiled up in him. "Fuck, yes, it was necessary! What do you think, I was just going to walk in there and ask them to go home like good little boys?"

She looked down at the ground. "Mac, don't yell at me. It wasn't my fault."

He felt an unreasoning rage start to well up inside him. "Are you saying that it was my fault?"

Her voice was unsteady, as if she were barely in control of herself. "I didn't say that, Mac. I didn't say that at all. I guess I know that you had to do it."

"Then what the hell are you saying? That if I had let them fuck with us all they wanted, they'd leave us alone afterwards? The hell they would! Those little bastards would have done for us both. They were nothing but a couple of vicious punks, and if we'd let them, they'd have killed us both." He looked down at her. "They'd have killed me. With you, it would have been different. They'd have had a little fun before they put your lights out."

She began to shake uncontrollably. She looked up at him, her eyes shining with tears. "I know they would," she said in a small, trembling voice. "Don't be mad. Don't take it out on me. I don't blame you for anything."

"Damn right you don't!" He stopped and clenched his jaws tightly together. He took a deep breath. "I'm sorry, Sue. I don't mean to be this way." He paused and went on, his voice low. "It's just that . . . hell, I'm not sure what it is. Delayed reaction, I guess. Come on, let's go in."

"I . . . I'm not sure that I can go in there. Are they still . . ." Her voice trailed off."

"Yes," he said gently, "they're still in there. I've got to get them out." He grasped her arm and squeezed her bicep. "You've got to help me, Sue. I know that it'll be tough, but I need your help."

"But . . . what can I do?"

"We've got to get rid of the bodies. And clean up the mess. I'll put them somewhere, but we can't leave any evidence lying around."

She stared at him. "But . . . aren't you going to call the police? I mean, in a case like this . . . they'll have to agree that it was self-defense, won't they? But if you try to cover it up, it will look like . . . murder. Won't it?"

"It's not going to look like anything, if I can help it. And if I call in the sheriff, you'll be involved. I won't be able to hide the fact that you're here. The news services will get hold of it, and the people that are looking for you are liable to pick up on it."

"Wh . . . What are you going to do?"

"Those clowns had enough booze and junk in them to fly under their own power. It won't be hard to make it look like an accident."

"An accident? What kind of accident? Nobody will believe that, and they'll still find out that there is someone living here with you, won't they? I mean, there'll have to be an investigation."

"Yeah, but it'll be a long way from here. I ought to be able to fake a pretty convincing wreck. Once they test for alcohol and drugs and find what they're going to find, they won't look any further."

She leaned against the wall. "What do you want me to do? I'm not sure that I can do very much. I don't think that I can hold together very well right now."

He pulled her toward him. "They made quite a mess in the house. I want you to clean up while I take care of the bodies."

She blinked. "Is it very . . . bad in there?"

"Bad enough." He stopped. "No. I see what you're getting at. They tore down the books and broke things, but there's not a lot of blood."

She swallowed and straightened her shoulders. "Okay. I'm ready."

He took her arm, and they walked together across the yard. As they stepped up on the little porch, he said, "The first one, the one with the pimples, is in the pantry, so don't be shocked when I open the door. The other one is in the middle of the living area. Ready?"

She nodded silently. He opened the door and went in. The pimple-faced intruder was lying as he had left him, on his back, with one arm lying limply across his chest. There was a big, dark puddle of blood under his head. MacGonigal paused, looking down at him. He heard Susan come in behind him and catch her breath. "Are you all right?"

"Y . . . yes. It's not as bad as I thought it was going to be. Is . . . is the other one any worse?"

"About the same. I hit him from in front, and he looks . . . battered. But he isn't bad. If you're ready, we'll go in and look at him. Be sure that you don't touch anything that belongs to them. I'll have to put everything they brought with them—guns and stuff—in the truck with them. We don't want any fingerprints on it."

They went through the pantry door, and Sue looked around the room. She avoided looking at the corpse. "I guess I can clean this mess up, Mac. But I can't touch . . . them."

"You won't have to. I'll take care of them. You just sit down for now. I've got a few preparations to make, and then I'll take them away." He stopped. "Will you be all right while I'm gone?"

She sat down on one of the dining table chairs. "I'll be okay. I think I'd rather do it this way. I need to be alone a little . . . to get control of myself. I'll be all right."

He left her like that while he went up into the loft. He came back down the stairs with an old Army blanket and a handful of large plastic bags. In his pocket he had a half-dozen rubber bands. A pair of ski gloves was thrust into his belt. He threw the blanket over a chair back and went to the first corpse. He lifted the head and slipped the bag over it, securing the bag with a rubber band.

"My God, how can you do that?"

He straightened up. "I've got to keep the blood off of things somehow. If it bothers you, don't watch."

He went into the pantry and did the same with the other corpse, then came back out and began to cut the blanket into strips with his pocket knife. Susan watched in spite of herself, irresistibly drawn to witness each action.

He unbuckled the first man's belt and passed a

strip of blanket down one side, between his pants
and belt, then across his buttocks and up the other
side, going under the belt again to form a sort of
sling. He knotted a second strip to the ends of the
first, transforming the sling into an endless loop.
With a piece of cord, he tied a knot around the seat
of the sling and led the cord up between the corpse's
legs, fastening it to the belt. A final strip of blanket
went around the body's chest, just below the armpits. He stepped back and looked at what he had
done. The body was securely encased in a crude
harness.

MacGonigal ran two more strips of cloth into the
harness and let them dangle. Then he heaved the
corpse up into a sitting position. "I'm going to need a
little help here," he said.

Susan rose and came over to him. "What do you
want me to do?"

"Just pass the sling over the top of my head."

She lifted the loop of blanket and dropped it
around his neck. He put his hand up and guided the
sling up to his forehead, where it formed a tumpline.
He reached back, grabbed the dangling strips of
blanket, and brought them around his chest and
knotted them. "Take my hands and help me up."

She came around in front of him and steadied him
while he rose from his squatting position, his thigh
muscles straining. The corpse, grotesque with the
plastic bag around its head, looked as if it were riding
piggyback.

"I'm going out now," he said. "You get started on
your part whenever you're ready." She didn't say
anything. "Be sure you don't touch anything of

theirs with your bare hands," he cautioned.

He took a couple of tentative steps. His walking stick leaned near the door, a six-foot length of inch-and-a-half-diameter bamboo with rubber crutch tips on each end. MacGonigal took up the stick and went out the door. "I'll be back in a little while for the other one," he called. Susan did not answer.

With some surprise, he realized that it was growing late. He glanced at his watch—only an hour and a half of useful daylight left. He would have time to do what he had to do, but he wouldn't have any to waste. He made his way slowly to the trail by the falls, then started down.

It was a long, torturous descent. A fine mist in the air made the going slippery. With the walking stick he constantly tested his footing, probing with the rubber tip, seating it firmly, then bracing himself against the stick as he moved forward. Step by step, he inched his way down the trail.

It seemed to take forever, but at last he emerged by the green pickup. He tried the door on the driver's side. Locked. He went around to the back of the truck and dumped the corpse unceremoniously. He stripped off the blanket harness and then went through the boy's pockets. He found the keys and opened the door, then wrestled the corpse into the seat. He went around to the other side and opened the passenger door, then came back and put the keys in the ignition.

Something was bothering him. MacGonigal realized his truck was blocking the road out. He'd have to move it. He hiked back along the entrance road, the mist thickening, and climbed into his truck. As he started it, he realized the flaw in his plan. He would drive the green pickup out, but would have to walk home. He sighed to himself. He'd have to ask Susan to help.

He pulled behind the green pickup and sat a moment, thinking. There wasn't any real choice: The spot he had selected for the "accident" was over thirty miles away. She would have to go. Damn! he thought, I hate to tell her that. She's been through enough already.

He made his way slowly up the trail, the blanket sling over one arm, his walking stick thumping the trail ahead of him. As he reached the head of the trail, he saw that Susan had lit a lamp inside. It was dark enough now so that it made a distinct difference. He'd have to hurry to get the other corpse down to the truck before it was too dark to trust his footing on the wet trail.

He came into the cabin to find Susan putting the books back in the shelves. She turned to him, her eyes shining with an unnatural, forced brightness. "They didn't do as much damage as you might think. Look!" She held up his pipes. They had been buried under an avalanche of books. He hadn't thought about them at all, but now he shuddered. He took the pipes and looked them over. It was the thin wood of the chanter that worried him. It could be broken so easily, and he could never find another antique Starke chanter. But there was no damage. He carefully laid the instrument on the top shelf.

"Sue," he said slowly, "I've got to have some

help. Someone's got to drive my truck while I drive theirs. I know I told you that I would take care of this end of things, but I guess I wasn't thinking straight."

"That's all right," she said. She seemed to have recovered from the shock of events with remarkable quickness. He marveled at her, thinking about how close he himself was to falling apart, making stupid mistakes like forgetting about having to get back afterward.

"We can't forget about the stuff they brought with them," he said. "Their guns and anything else, I mean."

"I've already taken care of it. The guns, a beer can, even the butt of a joint they left on the floor. It's all sacked up. Now you go get the other one ready," she said, gesturing toward the kitchen, "and I'll get my coat." She paused. "It's going to be dark soon. We'll have to hurry."

From inside the pantry he answered her. "That makes it easier for us. It's going to rain, and that's good, too. But I have to get this guy down the path while there's still a little light. I don't want to fall and break my neck."

He turned his attention to the corpse. She had moved it a little, dragging it aside so that she could sprinkle dry detergent on the bloodstains. It probably wouldn't fool a forensic pathologist, MacGonigal thought, but it would have to do for now. Later he would rip up the stained floorboards and burn them. He set about fashioning the harness for the corpse. As he was tying the last knot, Susan appeared at the door. "I'll help you get him up," she said.

Together, they got the corpse to a sitting position. She helped him slip his forehead into the tumpline and tugged at his hands while he struggled to stand up. He was getting tired. The trip with the other body had taken more out of him than he realized. She passed him the dangling strips, and he made them fast around his chest.

They went out the door together, but suddenly he turned back. "Go in there and get my Colt .357. Get a box of shells, too."

She stood there for a moment. "Why? Are you afraid that we'll run into the police?" She seemed genuinely alarmed.

"No. It's just that today I got caught without a gun when I needed one. I'm going to make sure that never happens again."

She turned and went in the cabin and came out with the holstered revolver. She threaded the heavy weapon on his belt buckle. "You know, if you'd had this thing today, we'd be in a fix. We couldn't fake an automobile wreck with bodies full of holes."

"Yeah, I know. But I'm going to keep this thing with me from now on, anyway. Shoot first when you're in trouble, and worry about the law afterwards."

She took a flashlight out of her parka pocket. "I thought we might need this," she said. "It's getting dark. I'll lead the way down."

"No," he said, "if I slip, I'll fall into you. Just follow me and use that thing to show me the path." She walked behind him a little stooped and shone the light at his feet while he tested each step with his stick. "It's getting dark. Can't you move any faster?"

"I can. I can fall all the way to the bottom and leave you to explain three bodies. Is that what you want?"

She didn't answer, and a pang of guilt flashed through him. "I'm sorry. I didn't mean to snap at you. It's just that I'm tired."

"I know," she said, "the strain is getting to me, too."

They soon reached the foot of the trail. MacGonigal dumped the second body on the hood of the truck and stripped the harness off. Together they heaved it into the passenger's seat next to the slumped form of the driver. "Okay," said MacGonigal, "you take my pickup and follow me. I'll go slow. Watch how I negotiate the tough spots —this is a tricky place to drive, especially in this weather."

He started the engine and switched on the lights, while she started up the other truck. Then he slowly eased forward. It was raining now, a gentle, freezing rain. A crust began to build up on the windshield. He turned on the heater and defroster and switched on the windshield wipers.

He drove slowly, one eye on the road ahead of him, the other on the lights of the truck behind him. He could feel the tires sliding on the wet, greasy surface of the dirt road. He was worried that they'd get stuck. His own pickup had hub winches, old tire rims bolted to the rear wheels, which would get them out if they got mired down, but it would take time and energy. He hoped that they didn't get stuck. He really didn't feel up to it.

They made it through the gate at the edge of his property and kept going, leaving it open. He kept watching the rear-view mirror. Sue was doing fine, keeping to the same ruts he chose, and driving with skill. She was one hell of a woman, he thought.

They turned out on the road where going was a little better. He felt encouraged, as if they had passed a major obstacle. The corpse of the driver kept falling against him, though, and he elbowed it roughly aside. It kept falling back. He tried to think of some way to tie it in place, but the mental effort was beyond him.

They came to the low water bridge. He stopped the pickup and got out, walking back in the lights of the other truck. He stuck his head in Sue's window. "This part is tricky. You have to gear down and keep the engine going. Don't stop, whatever you do, or you'll drown the engine out. Let me go through first. I'll wait for you on the other side." She nodded, and he went back to the green truck, shoving the driver's slumped body roughly aside as he got in. He put the engine in low and gunned it, jouncing through the stream, the two corpses falling all over him as he wrestled with the wheel.

He went a good hundred yards beyond the edge of the water, then stopped and put on his parking lights. Through the rear-view mirror, he could see his truck's lights moving erratically toward him. They dimmed as the water obscured them, but kept coming. At last she pulled up behind him and stopped. He got out again and walked back to her.

"Okay, the hardest part is over. Just stick close to me. I'll go slow." She nodded again. He went back and started up again.

The rain was coming down harder now, and freezing in earnest. The lights showed silver streaks, but little else, as they wound slowly up the switchbacks. MacGonigal concentrated on his driving and on keeping the two corpses from falling over on him. Several times he had to stop and push them over to the far side of the cab, but they soon crowded him again.

They reached the turnoff, and he signaled a left turn as he pulled out onto the wide gravel road. Ahead, he could see the lights of a house. For a moment, he thought irrationally that the occupants would notice the two vehicles and report them. He put the thought out of his mind. Two pickups on a back country road were nothing unusual. He drove past the first house and saw the dim glow of the windows of a second ahead through the rain.

At the highway they stopped and he got out again. "We'll take the highway for about twelve miles, then turn off again. Don't lose me, but if you do, just pull off on the shoulder and put your flashers on. I'll come looking for you."

He went back and pulled off onto the pavement. There was ice on the road, and he could feel the tires break free now and then. It was ticklish driving, and he had to force himself to concentrate. He was comforted by the sight of her lights clinging to his rear bumper.

The bridge at Turkey Creek was bad, and he

slowed down and put the truck in low. She followed without hesitation, and he began the climb up Brown Mountain. They passed a few more houses, their lights dim in the rain.

At Meadow Creek turnoff, he waited for her to close up to him, then steered onto the gravel road. It was narrow going, with the creek very close on the left and a rough rock wall on the right. He went slowly, to avoid sliding into the rock.

The one-lane timber-floored bridge across Meadow Creek was slick with ice, and the flooring rattled and heaved under his wheels. He was really angry at the two corpses now for the way they kept lurching into him. He pushed them angrily aside with one arm while with the other he struggled with the wheel.

Once across Meadow Creek, they began a long, steep ascent. Now and then, he had to stop, backing and filling to make the sharp hairpin turns at the switchbacks. At last he reached the top of the ridge. The road here was little more than a track, and he worried about it. They were so close. It would be hell to get stuck here.

He waited a minute at the top and looked for her lights. She was just negotiating the last turn. He watched as she came lurching up to the top, then started forward slowly again. They drove a mile along the unimproved narrow, one-lane road. He kept a sharp watch along the left shoulder for the big sycamore that would mark his destination. When he found it, he stopped. She pulled up behind him.

"Give me the things they left in the house." She passed the bundle out the window to him. "I'll take it from here. About a hundred yards in is an open place where you can turn around. I'll flash my lights when I pass it." He paused. "Maybe you ought to get out and check with the flashlight before you try it. I don't want to get stuck here."

He started the green pickup again and went on through the slashing rain for a quarter of a mile. When he reached the rocky spot where he intended for her to turn around, he flashed his lights and drove on slowly. As he went slowly on for another hundred yards he saw her vehicle halt. Then he stopped and set the brake. He waited in the truck with the engine running, watching the thin shaft of her flashlight inspecting the ground. After a long time, he heard a door slamming. He waited while the lights of the truck manuevered.

When he was sure she had made the turnaround, he got out and looked around. The track in front of the green pickup was nearly invisible—he could barely make it out in the lights of the truck. He walked forward, to the point where the dimly seen ground suddenly disappeared.

He had chosen the place well, he thought. Steamboat Rock, six hundred feet above Meadow Creek, and the drop was close to vertical. It was a fairly popular spot. In the spring and summer, people came here for picnics. Not many, of course, because it was hard to reach even in good weather, but the view was spectacular. At night, kids came up here to make out. But not in this weather. It was much too cold and wet. MacGonigal went back to the pickup and made his preparations.

He took the plastic bags off the bodies and emptied the contents of the bundle in the cab of the truck, careful to touch nothing with his bare hands. As a final touch, he fished the butt of the joint out of the bundle and put it in the driver's shirt pocket, then tugged him into position. He put the stiffening foot on the gas pedal, and the note of the engine rose. He turned off the lights and stepped back.

The door was still open on the driver's side. He could see the two corpses slumped over in the glow of the dome light. He bundled up the plastic bags and the strips of blanket and laid them aside. He stepped up to the vehicle, making sure there was nothing behind him to snag when it started moving. He leaned over the corpse and, nudging the lever into drive, jumped back.

Lights off, the truck jumped forward, leaving him barely enough time to get clear and slam the door. It rolled out of sight in the rain, and suddenly the note of the engine changed, rising to a high pitch as the rear wheels left the ground. He could hear the crash and crackle of brush as the truck plunged down.

It seemed to take a long time to reach the bottom. About halfway down, the engine quit, but he could still hear the clatter of breaking trees and smashing metal. It went on and on, and finally died away, far below. MacGonigal picked up the sodden bundle at his feet and turned away. With luck, they wouldn't be found for months.

He was committed now. He was sure he'd done the right thing. With Susan in his life now he couldn't take the chance of anybody finding out what had happened. But if they found the bodies and traced them back to him . . . He stood a long time in the dark. There was no sound but the steady drumming of the rain.

His eyes had adjusted to the dark, but the rain was falling harder now, a real downpour, and it was freezing cold. He felt cold clear through, as if the rain were seeping into his bones. He picked up the bundle and sloshed along the narrow trail, heading for the lights of his own pickup.

He opened the door and slid inside. Susan looked at him. "You're soaking wet, Mac. Better let me drive back."

"No," he said. "I know these roads. Besides, it'll keep me awake. I feel like I need about a year's sleep right now."

They drove back as slowly as they had come, with MacGonigal fighting the wheel all the way. It seemed worse going back. But, he realized, he'd had a lot of other things to think of on the trip out.

MacGonigal put the bundle down inside the door and grabbed a kerosene lamp. Its yellow light showed a depressing scene. Susan had done quite a bit to clean up, but there was still a lot to be done. He put the lamp down. "There are a few things I've got to do right now. You go on to bed."

"No, Mac, if you're going to be up, I'll stay up, too. Why don't I finish putting the books back in the shelves and picking up?"

He grunted and went back out into the rain again. In a few minutes he was back with an armload of lumber and a big tool box. Without a word, he began ripping out the bloodstained floorboards and throwing them into the fire. As the flames leaped up, he added the plastic bags, which melted at once, and the strips of blanket, which smouldered slowly. He looked at his ski gloves regretfully. They were good gloves, but he knew that glove prints could be lifted like finger prints.

As the fire burned, he measured and cut and nailed. At last he sat back and put his hands to the small of his back. He felt tired and sore all over. Susan came over with a broom and dustpan. "I'll clean up here. Why don't you go to bed?"

He was tired, incredibly tired, drained, but somehow the idea of sleep didn't appeal to him. He was too keyed up. "Want a drink?"

"Yes. But there isn't any. They finished it all, or else poured it out." He remembered the bottle of Irish Mist smashing into the fireplace and sighed. MacGonigal rarely drank, but he felt like a stiff one now.

He filled his pipe, stalling, while she puttered around, making a few adjustments here and there. The odor of burning wool and leather from the fireplace made her wrinkle her nose. He poked at the fire, stirring the coals, then added another log, making sure that all the evidence burned. Then he sat back on the sofa, puffing at his pipe. She had filled a plastic trash can with ripped books and broken glass and other reminders of the intruders. "Go through this and see if there's anything you want to keep."

He barely glanced at it. "No. I'll burn what will burn, and take the rest out in the morning."

She stood a moment longer. "Well," she said, "I'm going up to bed."

He watched her climb the stairs to the loft with a deep regret. There was something so final about it, as if it marked a watershed in their relationship. Over the past few weeks, there were times when she had simply gone up to the loft or slept on the sofa, and he had respected that, knowing her occasional need to be alone, and he had felt no sense of rejection. But tonight was somehow different.

He felt no deep sexual desire—he was too drained, too emotionally saturated. But as she disappeared up the stairs, he felt a great sadness. He wanted to sleep with her, with a longing more spiritual than physical. He sat there smoking, wrapped in a somber mood until his pipe went out. At last he rose and went into his own bedroom.

He lay staring into the darkness a long time, thinking disjointed thoughts. In his forty-odd years, MacGonigal had not been a stranger to violence. Slowly, the realization came to him; he had never until tonight hated any man he had killed. Mostly they had been faceless enemies, who wore a different uniform than he did, and were trying to kill him. But the two youths who now lay broken and smashed at the foot of Steamboat Rock had introduced him to violence on a newer, more personal plane. They had invaded his home out of hatred, and he had killed them in the same spirit.

* * *

Suddenly MacGonigal was fully awake, reaching under his pillow for the .45 automatic he had tucked there before undressing. He had no idea of what had roused him, but he knew with certainty that he was not alone. He eased the pistol out and silently slipped off the safety. He lay tense in the darkness, all his senses straining.

There was a tiny sound just outside the room. The door to his room slowly opened. He leveled the pistol.

"Mac," said a small voice, "I can't sleep." He pushed the safety back on and put the pistol on the bedside table. He could see her vaguely in the darkness as she silently crossed the floor. He pulled back the edge of the quilt for her. She slid under the covers and pressed against him. She was naked and cold. He put his arms around her and held her close. She was trembling. "Every time I close my eyes, I see . . . things."

He stroked her until the trembling stopped and her breathing grew deep and regular. He lay there in the darkness with her in his arms, staring into the blackness and keeping watch over her.

It was a bleak, dreary morning. The rain had frozen on the trees and on the eaves of the cabin, forming long icicles. Ice sheathed each branch of every tree. Looking out the window, MacGonigal could see that many large limbs had broken under the weight of the ice. There would be many farmhouses without electricity, he thought.

His left arm, under Sue's head, was asleep. He slowly withdrew it. She stirred and pressed herself closer to him, and he ran his hand gently over her back.

They lay like that a long time, drifting between waking and sleeping. His hands roamed over her, gently, not insistently. She shifted slightly to let him touch her small, perfect breasts, and he felt a quiet, but strong desire build.

When they were finished, he lay looking down at her. "Sue, I think I have something I have to tell you."

"I know what it is, you don't have to say it."

"I do have to say it." He looked down and put his lips to her ear. "I love you."

She moved a little away from him and looked at him. "I mean it," he said. "I love you." He stared at her. "I don't care if you feel differently, but I love you, and I have to tell you."

She put her hand gently on his cheek. "I love you, too, Mac, but I'm not sure how things are going to turn out for us."

"It doesn't matter. I love you now, and that's enough for me. I don't really even care if you love me. But I want you to know that I'll always love you."

MacGonigal pushed back his plate and leaned back in his chair. He felt a strange feeling of contentment, overlaid with a fierce joy. He looked at Susan as if he were seeing her for the first time. What was it that made her so beautiful? She was a damned attractive woman, he had known that from the first time he had seen her. She was trim, graceful, almost exotic, but he had never seen that quiet glow about her.

She looked at him thoughtfully and smiled. Then her expression changed. "Mac, what are we going to do about the horses?"

He had almost forgotten about the horses. Now the events of the previous day and night came flooding back. He pushed away from the table. "I'll take care of them. Don't worry about it." He pulled on his parka and looked for his gloves. Then he remembered that he had burned them in the fireplace. He went out the front door and stood a long time on the porch, his breath making clouds of steam.

The sun was out now, making the ice-coated woods sparkle like diamonds. He shoved his hands in the pockets of his parka and walked across the frozen ground to the paddock. Smoke lay there, his long, fluffy coat sheathed with ice. The sun struck multi-colored lights from it. MacGonigal turned and walked slowly back to the equipment shed and opened the double doors.

The settlement bowl on the Farmall Cub tractor was full of gas—no water or ice in it. He climbed up in the seat and put it in neutral, pulled out the choke and pressed the starter experimentally. The engine ground a moment and then caught. He let it warm up while he gathered up some chains and rope, then got his chainsaw. He climbed back into the seat and drove to the paddock gate. He went through and closed it behind him from habit.

He approached Smoke's carcass reverently. He felt full of sadness as he hooked the chains to the big horse's hocks and then to the drawbar of the tractor. He pulled him out of the paddock, closing the gate behind him again, and up into the woods, away from the cabin and the stream.

He unhooked the horse in a little hollow halfway up the ridge, put the chainsaw down beside him, and went back to the paddock.

Harry lay between two trees with his long legs stretched out. MacGonigal had a lot of trouble manuevering him out to where he could hook him up for dragging. As he worked, he saw a flash of motion in the trees at the end of the paddock. He looked carefully. It was Josephine, his little brood mare. She stood well back in the trees, her tail and head down. He got off the tractor and walked toward her, but she wouldn't let him approach her. She would roll her eyes and snort and move nervously away from him, her great, swollen belly swaying. He was afraid that he would panic her and drive her through the barbed wire fence, so he left her alone and went back to Harry.

He dragged Harry up beside Smoke, then took the chainsaw and began to cut dead limbs and fallen trees, heaping the wood over the two horses. He worked until the chainsaw coughed and died, out of fuel. Then he drove back to the shed, put the tractor up, and filled a three gallon gas can. He climbed back up to the two horses and sprinkled the wood with gasoline. He wasn't sure the icy wood would burn, but he stood back and tossed a match. The gas went up with a woof. He stood there until he saw the wood catch, then turned back toward the cabin.

As he came down out of the woods, he saw Josephine standing at the feed trough, eating quietly. Sue was standing next to her, stroking her neck and saying something private to her.

V.

For two days MacGonigal went up to the site where the two horses had been burned and cut more wood and rebuilt the pyre, burning them again and again until all trace of the carcasses was lost in a pile of ashes and charcoal. Susan accompanied him, although he was afraid that she would find it too depressing.

The second time, she sat on a log and watched as he built a mound of brushwood over the charred bones. "Why the hell did they have to shoot the horses? I can understand, just barely, how their warped little minds worked. You humiliated them, and they wanted to get back at you. But the horses didn't do anything to them. Why attack helpless animals?"

MacGonigal sat down beside her on the log and watched the flames. "Hell, I don't know. Why do bastards like that do anything? What's the point of harassing people, terrorizing them? The sons of bitches would have killed both of us, and probably bragged about it afterwards."

Sue moved over closer to him. "I'm just glad you came when you did, and that you had the sense to see that something was wrong right away. If you'd come right up to the cabin and walked in, they'd have killed you without blinking an eye. I don't even want to think what they'd have done to me if they'd found me."

MacGonigal was silent a moment. "Sue," he said slowly, "I've got something that I've got to tell you, but you don't have to listen to it."

She looked at him, puzzled. "What is it, some deep, dark confession?"

"Kind of," he said. "The black-haired one, the one that was driving when they scared the girls' horses—I killed him in cold blood." He stopped, looking for her reaction. "The pimply-faced one, he came into the pantry, and I just clubbed him down. The other one came looking for him—he had the shotgun. I knocked it out of his hand, broke his wrist. He couldn't have done anything then. He tried to get away from me, but I just stepped up to him and smashed his skull while he was trying to talk me out of it. I didn't have to kill him."

She sat there for a moment, then took his hand in hers. "You did the right thing, Mac. He'd have tried again some day. If I've learned anything, it's that the law can't ever prevent anything like what they tried, and after they've done it, the law usually can't catch them, and if it does catch them, it can't do anything to them."

"I guess that's right, but I can't help worrying about it. I've killed men before, but never with as much rage and hatred. It was never so personal, if you see what I mean."

"I think I do," she said, pressing closely against him.

"I was afraid that you'd see that, that you'd see what a deliberate thing I had done. And when I got you to help me get rid of the bodies, I thought you'd be disgusted with me, that you'd feel like I was the same sort that they were. I think you did, because it kept bothering you and you couldn't sleep."

"I couldn't sleep that night, but not because of what we'd done. It was the stress, the overload. I don't feel guilty about it, and I don't want you to, either. They came after us, and you took care of them—MacGonigal's way. I feel safe with you. Don't ever change."

Two days later MacGonigal came climbing up the trail to the top of the falls. Sue met him there. "Guess what I've got," he said, grinning.

"Horses," she said. "I heard you coming and looked out the upstairs window. I saw the trailer. Where did you get them?"

"Bought them from a fellow I know that raises good stock. Been friends with him for years, and when I told him that my horses had been shot by vandals, he made me a good offer on two of the best-looking geldings I've seen in a long time. Come down and look at them."

They went down the trail together, and Sue approached the big, double horse trailer. A brown eye, ringed with white and rolling in fear, looked back at her. "What kind of horses are they?"

"American Saddle Horses. That's a breed developed from the Arabian. These two fellows could be registered, but there's no point in registering a gelding."

"Why not?"

MacGonigal's jaw dropped. "Well . . . uh . . . they can't breed. I mean, they've been cut."

"They've been castrated! Why?"

MacGonigal was at a loss for words. He tried to find words to explain, but was overcome by laughter. At last, by sheer willpower, he straightened out his face and said, "Honey, only the best male horses are allowed to breed. All the rest are cut, gelded. That's how good bloodlines are perpetuated, and bad ones weeded out."

"Well, I still think it's a dirty trick!"

He laughed. "I'll tell you what, I'll get these fellows bedded down and adjusted to their new home, if you'll fix us something to eat."

He had just finished pitching hay down to the two horses when he heard the sound of an engine on the road to the falls. He jumped from the loft and sprinted for the house. As he clattered across the porch, the door opened and Susan stood there, ashen faced. "It's a police car! I saw it from the upstairs window!"

He reached out for her and gripped her by the shoulders. "It's probably nothing," he said, with an assurance he didn't feel. Harvey Siler is probably just out canvassing votes or something."

"You don't believe that," she said, her voice rising. "Mac, they've found the bodies, I know they have! We should never have tried to hide killing them."

"They can't have found them so soon, and even if they have, there's no definite connection with us. Maybe they know what the bastards did out on the highway, and they're just routinely checking leads." His voice was steely calm. "Now get your parka and go out to the barn and groom the horses. Stay out of sight of the cabin. I don't want them to know you're here, but I don't want to trap myself in a lie."

She went back inside and struggled with her parka. MacGonigal was ice-cold on the outside, but his guts were churning. What if they had found the bodies? Had anyone along the road seen and remembered the two pickups? He waited for her to go out, then deliberately composed himself. He picked up and charged his pipe, lit it with care and took out the manuscript of an article. Clearing a place at the table, he sat down and began to go over his writing, one ear cocked for the sound of footsteps.

He had an almost uncontrollable urge to run to the window. He struggled to suppress it, forcing himself to concentrate on the manuscript in front of him, going over it word by word. He found two typographical errors and swore at himself as he penciled in corrections.

His enforced concentration worked, and he was startled to hear boots on the porch. A moment later there was a rap on the door. "MacGonigal, are you home?"

He opened the door to see the sheriff standing there. Harvey Siler was a man in his mid-fifties, with a paunch that strained at his Sam Browne belt, bags underneath bloodshot eyes, and sagging jowls. He wore a wrinkled, semi-military, green whipcord uniform, with ankle boots in need of polish, and a bomber jacket. His campaign hat and Smith and Wesson Highway Patrolman revolver were the only really clean things about him.

"Come on in, Harvey. This business or pleasure?"

Siler was still panting from the exertion of the climb up from below the falls. "Damn it, Mac, you ought to put in a road all the way up to your place. Fella could have a heart attack just walking up here."

He looked around. "This is a nice place you've got here, Mac. Don't believe I've been inside since you got it finished."

MacGonigal pretended to think. "No, I don't believe you have, Harvey. You ought to come up now and then."

The older man snorted. "Huh! I'm gettin' too old to climb mountains. That walk up here just about did me in."

MacGonigal showed him to a chair. "Have a seat and catch your breath, Harvey. I was just going to have some coffee. Want some?"

The sheriff gratefully lowered his well-padded posterior into the chair, shifting his Smith and Wesson around to a more comfortable position. "I don't mind. Maybe you've got something a little stronger?"

MacGonigal grinned. "Wish I did. I had a bottle of some good stuff, but some kids got into the place the other day and drank it. Broke the bottle in the fireplace, too."

The sheriff's eyes widened slightly. He pulled out his notebook. "Kids, huh? Any idea who they were?" His pencil hovered over the page. He looked at MacGonigal closely. "You been havin' a lot of trouble with kids lately, I hear. Had quite a little set-to over west of town."

Here it comes, thought MacGonigal. "Wasn't anything to get upset about," he said, as calmly as he could. "A couple of little girls were riding along the shoulder of the road. These kids came by and deliberately frightened their horses. I set them straight."

The sheriff looked narrowly at him. "I heard that there was more to it than that. You roughed 'em up pretty bad."

MacGonigal forced himself to be noncommittal. "You hear all kinds of things, sheriff."

"Yeah," said the sheriff, "well, if these kids had made a complaint, I'd have had to come after you with a warrant. You want to be careful about that kind of stuff. You could get into a lot of trouble."

He paused, looking closely at MacGonigal. "You ain't thinking about doing something like that to the kids that broke in here, are you?"

"No," said MacGonigal. "I don't even know who they were. I doubt that they'll come back."

"Well, don't let that Irish temper carry you away if they do. You wanna make a complaint?"

MacGonigal poured two thick stoneware mugs full of coffee. "No. Don't see what good it would do. If I find out, I'll talk to their folks."

The sheriff sighed, returning the notebook to his pocket. "That's about all I could do, anyway. Law's awful soft on kids these days. Mistake in my opinion —teaches 'em they can get away with murder."

At the word "murder," MacGonigal's hackles rose. He forced his voice to be calm. "What do you want in this? cream? sugar?"

The sheriff made a wry face. "Black. I don't like it that way, but the doc tells me that's how I have to take it."

MacGonigal passed him the mug, then sat down across from him, clearing his manuscript out of the way. The sheriff eyed the paper momentarily. "Doin' some more writin', huh? I don't see how you do it, livin' up here all by yourself, writin' all the time. Couldn't do it, myself."

"It's not so bad," said MacGonigal. "I have a few friends, and some of them come up here now and then, despite the climb."

The sheriff took a tentative sip of the steaming liquid and made a face. "Just ain't the same without sugar." He went on, "Yeah, I heard that you got yourself a ladyfriend. Anybody I know?"

MacGonigal forced himself to smile. "That would be tellin', sheriff. You know my motto, 'Let people guess, and to hell with 'em.'"

The sheriff took another sip of coffee, made another face. "Yeah, you always did play your cards close to the chest." He put the heavy mug down on the table. "What I come up here to talk to you about is a fella named George Coxley. Know him?"

MacGonigal's face remained calm, even though his heart turned over at the question. Shit, he thought, they've found the bodies. His mind raced. "No," he said carefully, "I don't think I've ever heard of him."

The sheriff picked up the mug again and took a long pull. "Well, you might know him under another name, George Harris. That ring a bell with you?"

MacGonigal was caught completely off guard. His mind went completely blank. What the hell did George Harris have to do with this? To cover his confusion, he picked up his pipe and made an elaborate show of relighting it. At last he said, "Yeah, I know a guy named George Harris. Served with him in Vietnam."

"Heard from him lately?"

MacGonigal puffed at the pipe. He was completely lost. His instincts told him that there was a trap here somewhere, but he couldn't imagine where. Well, he thought, the best thing is to tell the truth, but not to volunteer information. "Yeah," he said, "he came by about a month or so ago."

The sheriff's eyes narrowed. "Was he drivin' a red CJ-5?"

MacGonigal pretended to try to think. "Yeah," he said slowly, "yeah. I think so." He paused. "What's old George done?"

It was the sheriff's turn to play coy. "What did he want?"

"I dunno. Old George is a strange one. Used to be with the CIA, I think. Anyway, in Vietnam he didn't wear a regular Army uniform. He never did get around to telling me what he wanted, just kind of hinted around."

The sheriff was definitely interested now. "What did he hint at?"

"Hard to say. These spooks are real good at not

saying anything that you can pin on them later. He just talked, mostly about 'Nam. I kind of got the idea that he was sounding me out about a job."

"What kind of a job? Did you take it?"

MacGonigal treated the sheriff to a condescending smile. "I can't work for the government, Harvey. I'd have to give up part of my pension, and it wouldn't be worth my while."

The sheriff's deep-set little eyes were glowing now. He leaned across the table. "Are you for sure that it was a government job? What was it?"

MacGonigal paused. "He didn't come right out with anything. He told me, more or less, that he was out of the government and that he was running some kind of security service outfit. When I turned him down, he wouldn't give me any details about the job."

The sheriff relaxed, disappointment evident in his sagging face. "Well, that checks with what the state police told me. How come you even bring up the government thing?"

"Well," said MacGonigal, "you never can tell with these spooks. One minute they're working for the government, and the next they're not. Or so they say. But I just told him I didn't want any part of whatever he was offering."

The sheriff nodded. "Any reason you know of somebody'd want to kill him?"

MacGonigal suddenly sat bolt upright in his chair. "Killed? George Harris? When?"

The sheriff pulled out his notebook. "Apparently not long after you saw him. According to the state police, he rented that CJ-5 in Fort Smith under the name of George Coxley. Had a driver's license and everything. When he didn't bring it back, they reported it stolen. Everything he gave them was phony—driver's license, address, insurance, everything. The state police had all that checked out.

"Anyhow, about a week later, the CJ-5 turned up over in Missouri. It was on the hot list, so the Missouri state police reported it. They checked it out, and there was bloodstains on the seats. So they went over it carefully and dusted it and all, and sent in all the prints they found. One set came back with a name to it, George Harris. They got to looking around, but couldn't find a body anywheres nearby.

"The Arkansas state police got a picture of Harris from the Feds and took it by the place that rented the CJ-5. They identified it as Coxley, the guy that rented the jeep.

"They got to checking around a little more, and found that a Mr. and Mrs. George Coxley checked into a motel near here just the day after the jeep was rented. Same fella, he put down the license number and everything. Gave the same phony address, too. Stayed there one night and checked out.

"The state police figured they were on to something. They asked me to see what I could find out about it. Well, not too long after I got their request, somebody over in Carrol County found a body. Fella had been shot and buried in the woods. The state crime lab managed to lift some fingerprints, and guess who it turned out to be?"

"George Harris," breathed MacGonigal.

"Yeah," said the sheriff, surprised. "Sounds like you kind of expected it."

"You'd make a lousy fiction writer, Harvey. You have no feeling for suspense."

The sheriff shifted his bulk in the chair. "That's your game, not mine. Anyhow, this guy Harris, or Coxley, is dead. I checked around. The fellow at the motel said that he asked about a guy that plays the bagpipes, seemed real anxious to find him, so that had to be you. Now the question is, who killed him, and what did they do with his wife?"

MacGonigal thought a minute. "I didn't know he had a wife. He was alone when he came by here."

"Well, he sure as hell had one when he stopped at the motel." He frowned. "The guy at the motel didn't get a look at her, and I was hoping to get a description from you."

MacGonigal directed a silent prayer of thanks to his guardian angel. If the motel manager hadn't seen Susan, it wasn't likely that anyone around could identify her. Harris had kept her in the motel while he was making contact and hadn't brought her out until time to make the drop-off. "Well, I'm afraid that I can't help you there, Harvey. Like I said, he was alone when he came by here. Didn't even mention that he'd gotten married."

"He wasn't, so far as we can tell. Which adds to our problems. Who was the woman, and where is she now?"

"'Fraid I can't be much help to you on that."

The sheriff sighed. "Any idea who might have wanted to kill him? Whoever it was wanted him bad, according to the autopsy report. They broke all his fingers and beat him up pretty good before they shot him. Did anybody hate him, that you know of?"

MacGonigal gave a wry smile. "Harvey, everybody that knew George Harris hated his guts. If you'd known him, you'd have wanted to kill him. I think his own mother, if he had one, would have put a contract out on him."

The sheriff's notebook appeared in his hand, as if by magic. "How come you hated him?"

"It's a long story, Harvey. In 'Nam, we got into a tight spot." He pulled open his shirt and pointed to the long scar that crossed his abdomen. "See that? I got that the last day I was with George Harris. We got into a tight spot, and I got shot up pretty bad. George ran off and left me."

"You hate him enough to kill him?"

"Harvey, I despised the bastard. But I didn't kill him. I wouldn't dirty my hands on George Harris. And as for who did, I haven't the vaguest idea."

The sheriff made a note in his book. "You say he wanted to hire you. Didn't it strike you as funny that a man would drive all the way from North Carolina to offer you a job? After all, he could have written a letter."

An alarm went off in MacGonigal's head. North Carolina wasn't where Harris had his security company, unless both Harris and Sue had lied to him. He didn't think that Sue had lied, but he wouldn't put anything past Harris. More likely, the sheriff was expecting him to correct that statement, revealing more than he had claimed to know about Harris's business. "I don't know how far he had come," he said slowly. "He claimed to be just passing through and stopped to look up an old buddy. But now that you mention it, it does seem strange."

"Yeah, strange. Why would he come all that way to offer a job to a man that hates his guts? A man that he knows hates his guts?"

MacGonigal shrugged. "I don't know. Like I told you, I figured that he still worked for the CIA, despite him claiming to be in business for himself."

"Uh huh. Where was it you said he was in business?"

The alarm bells rang again. "I didn't say. He didn't tell me. You said that he worked out of somewhere in North Carolina."

The old man didn't blink. "Uh huh. What sort of job was it?"

MacGonigal recognized the technique. Ask questions at random, get the suspect to lose track of the direction of the interrogation, and try to pick up inconsistencies. Well, Harvey Siler wouldn't get any inconsistencies out of Francis Xavier MacGonigal. "He didn't tell me. I didn't really ask. I just turned him down."

"Uh huh. You weren't even curious."

Anger flared. "No, damn it, I wasn't! I didn't want any part of George Harris, and he's damn lucky I didn't set the dogs on him, except that I don't have any dogs."

The sheriff changed direction suddenly. "He didn't mention his wife?"

"No, he didn't. But maybe if you tell me what she

looks like . . . it might be someone we both knew."

The sheriff shook his head, his flabby jowls wagging. "Don't know what she looks like. Nobody saw her, not at the motel, not at the place he rented the jeep."

MacGonigal, never one to pass up a tactical opportunity, leapt to the attack. "Then how do you know that there was a wife?"

The old man blinked both eyes, like an owl. He turned the proposition over slowly in his mind. "Hmm. Well, the motel operator said that both beds had been used . . ." His voice trailed off. "You mean, he could have been traveling with a woman who wasn't his wife?"

"Or with a man."

The sheriff pulled out his notebook and began scribbling. "A man. What makes you think so?"

MacGonigal leaned back and clasped his hands behind his head. "Well, for one thing, I'd never trust George Harris to tell the truth. If he said the sky was blue, I'd know without looking that it was red. If he registered a woman, then I'd figure he had a man with him. And another thing, if he had a woman, there would have been only one bed slept in. I know George, and that's the way it would have been, unless she held him at gunpoint all night."

The sheriff tapped his teeth with the eraser of his pencil. The motion made his jowls wobble. "So what happened to this man? What did the killers do with him?"

MacGonigal unclasped his hands and looked into the sheriff's little eyes. "Nothing. Maybe there was only one killer, and that was the guy that George was passing off as his wife. That's the most logical explanation."

"Hmm. Yeah," said the sheriff, "except that there was three killers, according to the state crime lab boys."

MacGonigal silently congratulated himself. Instead of luring old F.X. into a trap, you stepped into one yourself, you old bastard. He gave the sheriff an innocent look. "How do they know that, Harvey?"

The sheriff gave him a sudden, startled, guilty look. "I shouldn't have said that. Don't you go telling folks about that, Mac, because it's confidential. The newsmen aren't supposed to have it."

MacGonigal maintained his innocent look. "Oh, I won't, Harvey. You know me. I play my cards close to the chest, like you said. But how do they know that there was three killers?"

The sheriff looked at him. "If you tell anyone about this, I'll lock you up, Mac. I'm tellin' you, not a word to anybody."

"Not a word, Harvey." MacGonigal held up his right hand.

"Well, first of all, there was one guy who was left-handed. They could tell that by the way he was beaten. He was shot from behind, just back of the right ear, so the guy that actually pulled the trigger on him almost had to be right-handed. Something to do with the angle of the bullet. And there was two different kinds of cigarette butts around the body, along with a cigar butt they found in the grave. There were footprints in the bottom of the grave, and they were of three different sizes. It just had to be three men."

The sheriff leaned forward as far as his bulk would allow. "I shouldn't be telling you any of this, Mac, but they really did a job on that boy. He was beat all to hell. The medical examiner wrote a report that made me sick to read it, and I covered the pictures with my hand while I was reading."

His voice dropped to a hoarse whisper. "They burned him, that's how come there to be all kinds of cigarette butts around. Every bone they could break was broken. They jammed a stick this big," he held up his thick forearm for MacGonigal to regard, "up his ass. I mean, they did stuff to him I never imagined anybody would do to another person. Those boys, the ones who killed him, were poison-mean! They cut him open and gutted him like a hog, while he was still alive. They even cut his nuts off." He pulled out a handkerchief and mopped his fore-head. "I tell you, it was sickening what they did to him."

MacGonigal showed concern. "I didn't have any use for old George, and that's a fact, Harvey, but nobody should have to die like that."

"Yessir," said the sheriff, mopping his brow again, "they cut off his nuts and pecker and threw 'em away. The state boys couldn't find 'em. Most likely eat up by some varmint. Hell of a thing to happen to a man. Hell of a thing."

"How come they can do that, Harvey? What do the state boys think?"

"Well, at first, they thought it was a psycho, some

kind of a sex nut. But with three killers, well, either they really had it in for him, or he knew something, and wouldn't tell." He mopped his forehead again. "I'll tell you, if it was something they wanted him to tell, I'm betting he told."

MacGonigal felt a cold trickle of sweat running down from his armpits. Yeah, he thought, I'm with you, Harvey. Good ol' George told them everything. I wonder if he did burn that map, like I told him. Damn! I should have stood over him while he did it.

Aloud, he said, "Have they got any ideas at all who did it?"

The sheriff shook his head. "It's got them beat. If we can't find a witness, somebody who saw something or some kind of a lead, we're whipped. They figure," he said, leaning forward conspiratorially, "that it was organized crime. You know, the Mafia. That's their way of doing things," he said authoritatively.

"Is that really what the state boys tell you? There ain't any organized crime around here, not that I know of."

"You'd be surprised," said the sheriff, shaking a pudgy finger. "We get stuff all the time, FBI stuff, state bureau stuff. Organized crime is everywhere. Lots of 'em in Hot Springs. And there's the drug business, too. Lots of organized crime."

MacGonigal shook his head. "And you deal with that kind of stuff every day? I had no idea."

The sheriff leaned back, his pudgy hands clasped over his vast belly. "There's a lot of stuff goes on most folk don't know. Nobody has any idea what a sheriff gets into. I'll tell you," he said, shifting his bulk, "if folks knew what I got to do in this job, there wouldn't be anybody running against me in the next election."

MacGonigal smiled inwardly. Good old Harvey, the total politician. "Maybe you hide your light under a bushel, Harvey. Folks ought to know the kind of job you do, see what kind of sheriff we've got."

The sheriff looked pensive. "Yeah. I ought to see to it that folks are better informed." A sudden look crossed his face. "Now, if I was to solve this crime, why, it would be in all the papers. Folks would know for sure, then."

"You're right about that, Harvey. You need to get to work on this thing and solve it."

Siler heaved himself up out of the chair. "Yeah, I got to get on that." He picked up his hat and put it squarely on his head. "Thanks for the coffee, Mac. And you be thinkin'. If you remember anything, anything at all, you let me know, you hear?" He paused. "Just pass it on to me. To me directly. Don't go to the state boys with it, you hear?"

MacGonigal put his hand on the sheriff's well-padded shoulders. "I will, Harvey. If they come around here, I'll tell them I've talked to you, and that I've told you all I know."

He felt the sheriff stiffen under his hand. "Well," the sheriff said, "I don't think they'll be coming around here. I don't aim to give them all the leads I've uncovered, not by a long shot. This is my case."

"But if they do come," MacGonigal persisted, "I'll just tell them I've already talked to you."

The sheriff paused at the door. "No, don't do that. Lemesee now. . . . You tell 'em that you're a deputy. I'll put you on the books. Then tell them that they have to clear through me."

He walked the sheriff to the head of the trail leading down the falls, then stood listening to the fat old man stumbling and wheezing his way down. For a moment he smiled to himself, a self-satisfied smile. I've covered us pretty well, he thought. Now if the state boys start nosing around, they won't come here. His smile changed to a frown. George must have told them everything. A stronger man than he would have caved in under what they did to him. I'll bet he gave them detailed instructions on how to find us. Damn! Why didn't I make sure he burned that map?

He could still hear the sheriff scuffling down the trail. Maybe, he thought, George did burn the map. After all, he was killed a while ago, and no one has showed up here yet. He stood listening, letting his mind go blank. When he heard the engine start in the patrol car, he turned and went back. Susan was waiting for him in the cabin.

"I was watching from the barn. What did he want? Did they find the bodies?"

MacGonigal pulled up a chair to the table. "Pour me some coffee, honey. We've got to talk. Things have taken a new twist."

Impatiently she filled two mugs and placed them on the table. "What is it? Did they find those two you killed? Don't keep me in suspense."

He picked up his mug and took a sip. "No,

honey," he said slowly. "They found George Harris."

She started violently, the coffee slopping out of her mug onto the table. "George Harris?" Her voice rose in alarm. "Did he tell them about us, about me? Is that why he was here?" She bit her lower lip.

MacGonigal took a deep breath. "Sue, George is dead. They found him murdered not far from here. The sheriff checked the motel where the two of you stayed, and found that George had been asking about me. That's why he came here."

"Do they know who killed him?"

"They don't have any idea, but we do. George was tortured, obviously to get something out of him. The only thing that I know that anybody might have wanted to get out of George is where you are."

Susan's face was white. Her hand shook so much that she couldn't hold the cup. "Tortured? Did they say what they did to him?"

"Yeah, but you don't want to know about it. The state police say that it was three men. They beat him, broke a lot of bones, burned him, did other things, too."

She stared at him, her eyes like holes burned in a sheet. "What other things? I have to know."

He looked at her. "Don't blame yourself. It wasn't your fault."

She took the mug in both hands and swallowed a mouthful of coffee. It was hot, and she choked and sputtered, then rubbed her breastbone with her fist. "Mac, I have to know just what happened to him. I have to know. Tell me."

"Honey, it isn't your fault. George made the decision to get involved in this all by himself. You didn't have any choice."

"Damn it, tell me!" Her voice was almost a scream.

MacGonigal looked at her hard. Maybe it was best. Hit her hard with it and she might get over it. He said bluntly, "They rammed a stick up his ass, a big one, the sheriff said. They disemboweled him, and they castrated him." A shudder ran through her whole body, a sudden unsuppressible trembling.

"That's Nazario," she said. "He killed a man in upstate New York that way. People used to talk about it. That's one of the reasons everybody was so scared of him. When DeLisle would get nervous about something, he used to say 'Nazario's not going to stick a log up my ass!' He used to have nightmares about it." She shuddered again.

MacGonigal took another sip of coffee. "Well, he knows where you are now, that's for sure. And he knows about me, too. I'm surprised that they haven't been up here before now, but maybe they're not so bold out in country like this."

She put her face in her hands. In a moment, she looked up at him. "Mac, I've got to get out of here. They won't bother you—it's me they're after. I can't stay here and let you get caught up in this."

MacGonigal put his mug down with a thump. He reached across the table and took her hands. "Do you think that I'd leave you in the lurch now? I thought that you knew me better than that by now. Damn it, I love you!"

Tears were streaming down her face. "I love you, too, Mac. That's why I have to leave. I just can't have that happen to you . . . what happened to George . . ." Her voice broke.

He got up and came around the table and took her in his arms. Her legs wouldn't support her. He half led, half carried her to the sofa. He brushed her hair from her face. "Sue, dearest, I'm not leaving you, and you're not leaving me." When she started to protest, he shushed her. "Look, George talked. He told them everything. I know George. He'd have sold his mother under pressure. So they know about both of us. But it's me that they're looking for, my place, that is. When they find it, it really won't make any difference whether you're here or not, because if you're gone, they'll try the same thing on me that they tried on George."

"My God, no, Mac! I won't have it! They can't!"

His jaw was firm, the muscles standing out. "You're goddamn right they can't! They'll come here, that much they can do. But when they get here, it isn't George Harris they've got to deal with. It's MacGonigal, on his own territory."

She was a little calmer now. "Listen, Mac, let's get out of here, both of us. Let's get somewhere far away. I'll get the money somehow, and we'll be all right. But we've got to get out of here now."

"Any ideas where we should go?" he said grimly. "If they can find us here, they can find us anywhere. But we've got two big advantages. We know they've found us, and we're on our own ground. I'm not going to throw advantages like that away."

"But what can we do?"

He gave another grim smile. "Wait for 'em to come to us, and do the same thing that we did to the last bastards that came here. Only this time we'll do it better and easier, because we'll be ready for them."

VI.

Her face was swollen and tear-stained. She looked somehow much smaller and more helpless than he had ever seen her, but there was a new tone to her voice. "What do we do, Mac? How do we get ready for them?"

He released her and crossed the room to the hanging guns. "If they come for us, they'll almost surely come up the road, just like those two punks did. The first thing we do is make sure that we're never unarmed. I don't want us to get caught short again."

He began to take weapons down from the wall. "We'll carry handguns everywhere, and I mean everywhere. But handguns aren't really worth much for fighting, they're just handy to carry. So we'll make sure that we've always got something better close at hand." He handed her a short-barreled twelve-gauge pump shotgun. "This'll be our upstairs gun. From now on, we'll sleep in the loft, and this'll be right where we can reach it." He slammed the action open and began to unscrew the magazine tube cap.

"What are you doing?"

He pulled out the magazine spring and shook out a long wooden rod. "This is a magazine block," he said, holding up the wooden rod. "It isn't legal to hunt with a shotgun that holds more than three shells. This Ithaca holds five, so to be legal, you have to put in a magazine block. I don't particularly care about legal niceties now, so I'm taking it out." As he spoke, he reassembled the gun. "Get me some shells out of that drawer," he said, pointing. "Get one box of number fours, and one of slugs."

She opened the drawer and looked through the contents. "Is this what you want?" she said, holding up a box.

"Yeah. That's number-four shot. Look for a box labeled 'slugs'."

She looked again and produced a second box. He opened the box of number fours and began to load the shotgun, chambering a round and setting the safety before cramming in four more cartridges. "These fours aren't exactly what I want. Buckshot would be better, but I don't have any loaded up. Doesn't matter, really. Inside the house, a load of number fours is as deadly as anything else. The slugs are just for insurance, in case we have to shoot any farther than a dozen yards with this thing." He handed her the gun. "Watch it, now. It's loaded. From now on, everything's going to be loaded."

She took the gun hesitantly. "You'll have to teach me how to use it."

"First thing on the agenda, as soon as I'm finished here. Take it upstairs now, while I load a few more."

She carried the pump gun up the stairs, while he selected another weapon. When she came down, he

SOLDIER OF FORTUNE

INTRODUCTORY OFFER
9 issues for only $18.95

Save over 29% off the 1 year single copy price.*

☐ Payment enclosed (must accompany order)

☐ MasterCard   ☐ VISA

Card #: _____

Signature _____   Exp. Date _____

Name: _____

Address: _____

City: _____   State: _____   Zipcode: _____

*Savings based on 12 issue single copy price of $36.

Offer good in U.S. only. All other countries add $7.00 for additional postage. Please allow 6-8 weeks for delivery of first issue. Offer expires 12/31/87. U.S. funds only.

BTBKF7

BUSINESS REPLY MAIL

FIRST CLASS   **PERMIT NO. 8**   **MT. MORRIS, IL**

POSTAGE WILL BE PAID BY ADDRESSEE

SOLDIER OF FORTUNE

P.O. Box 348

Mt. Morris, IL 61054-9984

had them laid out in a neat row. The Savage 99 he had selected as a rifle for the truck, along with a .30-caliber carbine that someone had given him years ago. The carbine wasn't much of a gun, but it was handy and short. In an emergency, he could be sure that he could get it into action from inside the cab.

His .30-30 saddle gun, he decided, he would keep in the tack room. It wouldn't be hurt there, any more than it already had been by years of bumping around in a saddle boot, and it would naturally go in the boot when they were working with the horses.

An old Kar-98 rifle, a German Army issue, in 8mm Mauser, would do for the barn. A Springfield would go in another outbuilding. Beside each of these weapons was a plastic box with at least a hundred rounds.

"You look like you're getting ready to fight a war," she said.

He looked up. "I am. When your friend Nazario comes looking for Francis X. MacGonigal, he's going to have a war on his hands, a full-scale one."

He started to gather up the weapons, then put them down. "It might not be a bad idea to have something with a little range upstairs," he said. He took down the Ruger Model 77 and put it on the sofa.

They carried the weapons outside and stashed them in the various outbuildings, then came back to the cabin. The model 99 and the carbine lay on the floor, waiting to be taken down to the pickup. MacGonigal crossed over to the bookshelves and scooped up two pistols. He tossed one holstered weapon to her underhanded. "Catch. And put it on your belt. And don't let me catch you with it off, ever."

He slipped a pistol on his own belt as well, then handed her a box of .22 long-rifle hollow points. "Load that thing, and we'll have a little practice with it."

She unsnapped the holster and drew the little Colt Woodsman automatic. "How do you load it?"

He took it from her, unlatched the magazine, and handed the pistol back. "Simple, just slip cartridges in here," he said, demonstrating. He took the pistol back, inserted the magazine, pumped the slide, and set the safety. Then he handed it back to her. "It's loaded now. All you have to do is release the safety," he said, pointing to the lever, "and start pulling the trigger. But it takes a lot of practice to be effective with a pistol. We'll have to work on that."

He loaded his own revolver, a Colt Python, holstered it, and gathered up the two rifles, handing one to her. "Come on, we'll put these two in the pickup, and then we'll start your shooting lessons."

They went down the trail to the foot of the falls. At the bottom, MacGonigal dug in his pocket as he approached the truck. The lock buttons were down and the windows rolled up. "Damn! I forgot the keys. I'd better slow down and let my brain catch up, we can't afford mistakes now."

As he turned away, he saw Sue giving him a strange look. "Mac, you never lock anything. Are you sure that you locked the truck?"

"Of course I'm sure. Can't you see that it's locked . . ." His voice trailed away into silence. He backed away from the truck, sliding the rifle off his shoulder. "Get back into the brush, quick!" He pushed her off the trail and down behind a boulder. They lay together for a moment, then MacGonigal crawled a few yards to a new position. Motioning Sue to stay put, he gathered his legs under him and leaped to his feet, sprinting across the road, his rifle at the port.

There was no reaction. Nothing moved in the woods. He moved silently, slowly, scouting the brush. Three hundred yards from the point where he had crossed, he moved back to the road. He carefully examined the surface. Almost obliterated under the tred marks of the sheriff's car was a heel print. He looked at it closely. It was new, sharp and clear, with no frost marks in it. It had to have been made the same morning. He crossed the road and checked the other side. More tracks, some coming, some going.

He moved slowly through the brush. In a few yards, he saw something that made him pause, a cigarette butt, lying on the ground. He stepped forward and found an area of crushed down brush. There were footprints and cigarette butts all over. He stood a moment, searching the area with his eyes. A cigar butt caught his eye, and his expression deepened to a frown. So that's it, he thought, the same three who killed George. They're playing it cagey. He came back to Sue, circling through the brush. She didn't hear him coming until he was a few feet away. When she finally realized that someone was behind her, she jerked up, pointing the carbine at him. "My God, Mac, I almost shot you!"

He took the carbine out of her trembling hand.

"Not with this. You forgot to take the safety off." He pointed to the little rotary safety in the front of the trigger guard. "You've got to flip this forward to fire. But make sure that you know who you're firing at first."

She took the carbine back. "What did you find?"

"Plenty," he said. "They're here, the same ones who killed George, from the looks of things. At least there were three of them, two who smoked cigarettes, and one who smoked cigars. After they finished with whatever they did with the truck, they hid in the bushes just up the road and waited. I think the sheriff's car scared them off."

"What do we do now?"

He stopped a minute, thinking. "I guess the first thing is to put you where it's safe. I'll lock you into the cabin. Don't open the door for anybody but me. If somebody else comes, shoot through the door. I'll come back here and try to figure out what they did to the truck."

She set her mouth in a firm line. "Oh, no. I'm not waiting all by myself while you're down here. I'm staying with you."

He shrugged. "I guess it's six of one and a half-dozen of the other. Come on, let's go back up and get a few things."

They climbed back up the trail and collected a tool-box, a flashlight, and an old shaving mirror. Back at the truck, MacGonigal cut a small sapling with his knife, then taped the mirror to it at an angle with tape from the toolbox. While Susan held the light for him, he ran the mirror under the truck.

"There it is," he said. She held the light steady

and craned her head to look. A small, irregular shaped object was duct-taped to the bottom of the truck next to the clutch linkage.

"What is it?"

"I'm not sure," said MacGonigal, pulling off his parka, "but I'll bet money it's a bomb." He took the flashlight, slid under the truck and examined the parcel.

The tape concealed its actual contents, but two battery terminals projected from the tape. From these, two insulated wires led to the clutch linkage. The ends of the wire were stripped. One wire was attached to the frame, the other to the clutch linkage itself. The stripped ends were about an inch apart. Depressing the clutch would have completed the circuit.

"Hand me a pair of side cutters, then get away from here. There just might be one hell of a bang."

She put the tool in his hand, then scurried away. He waited until he heard her footsteps stop. "Get down behind something. I'm going to try to disarm it."

He played the flashlight over the package. One of the wires disappeared inside underneath the tape, then reappeared before joining the terminal. He held his breath and cut the loop between tape and terminal, then stripped the wire off the terminals. Nothing happened. He resumed breathing and began to unwind the tape. In a moment, he slid out from under the truck, the device in his hand.

"It's safe now. You can come and take a look."

She emerged from behind a large boulder and came over. He held the device up for her inspection.

"It's simple and crude, but it would have worked."

The device consisted of a short piece of pipe, capped at each end. Inside the pipe was an ordinary flash bulb, the plastic safety cover peeled off and the glass cracked. Wires were attached to the bulb. The rest of the pipe was filled with a black substance.

"Shotgun powder. It would have made a nice firecracker."

She looked at it. "Mac, why would they want to do this? I mean, if they killed us, they'd never find out where the money is."

"They didn't mean to kill us, that is, they didn't mean to kill us outright. This would have probably taken my foot off, but that's about it. They probably figured on coming up and rounding us up after it went off."

"What are you going to do now?"

"Put it back," he said. He walked some distance into the brush and scattered the contents of the pipe, then replaced the wire he had cut with a short length of about the same size and color from his toolbox. He wormed his way under the vehicle and retaped the device in position. Then he slid out and gathered up his tools. "Let's hide this stuff and find out where the bastards came from."

They hid the toolbox and other things in the back of the shed that sheltered the truck, and MacGonigal smoothed out the dirt floor until there was no sign that anyone had tampered with the device. He picked up the Savage. "Come on. I'll give you a lesson in tracking."

"Do you think we should? I mean, they could be

anywhere, waiting for us."

"They sure could. That's why we've got to find them. We'll watch them from now on, instead of them watching us."

He led her through the brush to the place where the three killers had waited. With the muzzle of the Savage, he parted the brush and showed her the site. "See? Just like I said, three of them. They sat here, smoking and waiting for their little trap to spring. Now let's see where they went from here."

They paralleled the road, with MacGonigal occasionally turning into it to check the tracks. The three men had kept to the road, never moving off it except to hide and wait—and all that was necessary was an occasional confirmation.

When they got to the county road, MacGonigal left Susan well back in the woods while he scouted the road. The three men were still on foot. Their tracks were a little more difficult to follow on this road, which had had a little traffic that day, but MacGonigal soon confirmed that they had headed down toward the low-water bridge. He went back to where he had left Susan.

"Come on. I know where they are."

They went across the road and deep into the woods, climbing a steep ridge. It was cold, but soon the exertion and the pace made them uncomfortably warm. MacGonigal allowed a grudging halt while they peeled off their outer garments and tied them around their waists. He turned along the spine of the ridge and set a blistering pace, zigzagging through the brush, bending low to avoid overhanging branches, picking his way among boulders, striding out in relatively open areas. Susan was hard-pressed to keep up with him, and the carbine, which had seemed a toy when she first picked it up, was now a heavy weight dragging at her shoulder from its sling.

The ridge had originally been capped by a thick layer of limestone, now eroded into isolated islands of stone that stood up along its spine. As MacGonigal was negotiating his way along the base of one of these stone islands he heard her call. "Wait, Mac. I've got to stop for a while." He stopped and stood impatiently while she caught up to him. "Can you go on a little farther? There's a resting place just up ahead, a little cave with a spring. She nodded. "I think I can make it a little farther, but not much more. I'm not used to this."

He grunted his satisfaction and swung out along the narrow path that bordered the sheer rock wall. He didn't move quite so fast as before, though, and he stopped occasionally to check on her progress.

Despite his shepherding, Susan at last lost sight of him. Her breath coming in gasps, she struggled to increase her pace. She rounded a bend in the trail and found him standing at the mouth of a low cave. A tiny trickle of clear, sparkling water ran from one corner of the cave mouth. MacGonigal looked relieved to see her. "I was getting a little worried about you. Are you okay?"

She gave him a murderous look and sank down beside the stream, unslinging the carbine and lying it aside. She stripped off her gloves and plunged her hands into the icy water. It was shockingly cold and sweet. It made her throat cramp and ache, but she couldn't stop drinking. It was like swallowing cold mountain air.

At last she satisfied herself, or simply reached the point where she couldn't swallow any more of the cold water—she couldn't tell which. She sat back and wiped her long, brown hair out of her face. MacGonigal took her hands in his. They were like ice. He unbuttoned his parka and pulling up his sweater, thrust her red hands into the warmth of his armpits.

She leaned up against him. "That feels good, but this isn't the time to start getting sexy, is it?" He smiled, his face close to her hair. "Any time is okay by me, if you're not too tired."

She said nothing. After a while she said, "I am too tired, but I'm not going to tell you until my hands are warm again."

He laughed, a low, throaty chuckle. "You're just full of those womanly ways, aren't you? How come somebody else didn't find you a long time before me?"

She wiggled her fingers, tickling him. "They did. Not all that many, but I've had a couple of husbands and an affair or two." She put her head on his chest. "Does it bother you, Mac?"

He stroked her hair. "Hell, no. I'd be a fool to think that a beautiful woman like you wouldn't have a man in her life now and then. What I can't figure out is how they let you get away."

Her voice was a little more sober now. "That's a long story, Mac. Long and dreary. I guess I was too smart, too . . . whatever. I haven't always had what you call these 'womanly ways.' I used to think that a girl could have brains and ambition, and it wouldn't matter, not to a real man."

MacGonigal slipped his arm farther around her. "It doesn't, not to a real man. You must have married some boys."

"I guess you're right, Mac. They couldn't take the pressure of being married to a woman who was smarter than they were. I couldn't take the constant childish competitiveness, and having to pretend to lose, to give in all the time." She was silent a long moment. "I couldn't take being punched, either, but only one of them did that. I left him the next day. I told all the others that if they tried it, I'd kill them while they were asleep."

"Is that a warning? Are you trying to tell me something, Sue?"

She pulled her hands out from under his sweater and preoccupied herself with pulling on her gloves. At last she looked directly into his eyes. "Yes. Not that I think that you'd do it, Mac, but if you ever do . . ."

He pulled down his sweater and rolled his parka, strapping it around his waist. "Well, I guess I know what not to do. Come on, if you're ready."

She looked up, a little dismayed. She got to her feet, using the carbine as a crutch. MacGonigal watched her with a little concern. "Think you can make it?"

She pulled herself fully erect. "That depends on where we're going, how far and how fast."

His brow furrowed with concern. "We can wait a little while longer. Move over here and you can see it."

She joined him and looked out over the valley. With the leaves now mostly off the trees, the county road could be seen for most of its course down the side of the far ridge. She followed it with her eyes as it zigzagged back and forth, one switchback after another, until it disappeared in the valley below.

MacGonigal pointed with the muzzle of the Savage. "That's the low-water bridge, right down there." He saw that she was puzzled. "That place where we crossed the creek on a slab of concrete, remember?"

She nodded and he went on, "You probably won't see it, but there's a little road, just a trail, really, that turns down the creek just this side of the slab. There's a fellow that has a hunting cabin there, and that's his way in. Usually nobody's there—he only spends a few weekends a year there.

"Now, as I see it, that fool, Harris, didn't destroy that map like I told him to. It was a Geological Survey map, 1 to 24,000, and it showed every wrinkle and boulder. And of course, he told them everything he knew before they killed him. So they know where we are. Exactly where we are. Except for one thing, they've got everything going for them.

"They probably can't use that map, not like it was meant to be used. They don't understand anything but road maps, and they're road-bound. That's probably why they didn't try for us in the cabin, that plus the fact that Harris was pretty impressed with the defensive possibilities. 'A fucking fortress,' he called it.

"He probably impressed them with the strength of our position, too. In fact, I can't see why these guys wouldn't drive up most of the way, like the city types they are, unless George told them that we can hear and see them coming."

He stretched out his arm, pointing down into the valley below. "All of this adds up to one thing; they're down there. They came as far as they could by vehicle, and hid the vehicle a short walk from the turn-off. That means down there by the hunting cabin."

She looked dubious. "How far away are they? Can they hear us?"

"Not likely! They're probably down at the hunting cabin, if they bothered to go in far enough to find it. That puts them a good quarter of a mile from here. We're above and behind them. I seriously doubt that they'll expect anyone to come from this direction."

"What do we do?"

He put his hand on her shoulder. "I didn't want you to come, remember? You just stay up here, and I'll go down and see if they're there."

"And if they are?"

"It depends. If I can't get a real good opening, I'll just sit down and wait. It may be three or four hours."

"And if you do get a good opening?"

"Then you'll probably hear it." He dug the extra magazines out of the pockets of his parka and checked them. "There won't be a lot of shooting. I won't go for them unless I've got them cold."

He stood up and started to move away, but stopped when she called to him. "Wait, Mac. I'm not staying up here. I can't stand the suspense."

He gave her a look of annoyance. "You'll do as well here as anywhere else. I'll have to leave you anyway while I'm scouting their position, and this is the safest place you could be."

"I don't care. I'm going down there with you."

He shrugged. "Okay. If we run into them, take cover first. Then make sure you've got the safety off that carbine. If anybody gets too close, point it at him, keep both eyes open, and blast him. Don't keep pulling the trigger, though. If you don't put him down on the first shot, go through the whole process again."

"All right. And I'll make sure not to shoot you."

"Right!" he said. "Let's get going."

They started down. From this point on, MacGonigal moved slowly, quietly. The side of the ridge was naturally terraced, with broad, flat benches like giant steps every thirty feet down the ridge side. MacGonigal led the way, keeping close into the ridgeside, rather than walking along the outer edges of the terraces. Occasionally he would halt, raising his hand for silence, and stand motionless, listening.

They moved along more slowly now, with MacGonigal moving slowly and quietly out to the edge of each terrace, keeping low and making sure that his silhouette was broken up by branches and limbs before descending. They slipped carefully down from one terrace to another, using boulders and slabs of rock, rather than the deer trails or the broken fans of scree. At last they could distinctly hear the rushing of the creek. MacGonigal went forward to the edge of the terrace and lay a long time on his belly, looking out and down. At last he turned and half crawled back to where Sue waited. He grasped her wrist. "Want to see where they are?"

She nodded and followed his directions, moving up behind the bole of a huge hickory tree and peering around it.

The cabin below was much smaller than MacGonigal's, made of logs that still had the bark on them. The bark had begun to rot and peel away, giving the cabin a scabrous appearance. Apparently there was neither a well nor a cistern, for a five-gallon can was upended on a stand just outside the cabin, with a tube running from it through the wall. There was no lawn, nor any kind of yard. Brush grew thick and dense around the walls, so that even reaching the cabin in summer would be difficult.

There was absolutely no sign of life around the cabin. Susan's eyes strained as she tried to will her vision to penetrate its dark windows. At last she slithered back to join MacGonigal. "Do you think they're inside?"

"No. There's no fire, no smoke coming out of the stovepipe. I don't think that these friends of yours would be the type to sit around in the cold."

"Where are they, then?"

"I don't know. I'm going to slip along this terrace and check the entrance road. And you're going to stay put—with no argument this time."

In a moment, he was gone, drifting among the trees and slowly disappearing from sight, as if he were a puff of slowly dissolving smoke. Susan turned her attention back to the cabin. It looked forlorn and deserted, as if no one had been there in ages. She began to worry. Suppose MacGonigal were wrong? Suppose the killers were back in their cabin, waiting for them, right now? Suppose that they had heard or seen them coming down the mountainside, and were even now stalking them. She shuddered and rotated the safety on the carbine's trigger guard.

MacGonigal moved with elaborate caution, as if stalking a deer. From time to time, he slipped up to the edge of the terrace to look down on the entrance road. He saw nothing, however, and eventually he came to the county road. Now he was puzzled and as apprehensive as Susan was. He had been so sure that they would be there. It was the only logical place to leave a vehicle hidden. At last he decided to take a small risk. He climbed down to the road and inspected it for tracks. At the turn-off, he saw something that confirmed his faith in himself. There were two sets of tire tracks leading into the entrance road. He examined them closely. One was apparently from an ordinary passenger car, the other from a four-wheel-drive vehicle. He could see where the passenger car had gotten stuck and had been pulled out with the other vehicle.

He clambered back up the terrace side and made his way back, taking care to make a little noise as he covered the last hundred yards to where Susan lay.

She backed away from her vantage point and stood up as she saw him coming. He could see the question forming on her lips. He pulled her down in the lee of a boulder. "They were here, but they've gone. They've got two vehicles, and they were both parked down there."

She just looked at him. "So we don't know where they are?"

"Not exactly. They've probably gone back into town for the night. It's a good bet that they'll come back to this same spot tomorrow. If they do, I'll be waiting for them."

He rose and dusted off his jeans. "Where are we going, back home?"

"No," he said, "I want to go down there and look around a little. Maybe I can find a real good ambush point and settle things with these boys from there."

He went bounding down the terrace face, heedless of the noise, and she followed more slowly. She caught up with him at the cabin door. "Look there," he said, grinning and pointing to the ground with the muzzle of his rifle. In front of the doorstep were a maze of footprints. "They were here, all right . . ." he broke off, puzzled.

"What's wrong, Mac? What is it?"

He frowned. "There's four of them. Damn! I was just getting comfortable with the idea of taking on three."

She looked at the jumble of footprints. "Are you sure? Maybe it's not the same three."

He gave her an annoyed look. "Of course I'm sure. Look." He pointed out the four different sets

of footprints with his rifle barrel, explaining the
differences so that she could see them. "And it's got
to be the same people. It all fits together. Who else
would come up here this morning and leave in the
afternoon? If it was hunters, they'd have spent the
night here, and there'd be frost working in some of
the tire tracks and footprints. But there's none."

He looked up and pointed at the cabin door.
"Look, they've pried the hasp off the door. That
proves that whoever was here wasn't the rightful
owner."

"You can't be sure of all this, Mac. You're just
guessing. It doesn't have to be Nazario and his
friends, it could be thieves or vandals."

"Well, it wasn't vandals. Those windows would be
an irresistible temptation. As for thieves, let's go in
and see if anything's been stolen."

The interior of the cabin was dark, with a musty
odor. MacGonigal lit a kerosene lamp and hung it
from a nail in a rafter. Susan looked around the
small, single room. It was as dreary as it could be,
with old, sagging overstuffed furniture, obviously
castoffs. A rough bar stretched across one corner,
and there were empty beer cans and bottles in a
plastic bucket. More empties littered the floor. A
sheet-metal stove stood in the center of the room.

There was an almost overpowering smell in the
room.

She wrinkled her nose. "Whoever owns this place
must be a pig! It stinks in here."

MacGonigal sniffed. "Yeah. It smells like somebody got a deer this year. Or maybe it's from last

year." He broke off. "Look there! Fresh cigarette and cigar butts!"

Susan followed his pointing hand, stepped over closer to look, and slipped on the floor. MacGonigal put out his hand to steady her. "Careful, honey, that floor's wet."

He stopped and looked down at the wet spot. He took three quick strides across the room and laid his hand on the sheet-metal stove. It was cold. Frowning, he opened the fire door and looked inside. Nothing. It had been cleaned out, long ago, by the looks of it.

"What's wrong, Mac?"

"I'm not sure. Except . . . why would the floor be wet?"

"Maybe the roof leaks. Or maybe they spilled something."

His frown deepened. "Maybe. But there's no signs of a leak. And as cold as it's been lately, you'd think that it would be ice . . ." He took the lantern from it's nail and shown it on the ceiling and wall. "Funny that they had time to spill something, but didn't light the stove. What would they be doing that they would spill something?" He bent down with the lantern and examined the wet spot. There were some dark spots near it. He put his finger to one and sniffed it.

"Blood," he said.

"Are you sure?"

He didn't answer, but picked up his rifle and went out the door. Susan followed him. "Look at that," he said, pointing to a dark spot on a small bush. He walked a few steps further, going down toward the creek. He stopped and pointed again, wordlessly. Susan saw a dark red spot on a stone. A few feet farther on there was another. He followed them, his eyes on the ground. At the creek bank, he lost the trail. He wandered slowly up and down the bank, his eyes riveted to the ground. "They must have crossed over," he said. He stepped out on the stones that formed a rough crossing, walking gingerly on the moss-slick rocks. Susan watched him cross, then range up and down the bank on the other side. He stopped and touched a small hazel bush with the rifle barrel. Susan, watching from the other side, called to him. "What is it?"

He looked up, startled, as if he had forgotten all about her. "More blood," he said, laconically.

"Wait for me. I'm coming over." She stepped out on the rocks, balancing herself precariously with the carbine. Halfway across, she lost confidence and almost fell, but recovered and finished the crossing in a rush. MacGonigal stood motionless, as if afraid that the spoor would vanish if he left it. When she came up, he pointed out to the dark splash on the hazel bush, then began to cast around for more sign.

A dozen yards farther on, he found a single drop of darkening red, splattered on a stone. Beyond that was another, a few yards more a third. He followed the trail intently, with Susan following wordlessly at his heels. For a hundred yards, she kept close behind him, until he motioned her to keep back. They were approaching a clump of boulders lying in a disordered jumble some fifty feet above the stream. He slipped the safety off his rifle and cracked the lever slightly, opening the breech just enough to see the reassuring brass glow of the cartridge. He stepped up to the pile of boulders, then suddenly stopped.

"Now I know why there were four sets of tracks."

Susan joined him. Just ahead, she could see a boot protruding from behind a rock. MacGonigal went up to it and looked. He squatted down, disappearing from her view, and then stood again, shaking his head. "It's Henry Carberry, the fellow who owns the cabin. Poor Henry. He must have been out here when they came. They just killed him and dragged his body off into the woods."

He stepped away from the corpse. "Come on. We've got to make sure that we haven't left any fingerprints or other traces in the cabin."

She didn't move. He was already striding back toward the cabin. At last she hurried to catch up with him and tug at his arm. "Why, Mac? Why don't we just call the police? We didn't kill him, Nazario did. If they arrest Nazario, our problems are over."

He stopped and looked at her. "Didn't you tell me that Nazario had killed other people?"

"Yes . . . but . . ."

"But nothing! He got away with it before, and he'll get away with this killing. What kind of evidence have we got to prove who did it? Tire tracks? Cigar butts? What have we got that will stand up in court, even if they catch him?"

"But, Mac, he was here! He did it!"

"Sure, he did it. You know that he did it, and I know it. Try and prove it!"

"But, Mac, we can't just go off and not do

something! That poor man probably had a family. Somebody has to tell the police or somebody about him."

MacGonigal's face was bleak. "Damn right he had a family! And the bastards killed him like a dog, just because he got in their way."

She grabbed his arm and pulled him half around. "Mac, I'll go to the police if you won't! I won't leave that man lying there like that!"

MacGonigal grabbed her by the shoulders. "Look, Sue, I don't like this any more than you do. But listen to reason. Those bastards know where we live. They're after us. And they're going to get us, if we're not damn careful."

He sat on the doorstep of the cabin and pulled her down beside him. "If we report this, the police will ask questions. At the very least, I'll have to go in and make a statement. That'll leave you alone. Any bets as to what will happen to you while I'm gone?"

Her face, windburned and ruddy, suddenly went pale. He went on. "If the police find out about you, at the least they'll pick you up as a material witness. They may even hold you as a suspect. There are several murders in this thing now, Blue Larry, George, and now Henry Carberry. Look at it their way—a lot of people in your vicinity are suddenly dead."

She didn't reply, and he continued. "They'll certainly charge me with withholding evidence and obstructing justice. If they find out about those two punks, there'll be a murder charge for both of us.

"Now, it doesn't matter how you slice it, if they

connect us with this thing, we're both going to jail. Don't you think that Nazario's kind can't get to someone who's locked up?"

"What are we going to do, Mac?" she said in a small, defeated voice.

"We're going to clean up all evidence of being here . . . No, wait. I've got a better idea. We'll stop off just over the ridge from Lloyd MacCorkle's. Lloyd's got a phone. I'll go down and say I was hunting and noticed that someone had broken into Carberry's hunting cabin and ask Lloyd to call and tell him. That'll explain me being there."

"But, Mac, Carberry is dead . . ."

"Not officially, he isn't. Right now, he isn't even missing. But his family will be calling the sheriff sooner or later, and that will give them some clue of where to look. They'll find him, just like we did, but it won't involve us. Harvey will come out again, most likely, but I'll just tell him that I was squirrel hunting and noticed that the lock was broken."

He gripped her arm and lifted her to her feet. "We've got a ways to go before dark. We'd better get moving."

They went down the entrance road and up an old logging track, now grown over and barely visible. MacGonigal moved quickly, but stopped frequently to allow Susan to keep up with him. The road they followed—it was really not more than a faint trace —was not so exhausting as the hike into Carberry's cabin.

At last the old road gained the ridgetop and followed it for a mile or more. It continually forked and branched off where the old loggers had followed finger ridges down into the valleys, and Susan quickly lost her sense of where they were. But MacGonigal had traveled this way many times and held to the true course. At last he came to a halt near a jumble of boulders which the road skirted. "It forks here," he said, pointing. "That way leads back to within a mile of the cabin. If anything happens, just stay on the high ground. Follow the road until it peters out. You'll be on a high knob. Go down and cross the valley to the west, climb the ridge there and keep going west. You'll hit Bear Pen Creek. Follow it downstream to the falls, and you'll be home."

He started down the opposite fork, then turned back. "I can't go down there with a .308 and tell them I'm squirrel hunting. Give me your pistol." He put the Savage down and unbuckled his belt, passing her the big Python and taking the little Woodsman in its place. He rebuckled his belt. "Wait here an hour. I'll be back by then."

He went on down the trail, moving at an easy, swinging gait. Five minutes brought him to MacCorkle's back pasture. He slid through the wires of the fence, disdaining the gate, and strode over to the house. He knocked loudly on the door. For a moment he could hear no sound at all from within, then a voice said, "Who's there?"

"It's me, Lloyd, Francis MacGonigal."

There was a slow shuffling of feet within and the door swung open. Lloyd was a man of about fifty, beefy and sunburned, with sparse red hair. His scalp was shockingly white, in contrast to his face and neck, with the sweatband of his straw hat permanently engraved in his forehead. He carried a shotgun in his left hand, and stuck out one freckled, hairy arm to welcome his visitor.

"Lord, Francis, you could get yourself shot, comin' up the back way like that! Everybody's edgy since they found that fellow killed the other day."

MacGonigal forced himself to be at ease. "Yeah, I heard about that, Lloyd. Strange things happening in these hills these days."

MacCorkle grunted and waved MacGonigal to a chair. What brings you by this time of day?" Without waiting for an answer, he called to his wife, a tiny, birdlike woman, "Elsie, bring us some coffee, if you don't mind."

MacGonigal sat in the proffered chair, his elbows on the kitchen table. "I can't stay, Lloyd, although I will miss Elsie's fine cooking. What I came by for was to tell you that someone has broken into Henry Carberry's hunting cabin. I was just over there, and the lock was broken off. I went in and looked around. There didn't seem to be anything missing or any damage, but maybe you wouldn't mind giving Henry a call?"

"No, I wouldn't mind at all, Francis. But what was you doin' clear over there?"

MacGonigal grinned easily. "Huntin'. Or more truthfully, just bummin' around in the woods."

MacCorkle sighed. "I wish I was you, Francis. No work to do, no worries, just sit back and draw my pension and hunt and fish, and do whatever I damn well please."

"Francis MacGonigal, you need to find yourself a good woman and get yourself an honest job," said Elsie, as she put the coffee cups on the table.

MacGonigal grinned again. "I work, Elsie. I write. That's hard work. As for a good woman, I'm afraid they're all taken up, unless you're planning to get rid of Lloyd, here."

Elsie made a clicking sound with her tongue. "Some work you do! And I'll tell you one thing, Francis MacGonigal, if I was your wife, I'd put a stop to your shiftless ways."

MacGonigal laughed. "Your life must be hell, Lloyd!"

Lloyd grinned and put an encircling arm around Elsie, who was grinning as broadly as he. "There are compensations, Francis. There are compensations!"

MacGonigal drained his coffee cup and pushed his chair back. "I've got to go now, if I'm going to make it home before dark. I just came by to tell you about Henry's cabin."

MacCorkle stood with him. "I'll call Henry right now." He showed MacGonigal to the door. "You take care of yourself, Francis, you hear?"

"I hear," said MacGonigal, "and the same to the both of you. You take care of each other." He leered at Elsie. "If he won't take care of you, you know where to come."

She blushed and made a half-delighted, half-exasperated sound. "Francis, you're the worst in these hills."

"I know," said MacGonigal, smiling, as he went through the gate and into the pasture.

He went back up the logging road to where he had left Susan. She sat huddled in her parka, the Savage and the carbine leaning on the log beside her. "God, Mac, I thought you'd never come back. It's starting to get late. We'll never find our way home in the dark."

She was right, MacGonigal realized. There wasn't more than a half-hour's light left. He helped her to her feet. "We'll hurry, but don't worry; we'll find our way with no problem."

They went along the old road, making good time, although the light was going fast. By the time they reached the end of the road, it was nearly dark. "I wish we had had sense enough to take that flashlight with us," said Susan.

"We don't need it. I can see in the dark like a cat," said MacGonigal. "Besides, if we had it, we'd be tempted to use it, and that might not be such a good idea."

"What do you mean by that?" Her voice had an edge to it.

"I mean that we know where our friends were, but they were there a long time ago. They won't go back now. They've got as much sense as anybody, and they'll know that Henry Carberry's family will get worried when he doesn't come home. Somebody, probably the sheriff, will come out to check. They know that, even if they don't know about the phone call I had Lloyd make. They won't come back there, so they'll have to figure out some other course of action."

She had hold of his sleeve now, letting him guide

her through the dark woods. "And what do you think that they'll do?"

"Well, I don't know for sure. But we went looking for them. It's reasonable to expect that they'd go looking for us, especially since they know where we live."

She stumbled and he caught her. "My God, Mac! Do you think that they're waiting at the cabin for us?"

"They could be," he said. "They sure could be. But we won't be taken by surprise. We'll act as if they are."

They spoke no more, but concentrated on making their way through the woods. It had been pitch black, but there was an early-rising moon, and that soon gave them the faintest illumination. Coming down over the ridge, they could see the roofs of the cabin and outbuildings shining silver.

"It looks so peaceful, Mac."

"I hope it's as peaceful as it looks." He pulled her close to him for a minute. "But I know what you mean. That's why I decided to settle here." They went on down, and as they came up to the paddock, they could see the horses, standing under the trees on the far side of the fields, dim shapes in the moonlight. "At least the horses are all right," said Susan, with a shudder, remembering how she had hid while Harry and Smoke were killed. "Yeah," said MacGonigal, "that's a point for them. They're going to need points if I catch them inside my house." He put his gloved finger against Susan's lips to signal her to be quiet, and slipped away from her.

She could see him, a wraith in the moonlight, his rifle jutting forward, as he approached the tack room.

He crouched at the door, listening, for a full five minutes, then went in. There was no light, but he searched carefully, moving silently among the jumbled tack, checking the feed room, assuring himself that the place was clear. He went back out and waved to Susan.

She came across the open ground quickly, keeping the tack room between herself and the cabin. MacGonigal noted with approval that she took care to keep the carbine pointed up and under control. She was trembling when she joined him.

"Are you all right?"

"I'm cold and scared, but other than that, I'm just fine. Do you really think that they're here? There's no light showing from the cabin."

"You wouldn't expect them to advertise, would you?"

"No," she said, "I guess I was just hoping. Are they really down there?"

"There's only one way to tell, and that's go down and check it out. Will you be all right here?"

"I'll be fine. It's you I'm worried about."

"I'll be okay. I'm going to scout out the cabin as carefully as I know how. I want you to stay here. If I'm not back in twenty minutes, get the hell out of here. If anybody comes this way, let them get close, really close, and let them have it. Otherwise, don't get involved in any shooting."

She nodded, took a deep breath, and gripped the carbine. He brushed his lips lightly against hers and slipped out of the shelter of the tack room.

The cabin loomed ahead, black and lifeless, its roof shining a dim silver-gray in the moonlight. MacGonigal weighed the need for speed in covering the open ground against the need for silence. He decided that silence was preferable. They wouldn't be likely to hit him in the dark, even if he were moving slowly, and if he could come upon them unawares, they wouldn't even get to fire on him.

He reached the back porch and pressed himself against the wall, listening. With his ear to the logs, he could hear any sound in the cabin. The hum of the refrigerator and freezer were distinct through the logs. He couldn't hear anything else. He waited a long, agonizing five minutes, timed by his watch, before admitting to himself that the cabin was empty.

Well, MacGonigal, me boyo, he thought to himself, what next? The bastards may have boobytrapped the cabin like they did the truck. Hell, they may be just a little ways off, waiting for the bang. He stood thinking for another few minutes. He remembered that he had told Susan to leave if he wasn't back in twenty minutes. It was time to get back to her and reassure her. He reluctantly left the cabin and started back to the tack room, a plan forming in his mind.

"Mac, is that you?"

"That it is. I don't think that they're up at the house, but I'm going to need your help."

"Anything's better than waiting here."

"I'm afraid that you're going to have to do a bit

more of that. I've been thinking that maybe they've boobytrapped the cabin." He heard her take in her breath sharply. "Now, I don't know that they've done it. In fact, they probably haven't. But it doesn't hurt to assume that they have."

"I know, Mac. Don't worry about me. I just hadn't thought of it. When you went down to the cabin, I thought you were going down there and walk in, like you did on those other three. I'm glad that you thought a little further along than I have."

"I haven't, really. I was going to go in there, but something stopped me. It took me a while to figure out what it was."

He stopped a minute. "Now, here's what we're going to do: You stay here, just like you did when I scouted out the cabin. I'm going to check out the barn, then I'll come back for you.

"There's a ladder in the barn. I'll carry it across the yard and put it against the north gable window. You'll have to cover me, and steady the ladder while I go up. I don't think that it's likely they've boobytrapped the gable windows."

She took up a position where she could peer around the corner toward the barn. "Okay, Mac. Same rules as last time. I wait twenty minutes, and I shoot anyone who gets close to me."

"What a girl! I'm glad I've got you on my side." He started across the yard, rifle ready, but already telling himself that there was nothing to worry about in the barn. Careful about that, me boyo, he cautioned himself. When you don't think they're there, then that's when they're most likely to show up.

The cavernous interior of the barn was as black as if it were underground. There was absolutely no light. MacGonigal listened a while, but could make out no sounds other than the occasional creaking of the structure in the wind. He began to feel his way around the inside, working along the walls, foot by foot, and stopping to listen every few steps. There was nothing. He reached the foot of the ladder to the loft and drew his pistol, the little Woodsman. For a moment he debated going back and exchanging it for the Python, but decided against wasting the time. Pistol in hand, he began his climb into the loft.

He felt horribly vulnerable as he came through the hole in the floor, but as he scrambled to his feet, there was no sign of any presence other than his own. He moved slowly among the stacked, baled hay, the little .22 pistol at the ready. At the far end of the loft, he could see the pale square of the loading platform. MacGonigal worked his way around the loft toward the platform. A shaft of moonlight streamed in and gently illuminated a patch of flooring. A dozen feet from that patch, MacGonigal halted and sucked in his breath. A small object lay just in the edge of the moonlight. MacGonigal crept forward and picked it up. It was a cigarette butt.

He squatted there, just outside the range of the moonlight, the butt held between thumb and forefinger. They were there, or had been there. It couldn't be anyone else. Nobody in his right mind would smoke a cigarette in a hayloft, unless it was someone who knew nothing about haylofts. MacGonigal remained on his haunches, thinking. They had been there, all right. Up here in the loft. The loading platform provided a good, clear field of fire toward the trail coming up from the falls. A man here with a rifle could easily pick off anyone coming up from below. They must have come back after the sheriff left and decided to investigate the house. Finding no one home, they laid an ambush, but abandoned it when night fell. The question was, where were they now?

A dozen questions buzzed in his head. What about the booby trap on the pickup? Had they found that he had disarmed it? If they had, then they were a step ahead, for they would know that they were dealing with a professional. Maybe I should have left it, he thought. Maybe if I had, they'd have checked and blown themselves sky high. He shook his head, regretfully. I should have counter-boobytrapped, left the damn thing where they put it, but rigged it to go off when they touched it.

Well, Francis, he said to himself, that's enough crying over spilt milk. The question now is, are the bastards in the woodline with a starlight scope? It would be so easy for them to pick off the both of us. He shook his head. No, he told himself, they won't have anything so sophisticated. Even their bomb was crude. The components could be bought in any hardware shop. He himself would have made something much more effective without using anything more complex than the materials they had. All their actions to date showed that they favored the direct, simple approach. They weren't any the less dangerous for that, of course.

With a start, he remembered Susan. He looked at his watch. He'd been gone eighteen minutes. He crossed the floor of the loft swiftly and slid down the ladder, running back across the yard to the tack room.

"All clear?"

"It's all clear now, but they've been here. I found a cigarette butt in the hayloft."

He could feel the sudden tension. "Are you sure they're gone now?" she said.

"Hell, no, I'm not sure. But they're not in the tack room, and they're not in the barn, and I don't think they're in the house. But I won't know that for sure until I get in and look around. So let's get the ladder."

They went into the barn, and Susan posted herself at the entrance while MacGonigal manuevered the heavy extension ladder off its hooks. "Take the Savage and stand away from the door. I can't be sure that I won't clobber you with this thing," he said, as he struggled to bring it around so that he could get it through the door.

She let him get a little way ahead with the ladder, and only came out of cover when he actually reached the cabin. MacGonigal set the ladder against the end of the cabin and turned to look for her. "Where've you been?"

"I stayed by the corner of the barn. I figured that if they were around somewhere, they couldn't help hearing or seeing you with that ladder, so I thought I'd wait and see what happened."

MacGonigal grinned in the darkness. "That's my girl. You're starting to think like me."

She kissed him quickly. "Now get up that ladder. I'm freezing out here."

He tested the positioning of the ladder. "Hold it steady for me. I'm going up."

The windows at the top gave him a little trouble. He got the storm windows off easily enough, but the inner windows wouldn't budge. At last, swearing softly to himself, MacGonigal cracked a pane with the barrel of the Woodsman. He rolled the barrel around the frame, clearing splinters and shards of glass away, then reached in and freed the latch. Heaving, he pushed the window open and clambered inside the house.

The loft was as black as the hayloft had been, perhaps even more so. MacGonigal felt his way around the open space, his hands encountering familiar objects—his desk, the spare bed, the rustic rail at the top of the stairs. At last, satisfied that there was no one in the loft, he opened the storage room door and scrabbled among his camping gear. He dug out a small, double-bulbed flashlight. One of the two bulbs was red-shielded, and would be difficult for anyone outside to see. With the flashlight, off, in one hand and the Colt Woodsman in the other, he started down.

There was no sound or sign of another person downstairs. MacGonigal went into the pantry and closed the door behind him. Then, holding his breath, he switched the red light on. It barely gave enough light for him to tell that it was working, but when he held it a few inches from an object, he could make out its outlines. He went down on his hands and knees and carefully searched the area around the outside pantry door. That done, he ran the light over the door itself, paying particular attention to the latch and the edges of the door. There was nothing there that appeared out of place. Telling himself that the workmanship on the earlier booby trap indicated that he didn't have a highly skilled opponent, he slipped the bolt, grabbed the knob and opened the back door quietly, calling softly to Susan. She materialized out of the blackness and stepped into the darker blackness of the interior. "My God, Mac, can't you at least get a flash-light?"

"I've got one, a red light, but it's very dim. I don't think anything brighter would be safe. Close the door and I'll switch it back on." She pulled the door to, and he flicked on the tiny light. "Don't touch anything. I haven't checked for booby traps yet, except right around here."

"Thanks a lot," she said sarcastically. "I'll just stand here without breathing and hope nothing goes boom!"

He was already halfway into the living area. "Don't worry, you're probably safe in there. If there's a booby trap, it's probably either attached to the front door, or wired into the electrical system."

He played the dim light across the floor, checking for trip wires or other traps. As soon as he got to the front door, he saw it. It was a lot more sophisticated than the one in the truck, but still crudely made. It consisted of a plastic tube, probably from a high-priced cigar, taped to the doorknob. Two wires led from the cap of the tube down to the floor, where they were hooked to a six-volt dry cell battery. On the way down, one of the wires detoured into a package that was taped just below the knob. MacGonigal looked the contraption over closely. Behind him, he could hear Susan stirring.

"What is it, Mac? Have you found something?"

"I sure have. Stay back." He slowly rose from the floor and backed across the floor. "Just get back in the pantry. Close the door, sit down behind the freezer, and don't move."

"What have you found? Is it bad?"

"Bad enough. It's an anti-handling device. I'm not sure, but what it looks like they've done is strap a tube with a ball bearing in it to the doorknob. When the tube is disturbed, the ball rolls and completes the firing circuit."

"Can you disarm it?"

"I think so. It looks like there's only one battery, and that's in plain sight. But I want you well out of the way before I try it."

He waited until he heard the door close behind him, then counted patiently to a hundred to give her plenty of time to get under cover. With the little flashlight in his teeth, he crawled across the floor. The battery was there in plain sight, as he had said. All that he had to do was disconnect it. He was sweating, even though it was cold, and his hand trembled as he reached out. Damn you for a simple, blundering, heavy-footed Irishman, he said to himself. This thing is too simple. There's got to be more to it than that. He pulled his hand back and studied the arrangement.

It just looked too easy. He got up on his knees and traced the wires again with the flashlight. They were as he remembered. He rocked back on his heels and thought about it. Something wasn't right. They had waited for the first bomb, hidden in the brush, smoking while they killed time. But they weren't waiting for this one—unless they were waiting awfully quietly.

He thought a little longer. The first bomb had been a small affair, with a charge only about half the size of this one. He studied the charge again. It was large, big enough to hold a pound of powder. Now, they obviously didn't intend to kill with the first one, so why should they make this one so large? Unless they were sure that it wouldn't get Sue.

That had to be it. They had set this bomb for him alone. They had known that Susan wouldn't be the victim. Now, Francis, me boyo, he thought, how would they know that? Because they found that you'd disarmed the first one, that's how. They have a good idea of the sort of man they're dealing with, and they're playing on that.

Okay, he thought, mull that over awhile. They expect you to protect her. But unless they expect you to find the bomb, they can't be sure that she won't be the one to open that door. So they expect it to be found.

He could feel the hackles on his neck rising. If they expect it to be found, they must expect you to try to disarm it. And they've got a surprise for you. He went over the bomb again. Nothing. Then suddenly he saw it.

VII.

It was almost a fluke that he noticed it. The wire that ran from the tube into the charge was slightly thicker than the other wires. Other than that, there was no clue that the device was other than what it seemed—a crude, but deadly, tilt switch. MacGonigal held the light close to the wire in question. At first, he had wondered if it might be some trick of vision, but there was no doubt about it—it was just slightly thicker than the other wires. So that's it, he said to himself, that's why they left the battery so casually in sight, to lead you to believe that all you had to do is to disconnect the wires.

He studied the device again. Devilishly clever, me boyo, he thought. The battery on the floor's a fake, a decoy. The real battery is inside the tube, along with the little steel ball. The only thing that gives it away is that they need three wires coming from the tube, instead of two, because one of the wires is a dummy. So they use a piece of double lead that looks almost exactly like the single lead stuff they used for the rest of the wiring. Very clever. Big, dumb, Irish MacGonigal pulls the wires loose, and starts to disassemble the thing. And blows himself to hell in the process. They had you figured out, me boyo. They had you figured out to the last digit.

He backed slowly away from the device. Feeling for the knob behind him, he opened the door to the pantry. "Is it safe now, Mac?"

"No, it isn't. Your friends are a bunch of damn clever bastards. They meant for me to find that thing and try to disarm it."

"You mean that they boobytrapped the booby trap?"

"That's exactly what they did. And it damned near worked. I was just an impulse away from being dead meat."

She reached out for him in the dim red glow of the little flashlight. "We've got to get out of here, Mac."

"I thought we'd been through that before. There's no place to go. They'll find us, wherever we go, and they'll be able to deal with us a lot easier if we're on unfamiliar ground."

She tugged his sleeve angrily. "I don't mean run. I mean get away from this cabin. This is the only place they know. If we move away, they'll be at a loss as to where to find us, and they won't be able to set any more traps for us. Then we can set traps for them."

"Now you're thinking like MacGonigal. I wonder why MacGonigal isn't thinking like MacGonigal these days?"

"You're thinking fine, it's just that we do better as a team."

"Thank you for the vote of confidence," he said gravely. "Did you have any particular traps in mind for our friends?"

"No," she said, "I thought I'd leave that up to you. After all, what am I paying you for?"

MacGonigal grinned in the darkness. "I thought it was for my magnificent body. Do you mean to tell me that I have to use my brain, too?"

"If it wouldn't be too much of a strain."

"I'll manage," he said solemnly. "I pity these bastards. They've run up against the first team, MacGonigal and Ennis."

"While you're bragging, how about coming up with something to brag about?"

MacGonigal thought a minute. There was a half-formed idea in his mind, and he grappled with it for a few moments. "Okay, here's what we'll do; I'll go up and get a camp stove while you mix up some dough. Make enough to fill a pie pan."

"Dough? What kind of dough?"

"Doesn't matter. We're not going to eat it. But it should be fairly stiff, and bake up hard. A thick mixture of flour and water will do."

He left her mystified while he went upstairs and began to sort through all his camping gear. He pulled everything out and piled it on the floor, then came downstairs with the stove. By then, she had a gooey mass of flour and water in a bowl. He looked at it in the glow of the little flashlight. "Good. Just wait a minute longer and it'll be ready for cooking." He went out the pantry door, and was back in a few minutes with a large empty cookie can and a couple of coffee cans full of nails and assorted hardware.

"Mix this stuff with the dough and pour it all in the cookie can. Be sure you get an even layer on the bottom, then cook it."

She stared at the mess of rusty metal in the cans. "Mac, what is this?"

"Shrapnel, or langridge, if you want to be technical. We're going to make us a claymore."

"That doesn't tell me anything. What's a claymore?"

He was busy pumping up the camp stove. He put it on the floor of the pantry and lit it, nursing it until it gave off a steady blue flame. "It's a directional mine. We used them in Vietnam all the time. It works like this: The dough holds the metal bits, the nails, and screws and stuff in place. Once it has cooked, we cool it off and add explosives until the can is full. Then we turn it up on its side, with the bottom pointing toward the bad guys, and when it goes off . . . blam! Goodbye Nazario and company!"

"How are you going to set it off?"

"Let me worry about that. I know more tricks with explosives than our friends ever thought of. You just cook it up nicely. We wouldn't want our guests to get indigestion." He ducked out the door and made for the shed, where the tractor was stored. Without any preliminary scouting, he slipped into the little structure and went to the back. There were several sacks of nitrogen fertilizer piled there. He took an empty gunny sack and put several shovels full of fertilizer in it, then picked up a gas can. He heard it slosh—there was enough for his purposes. He headed back toward the house and deposited the sack and can on the back porch.

He next went down into his shop and collected a mass of things: a couple of rolls of insulated wire, a roll of thin steel wire, a few tools, a spool of fishing line, some tape, a can of FFFG black powder and a trio of large, electric lantern batteries. He poked around a few places, looking for other odds and ends, then came back to the pantry and looked in. He could just see Sue's face in the dim glow of the camp stove as she bent over the concoction. "How's it going?"

"I think that it's about done. Come and see what you think."

He came in and examined the lumpy, crusted mass in the can. "Good. Put the lid on it and put it under the pump. Just cool it off, but don't let any water get inside."

As she went into the living area, he followed her and checked the windows. "So that's how they got in and out," he said, holding the dim glow of the red light on the window next to the door. "They didn't show a lot of originality, did they? Well, let's hope they don't do any better tomorrow."

He took down his bagpipe case and dug through it, coming up with an olive jar full of reeds and a tin box. He took these into the pantry with him and laid them down on the floor near the stove, which he turned off. He went out and gathered up the things he had left on the porch, then called to Susan. "Come here and hold the light for me."

She took up the light and held it steady, so that its glow illuminated his hands and the things he worked with. First he opened the olive jar and shook out the reeds, selecting three bass drone reeds, pieces of cane larger than his index finger. Opening the tin box, he took out a stick of sealing wax and softened its end on the still hot burner of the camp stove.

With this, he carefully sealed the tongues of the three reeds, setting them carefully on end while the wax hardened.

That done, he cut three lengths of insulated wire, stripped the ends a little, and wired together one set of ends of each wire, using the steel wire.

"What's that for, Mac?"

He grunted. "It's called a bridge. The steel wire is too small and has too much resistance to carry the current. So when the current is switched on, it'll glow red-hot. Probably melt, if the current flows long enough, which it won't."

He took up the can of FFFG gunpowder and filled each drone reed with it, then carefully stuck the bridged ends of the insulated wires into them. He then picked up the sealing wax and melted it against the burners again and sealed the end of each open reed, making a waterproof package of each reed. "There," he said, "—blasting caps as good as Hercules Powder Company ever made."

He went back out and brought in the sack and can. He poured the fertilizer into the can, then dribbled gasoline into it, stirring the mixture into a pasty mess. "So much for that," he said. "There's our claymore, with three blasting caps to set it off. Let's let the gas evaporate a little before we assemble it."

He drew her up and led her up the stairs. "Now," he said, "we're likely to be in the woods awhile, so we'd better get ready for it." He began to go through the pile of stuff on the floor, sorting it, directing her to put articles into either a rucksack or a large expedition pack. They packed food for two weeks, a tent, sleeping bags, stove, cooking gear, and spare clothes. At last he stopped and strapped up the two packs. "Grab the rucksack and let's haul this stuff outside," he said. She did as he directed, finding the rucksack a solid, but manageable load. MacGonigal picked up the heavy expedition pack and hoisted it onto his shoulders, then took his binoculars off the peg and slung them from the top of the frame. By that time, Susan was halfway downstairs. He followed her, the unfastened waist belt of the pack clacking against the bannisters.

They put the packs outside, and MacGonigal took up the cookie can and inserted the three reeds, leaving the wires hanging out a bent-down section of the rim. Then he closed the lid. He stuffed a few objects in his pocket and said, "Let's set our trap now."

He led Susan around to the front of the cabin and had her stand up on the porch next to the window, holding the red light. Pacing off fifteen yards, he selected a small tree and strapped the makeshift directional mine with the wire between the trunk and one limb. Sighting over the top of the cookie can, he made minute adjustments until it was aimed directly at the tiny red spark of the flashlight, then firmly wired it in place. With his pocketknife, he cut small branches from nearby bushes, arranged them in front of the mine and wired them in place. It was too dark to check his handiwork effectively, but he hoped he had concealed the device well enough to escape detection.

The next item on the agenda was to rig the triggering devices. Taking a reel of insulated wire, he led it through the leaves, along the foundation of the cabin and under the porch. With a crow bar, he pried up a board just in front of the window and placed a small contact switch under the board. He pressed down on it and listened for the click, then took it out, reset it, fished out the wire from under the porch and attached the switch to it, then put it gently in place.

Going back to the mine, he spliced a second length of wire into the dangling leads and led that forward to the path that ran around the house. He wrapped foil around the jaws of a spring-type clothespin, then inserted a small piece of wood between the jaws to keep them apart. This piece of wood was attached to a length of fishing line stretched tightly across the path at ankle height. A man tripping over the fishing line would twitch the sliver of wood out, the foil covered jaws would make contact, and the device would detonate. The location of the trip line put it just in the edge of the expected fan of flying metal from the claymore. MacGonigal hoped that if the killers went past the porch, they would be close enough together for the mine to get them all if the first one tripped the fish line.

Back at the tree, MacGonigal fashioned a third trigger, this one from a mousetrap. He put two of the batteries down on the mousetrap and delicately released the trigger. The weight of the batteries held the trap open, but when the batteries were moved, the trap would snap shut, completing a third circuit. MacGonigal left the wire leading to the two batteries on the mousetrap in plain sight, but concealed the wire to the third, and hid that battery under a stone.

His work done, he backed slowly away and made a

long detour around the cabin. Susan waited for him at the back door. "We're all set," he said. "I'll go in and bolt the back door from the inside, and go out the same way I came in. It'll take awhile, because I've got a few things to do before I leave. Be patient."

He went in and bolted the door, then looked over the room. The window the killers had used was across from his gun rack, and there were a few nice pieces left hanging there. He took them down and moved them to the chimney corner, where the massive stone fireplace would offer protection from the flying fragments of metal. Then he climbed up the stairs and came down with an old alarm clock. He pried off the plastic cover and laid it aside while he broke off the large hand and discarded it, then bent the hour hand away from the face at an angle. He put the crystal back in place to verify that the hour hand almost touched it, but still had clearance to move. He set the hand at twelve and wound the clock. He bored a tiny hole through the plastic with the point of his knife, then screwed a wood screw in and replaced the plastic cover. He positioned it so that the screw was at about one-thirty. He took a length of insulated wire from his pocket and stripped the ends. One wire he hooked to the bell of the clock, the other to the wood screw. Then, holding his breath, he snipped the key lead wire of the booby trap attached to his front door. He spliced the wires from the clock into the circuit and hooked them to the battery on the floor, then hurried up the stairs and went through the window.

"Are you down there, Sue?"

She called up to him. He peered down into the darkness and said, "Pass up the storm window. I want to put it back, so they won't get suspicious if they approach the cabin from this direction."

He wrestled the window into place, then came down the ladder and collapsed it and hoisted it onto his shoulder. "Where are you taking that?" she said.

"Back where I got it. I don't intend to leave any evidence that might tip the bastards off." He carried the heavy ladder across the open yard and maneuevered it back onto its pegs, then went back for his pack. It was leaning against one of the porch uprights. As he lifted it, he realized how tired he was. He checked his watch. It was almost two in the morning. "My God," he said, "we've been up all night. Let's find a place to camp and unroll these sleeping bags."

Behind him Susan answered, "I was wondering when you'd think of that. How far do we have to go?"

He hunched the pack up on his shoulders and fastened the waist belt, then picked up his rifle. "Not all that far. Over the ridge, and down it a ways. There's a nice sheltered spot there. It's as good as any place farther on."

They trudged away from the little cluster of buildings without looking back and started up the ridge, trudging up the path toward the place where they had burned the horses. It was hard going in the dark. The slope was littered with loose rock, they were tired, and the packs were heavy. They stumbled again and again. The odor of the burning was in their nostrils, a dead, musty, but faintly acrid smell. It was depressing, and it weighed them down.

The packs were heavy, much heavier than those MacGonigal usually carried, and they were loaded inconveniently. The binoculars swung annoyingly on their strap, and MacGonigal took them down and hung them around his neck. It was no improvement. He unzipped his parka and thrust the cased instrument inside. They were too bulky to allow him to rezip the parka, and they restricted his movement. At last he stopped and lowered the pack to the ground.

"Thank God! I was wondering when you were going to call a halt."

"We're not there yet. This is just a rest stop."

"Just a rest stop?" she said, her voice rising. "How much farther is it?"

"Maybe a mile. Just over the top of this ridge and down the other side. There's a bluff that hangs out a little and provides good shelter. There's a spring, too." He was unstrapping the pack and stowing the binoculars as he spoke.

"Mac, I'm not sure I can make it. Do you know how far we've walked today?"

He thought a moment. "About twenty miles, I'd guess. Might be a little less."

"Twenty miles! No wonder my feet feel like raw meat!"

He showed concern. "Have you got blisters? Pull those boots off."

He knelt beside her, the flashlight playing its red glow over her feet as she slowly pulled off the heavy hiking boots. He peeled her socks down and whistled softly when he saw the blisters. One on her right foot ran clear around the heel, a thick doughnut of serum-filled skin, while the left foot had a complex of smaller blisters clustered around the heel and outside of the foot. Running his fingers gently between her toes, he could feel blisters there too.

He gently rested her feet on her rucksack and dug in a side pocket of the big expedition pack and pulled out a large plastic bag held closed with a rubber band.

"MacGonigal's patent disaster kit," he said, holding it up. He opened it up and shook out a waterproof match case. From that he extracted a needle, which he sterilized with a match, then used it to lance her blisters.

"You should have told me when you first felt them. They're really big now."

He stopped, aware that he was disheartening her. "I can fix them, though. You won't even know that you have them when I'm done. Old Doctor MacGonigal will fix you right up."

He gently squeezed the blisters, draining the smaller ones and covering them with bandaids. But with the larger ones, he was not so successful. He lanced them too, but the fluid flowed slowly, a drop at a time. At last, he drew his pocket knife and slit each blister. The fluid ran out like warm water, gushing over his fingers. He took gauze from the plastic bag and moistened it with antiseptic, then placed it over the now deflated blisters on her left foot. Finally, he took a whole square of moleskin and put it over the gauze. He did the same with the other foot, then rolled her socks back up, taking care not to disturb the lay of the moleskin, and pulled on her boots. "There. That's fixed it. Stand up and see how it feels."

Holding his hand, she pulled herself up. "It's like pins and needles."

"It'll feel like that for a while. By tomorrow, you won't even notice it."

He picked up her pack and helped her put it on, then handed her the carbine. Finally, regretfully, he heaved up his own pack and buckled the waist belt. As he was squatting to pick up the Savage, there was a loud thump from the direction of the cabin.

"What was that? It sounded like . . . Mac, we got them!"

He shook his head. "No, baby, that was the booby trap they put on the front door. I rigged a timer to it before I left the house."

"You blew it up? Your own house? But, Mac, why?"

"Don't worry, the house will be fine. I'll have to replace the door and frame, and there'll be a little damage inside, but it shouldn't be anything major."

"But why did you do it?"

"Well, they're hoping that we'll come home and set the damn thing off. The way I figure it, they meant for me to find it and try to disarm it, like I told you. So when they come tomorrow, and see the front door blown out into the yard they'll figure that's what happened, and they may just be dumb enough to walk right in."

He turned and resumed the slow climb up the ridge, with Susan limping along behind him. They zigzagged slowly up the steep slope, following a meandering trail that was barely visible even to

MacGonigal, for all his boasting about his ability to see in the dark. The moon was down, and it was too black for him to do more than maintain a general sense of direction as he plodded along, feeling for the trail with his booted feet. The loose rock slid annoyingly under his feet, and he slipped several times, regaining his balance with a muttered curse each time.

At last he reached the crest. The weight of the expedition pack was dragging him down, and he realized that the long hours, the exertion, the lack of food—for they had not eaten since breakfast—had sapped his strength almost completely. His legs felt like rubber, with red-hot wires running through the thigh muscles, and his knees trembled each time he moved his feet. He sat down and began to massage his legs, concentrating on his thighs, calves, and knees. Below him he could hear Susan struggling up the slope. Her boots rattled against the loose stones, and his feet ached in sympathy for her. His conscience bothered him, for he knew that she was in worse condition than he was. With a sigh, he slipped his big pack off and started back down the hill.

"Let me carry that thing for a while," he said, unfastening the waist belt of the rucksack and pulling it from her shoulders. She protested feebly. "I can carry it, Mac. You've got your own load to carry."

He ignored her protest and shouldered the rucksack, shuffling up the trail, putting one foot in front of the other mechanically. The damn thing was heavy, much too heavy for someone as slim as she. I should have realized it when I was packing, he thought. He slipped on the loose rock and almost went down, saving himself by grabbing a sapling that grew beside the trail. The force of the slide swung him half around and he collided with Susan.

"Mac, you're worse off than I am! Give me that pack."

He shrugged her off. "I'm just taking it easy. I'll carry it to the top of the ridge, and you can take it the rest of the way. It isn't far now, less than a quarter of a mile."

At the top, he lowered the rucksack beside his pack and sat down, his back against a boulder. He pulled the canteen from the shoulder pouch on the expedition pack and unscrewed the cap. "Want some water?"

She took the canteen from him without a word and drank greedily. At last she lowered it. "I haven't left much for you," she said, guiltily.

"That's okay. All I need is to moisten my lips. There's a spring up ahead, like I told you, and there'll be plenty of water when we get there."

He took the canteen and sipped slowly. There were a couple of mouthfuls left, he estimated. He swallowed slowly and regretfully put the cap back on the plastic bottle. It wasn't far to the camp spot he had chosen, but he was worried about Susan. A short break halfway there, a swallow of water, might be what she needed to keep up her morale. He thought about that for a moment, sardonically. His own morale was pretty low. Here he was, out in the open on a cold fall night, driven out of his own cabin by a bunch of killers. His expression was grim. Either they'd do for him, or he'd do for them.

Tomorrow would be a hell of a day.

At last he heaved himself to his feet. He worked the expedition pack onto his back, leaning forward to shift its weight upward while he fastened the waist belt. He picked up the Savage and slung it upside down from the frame of the pack, making sure that the scope didn't bang against the frame. He would probably need that scope tomorrow. He checked his load by leaning sideways, swiveling his body in a small circle, then picked up Susan's rucksack.

"Give me that, Mac. I can carry it!"

In the darkness, it was difficult to tell, but he got the impression that she could barely walk. The short rest had allowed her to stiffen up, and circulation had increased in her raw, flayed feet. MacGonigal knew how she felt. The next hundred yards would be agony for her. After that, her feet would be numb again, and she would be able to walk more or less normally. But she didn't know that, and MacGonigal sympathized with her.

"I'll carry it. It's only a little ways. Besides, your feet are probably hurting now. They always do after a break. I'll carry the rucksack until your feet feel better."

He started slowly down the ridge, bent almost double under the load. He tried to estimate how much he was carrying. A fanatic backpacker, MacGonigal held his loads to the minimum. The expedition pack, he knew, normally weighed about fifty pounds, the rucksack about twenty. With the tent, extra gear, clothing and rations, he supposed they weighed a little less than ninety pounds. With the rifle, pistol and ammunition, he thought, call it an even hundred. The thought made his knees sag. The damn campsite had better be close!

The trail was going down sharply, and it was difficult to keep his balance. He shuffled along, the rucksack dangling from his left hand, his right steadying the rifle as it swung gently in time with his step. He could hear Susan's irregular step behind him. "How're you doing back there?"

"I'm fine. I can take the rucksack now."

"That's okay," he said, "it would be more trouble to put it on than it's worth."

"How much farther?" There was a note of desperation in her voice.

"It's only a few more yards. I can hear the spring," he lied.

He stopped momentarily to allow her to catch up with him. "Want some more water?" he asked.

"No. Let's just keep going until we find that campsite. Don't stop again. I don't think I'll be able to get started again if I ever stop."

He plodded on. On his right, he could feel a rock wall loom. They really weren't far now. His ears strained for the murmur of the spring, and at last he heard it faintly. "Almost there. Just a few more steps," he muttered over his shoulder. She made no reply, but he could hear the steady scuffling of her boots. She was walking a little better now.

Suddenly, just a few yards ahead, was the little spring. He reached up and touched the overhanging rock ledge. "We're here," he said. Behind him, she sank down on the bare ground. He put the rucksack down and shrugged out of the expedition pack. When he turned back to Susan, she was trembling uncontrollably. "Mac, I'm so cold."

Exposure, he thought to himself. MacGonigal, the lass is in a bad way. He began unstrapping the packs, laying out a plastic groundsheet first, then the closed cell foam pads. He pulled a light goose-down mummy bag out of its stuff bag and shook it out, fluffing it up to increase its insulating effect. "Get those boots off and crawl in here. You'll be all right."

Her hands trembled and her coordination was so bad she couldn't manage the laces. MacGonigal got the boots off for her and slid her into the sleeping bag. Her slim body felt like ice. He pulled the hood up around her head and tightened the lacing, then put a stuff bag full of spare clothing under her head. "We've got to get something into your stomach, girl. Your body needs fuel to warm that bag up."

He pulled out the little Svea stove, about as big as a coffee mug, and primed and lit it. It sputtered a moment, then settled into a steady, satisfying roar. He filled an aluminum pot at the little spring and put it on to boil while he searched the bags for food. By the time the water was boiling, he had ready a mug full of water-soluble chocolate reinforced with dried milk and a plastic bowl full of oatmeal. He poured boiling water into both and stirred them. He took a plastic jar full of honey and laced the oatmeal liberally with it, adding margarine from a tube. "Here's a little something that will stick to your ribs."

He helped her into a sitting position, with her arms still inside the bag, the hood coming down low over her head. He gave her a sip of the chocolate, being careful not to burn her. Then he spooned the oatmeal into her mouth.

"I don't want to take it all. Leave some for yourself."

"There's plenty. Eat all you want. You need to eat a lot to make up for the effort you put out today. I'll make another batch when you've finished this one."

She ate more greedily, and MacGonigal interrupted his task to put more water on to boil. He continued feeding her and giving her sips of chocolate. At last she said, "That's enough, Mac. I can't hold any more. All I want to do now is sleep."

He lowered her and made sure that the bag was comfortable, that the foam pad and the clothing bag insulated her from the ground. By the time he finished, she was asleep. He flashed the dim red light in her face. It was drawn and thin, worn-looking, and slack in response. Her long brown hair straggled from the hood, and he pushed a wisp of it back. He kissed her eyes gently. "Poor Susan. Let's hope we make it through tomorrow."

The pot was bubbling, and he took the mug and plate and fixed himself a meal, consuming it slowly. Afterwards, he filled the mug and plate with cold water from the spring and left them to soak. He turned off the Svea stove, unrolled his own sleeping bag and fluffed it up, then pulled off his boots and slipped into it, zipping it up and pulling the hood closed.

At first, he couldn't sleep. He wriggled in the bag until he was close to Susan. He could feel her body next to him, pressing against him through the layers of goose down and nylon. He pressed even closer to her, and she reflexively moved against him. He lay a long time with his open eyes staring out into the black night, despite his fatigue. Somewhere out there in the darkness were three killers, searching for him and this woman. They wouldn't rest until they found them, or until he stopped them. He thought about the claymore he had set for them. That third trigger made him feel good. One way or another, they'd probably set it off. It might not get them all, but it would be a start. Slowly, his tense muscles began to relax, and he closed his eyes and drifted off.

His dreams were troubled, and he woke several times during the night. He felt as if some dark, sinister force were arrayed against him, watching him from the surrounding blackness, waiting to strike. Try as he might, he couldn't shake a sense of foreboding. He felt naked and vulnerable. At last he forced himself out of the sleeping bag and rummaged around through the piled gear until he found the Colt Python. He took the big revolver into the sleeping bag with him and felt better.

Toward dawn, he finally drifted off into a deep, dreamless sleep. He was aroused by a frantic shaking. Half drugged, he struggled up through heavy layers of sleep. "Wake up, Mac! Wake up!"

His eyes wouldn't focus, and he kept blinking to clear his blurred vision. He groped in the sleeping bag for the heavy revolver. "Wh . . . What is it? Somebody coming?"

She shook him again, hard and persistent. "Wake up! It went off! I heard it!"

It took a moment for the words to seep through to his confused brain. "Heard what? You mean the claymore? You heard it?"

"My God, yes! Didn't you hear it? It was like thunder!"

He fumbled with the lacing of the hood and worried down the zipper of the sleeping bag. He was fully clothed, except for his boots and parka. The morning cold bit deeply and cleared his head. He sat up, the sleeping bag still around his legs. "Did it just go off? Just now?"

"Yes! That's what I'm trying to tell you! Oh, Mac, do you think we got them?"

He shook his head violently to clear it of the last dregs of sleep and dragged in a deep breath of cold, bracing morning air. "I don't know. We'd better go see." He looked at his watch. It was just seven o'clock. He crawled out of the bag and reached for his boots. They were stiff with cold. He pulled them on, trying to make his stiffening hands obey him as he fumbled with the laces. He pulled on his gloves and stood up. His joints cracked. He felt stiff all over. Susan was out of her sleeping bag, on all fours in the tangle of nylon and down that encumbered the place where they had slept. "Can you make it?"

She got to her feet, slowly. She was still in her socks. "I don't know if I can get my boots on . . . I suppose I'll have to, somehow. Mac, if they're down there, we can't let them get away!"

MacGonigal was sorting things out, buckling on the big Python, checking the Savage to make sure that it was loaded, a round in the chamber. He shoved spare magazines into his pocket and dipped a cup of icy water out of the spring. He drank deeply, then refilled the cup and passed it to her. "Have a drink, and I'll see if I can get your boots on."

She sat back, and he tried to force the stiff leather over her swollen feet. "No go," he said. "Maybe if I take off those thick socks . . ." He stripped them off and looked at her feet. They were swollen two full sizes. He pushed his thumb into the flesh of her ankle. It left a dent that only slowly disappeared when he took his thumb away. He dug in her rucksack for a thinner pair of socks and rolled them on, then tried the boots again. They went on reluctantly. "It's not going to be comfortable, honey. Maybe you ought to stay here. I'll go see what's happened."

She glared at him. "I don't care how uncomfortable it is, I'm going with you. I can't stay here, waiting. I've got to know what's happening."

He helped her to her feet and gave her the .22 Woodsman and the carbine, then pulled the cased binoculars out of his pack. "Think you can make it?"

"Yes! Don't worry about me. Let's get going."

He slung the binoculars under his left arm and took up the Savage. Stiffly, he walked a few yards up the trail, leaving their gear as it was. He felt sore and used up, but knew that the stiffness would work itself out. His body ached for more sleep, and his eyes felt gritty, but he resolutely put the feeling aside. He looked back at Susan, who was hobbling along behind him. "Go on," she said. "I can make it. I'll catch up with you in a minute."

He went around the bend in the wall of the bluff and waited, listening to her slow, shuffling limp as she struggled to catch up with him. In a minute she came into view. She was walking strangely, putting one foot directly in front of the other, without toeing out. He knew that her feet were excruciatingly painful. He waited for her to catch up to him. "You don't have to come with me."

"I'm going. Don't worry, I'll be all right in a minute. Wait until my feet warm up."

He grunted and went ahead slowly, looking back at her limping along behind. She waved him on, but he held his pace down. "No need for us to run. If we got them, they'll still be there when we get there. If not, they'll be gone."

They followed a dim trail, a deer trace that ran just below the top of the ridge line, keeping to the cover of the bluff. Ahead of them a rocky knob thrust up above the leafless trees. "We'll climb up there," said MacGonigal. "We should be able to see what's going on from the top."

It took five or six minutes to cover the hundred yards to the knob, and MacGonigal slung the Savage, looking up at the jumble of stone, planning a route up. It wasn't high, only about fifty feet or so, but it would be a difficult climb for someone who was stiff, sore, and still exhausted from the day before. "I'm going up that crack. Do you think you can follow me?"

She looked up at the mass of rock, her expression of dismay barely concealed. "If you can do it, I can."

He looked at her and started up, the Savage slung across his back. It was easy at first, wedging himself into the crack and hitching his body higher, but his cramped muscles soon began to protest. He found a stopping place about ten feet up, and managed to get himself braced in a sitting position. He looked down. Susan stood looking up at him, confusion in her face. He unslung the rifle and made a long strap of the military style sling. He dangled it down the crack. "Grab this. I'll give you a boost."

She pulled herself up and took a moment to collect herself, then looked up. "Does it get any easier?"

"I hope so. But stay out from directly under me. No sense both of us getting smashed up if I fall." He rethreaded the sling through the swivels, slung the rifle and began the climb again, wedging and levering his way up. He gained another ten feet and came to a sloping gully that led to the top. He called down to her, "Once you get this high, you've got it made." She looked up, biting her lip, and waited while he rigged the sling again. It took longer this time, and once he thought he had lost her. Her feet lost their purchase, and she swung away from the rock face, her grip on the leather strap the only thing between her and a fall. She hung with her arms stretched full length over her head, her legs scissoring wildly as she sought to secure some kind of purchase. In a sick flash, MacGonigal thought that she would lose her grip and plummet to the bottom of the crack, a bone-breaking fall, but she managed to get back to the face. She paused there for a long time. MacGonigal, looking down at her pale, pinched face, was afraid that she had flamed out, lost the ability to move. Finally, she took a deep breath and started up again. At last she joined him. He pointed up the gully. "This goes all the way up. Why don't you lead? If you slip, I should be able to hold you."

She hobbled up, leaning on the rough rock sides of the gully, with MacGonigal giving her an occasional boost from below. After twenty feet or so, it got easier, and they soon came to the top, a bare expanse of rock about ten feet on a side forming a rough triangle. From there, they could look over the valley of Bear Pen Creek and see far down the county road. "It's beautiful up here, Mac. You should think about putting in handholds, or something to make the climb easier."

He snorted. "If it was easy, you wouldn't appreciate it. Besides, we came here for a reason." He unslung the binoculars and focused them on the valley. The cabin was in plain view, as were its outbuildings. MacGonigal carefully scanned the scene below, the 10×50s bringing everything in close.

He looked over the yard and outbuildings, remembering the man who had been stationed in the hayloft. Up here, he reminded himself, they would be a mark for a sniper, if anyone happened to glance their way. The thought made him crouch lower to the stone, and he turned to Susan. "Move back. Get down in the gully. We don't want them to pick us off."

She slid back and concealed herself behind a jutting piece of sandstone. MacGonigal resumed his search. There was nothing moving, at least nothing that he could see. The front door of the cabin lay broken and splintered on the front porch. He turned the focus wheel carefully until the scene was needle sharp. He could see that the frame was splintered and hanging loose in the door opening. The windows were all broken on that side of the cabin, and there were bright marks, splinters of fresh wood, showing up against the weathered surface of the logs, giving the cabin a freckled appearance. Well, he said to himself, at least the damn thing worked.

The little tree to which the claymore had been strapped was cut in half. He could clearly see its stump, splayed and splintered like a broken broom, standing in front of the cabin. He searched the area of the blast carefully, but other than the obvious damage to the cabin itself and to the surrounding shrubbery, he could see no result from the claymore.

"What do you see?" said Susan, impatiently. "Did we get them?"

He lowered the binoculars slowly. "I don't know. There aren't any bodies in sight. Maybe . . . maybe an animal blundered into the trap, or maybe the wind set it off . . ."

She wriggled up beside him and snatched the glasses from his hands. "Let me see!" She twisted the focus wheel and swept the binoculars around the cabin. "I don't see anything!"

"Look at the front door. You can see where it's blasted away. See the marks on the wall? That's from the claymore. You can see the tree we wired it to. It's cut in two."

She was silent for a long time, bracing the binoculars with her elbows wedged into the sandstone under her. At last she said, "Mac, if it was an animal, wouldn't it be lying there?"

"Maybe it got away. Maybe it was the wind, a

branch blowing against the trip wire . . . it could have been anything."

She struck the unyielding rock with her little fist. "It wasn't 'anything,' Mac. It was Nazario. Or some of his men. It had to be."

MacGonigal took the glasses from her. "Maybe it was. But what happened to him?" He stared at the scarred cabin wall through the powerful glasses. "It had to get them, at least one of them. That pattern is too dense for a man to escape unhurt."

"Maybe . . ." The sound of a motor starting interrupted her. MacGonigal swept the binoculars around, searching for the source of the sound. In a moment, a flash of motion attracted him, a four-wheel-drive vehicle, a gray Scout, was pulling out of the brush about a half mile down the valley. He stared intently at it as it swung onto the access road going away from his property. He put down the binoculars and took up the Savage, planting his elbows solidly and spreading his legs, heels flat on the rock. It was too far, more than nine hundred yards, maybe even a thousand yards. He couldn't make it, not on a fast-moving target like the Scout. Reluctantly, he lowered the muzzle of the Savage.

He reached for the binoculars, but Susan had them. "Shoot, Mac! Shoot! It's them, I know it is!"

He took the binoculars from her. "Too far, honey. I wouldn't have a chance of hitting them. Besides, we really don't know that it was them." He watched the Scout pull out onto the county road and turn south, a long plume of dust rising behind it. He lay motionless until it was out of sight. When it finally disappeared behind one of the far hills, he rolled over on his back and looked up at Susan.

"You should have shot at them, Mac. At least then they'd know that they can't play games without some risk to themselves."

"If it was one of them that detonated the claymore, they already know that. But there was no point in shooting and missing. And if I'd hit them, sure as hell, it would have turned out to be some family looking for a place to hold a picnic."

"I suppose you're right. But I know that it was them. I was just waiting for you to fill them full of holes—I was so disappointed when you put the rifle down."

"Yeah. Well, we better get down from here. Let's go back to camp and have some breakfast, then we'll figure out what our next move is."

They made their way down the gully, MacGonigal leading and keeping himself braced to catch Susan should she slip and come cannoning into him. At the end of the gully, he sat down and rigged the rifle sling, lowering her slowly to the ledge below. When they stood on the ground at last, looking up at the knob rising above them, Susan said, "Maybe we shouldn't have come down. Don't you think that one of us should stay up there and keep watch?"

MacGonigal shrugged. "Maybe. But we're too far away up there to do anything, unless they give us a clear shot. And it's exposed. Down at the cabin, you can see anyone up there. They stand out against the skyline. We were taking a risk going up there, and I don't think that we should take that risk again."

They trudged back to their impromptu camp.

MacGonigal drew water from the spring and made a new batch of hot chocolate and oatmeal while Susan packed the sleeping bags back into their stuff bags. Over his shoulder MacGonigal said, "Don't put them away yet. We'll probably sleep here tonight, and anyway, I think you need to spend the day in camp."

She looked up at him, her eyes snapping. "Just what does that mean? I told you that I'm not staying here while you go off. And that's final."

MacGonigal reasoned with her. "Look, Sue, your feet won't take a lot of hiking. You'll slow me down, and I won't be able to go places because of you. Besides, what about tomorrow? If you rest and let those feet start to heal, you'll be able to get around tomorrow. If not, you'll be completely immobilized. Then what will we do?"

"What will you do if you get in trouble? You need me to watch out and to cover your back."

"Yeah, I do. But today I probably won't. I think they've gone for the day. Tomorrow I'll need you, and I want you in top shape then."

She didn't answer, but watched him while he ladled porridge, thick with honey, into a bowl for her. "Look at it this way," he said, "we don't know what they'll try next. They probably won't try anything today, but tomorrow will be another story. We've got to be ready for them, and we won't be if we run ourselves into the ground."

She took up her spoon, sitting cross-legged with the bowl in her lap. "All right, Mac. I'll stay here like a good little girl. But what are you going to do?"

He swallowed a mouthful of porridge. "I guess I'll go down and check out the cabin, try to figure out what happened there, what they're most likely to do next."

He finished his breakfast and gathered up the dishes. "I'll do those," she said.

"Oh, no. You climb back in that sleeping bag and elevate those feet. I'll clean up. I want you rested and ready to go tomorrow."

Obediently, she stripped off her outer garments and slid into the bag. MacGonigal watched, feeling himself stir with the sight of her. When she was in the bag, he zipped it up for her, then put a stuff bag under her head and the rucksack under her feet. He brushed her forehead with his lips. "Sleep tight. I'll be back in a little while."

He picked up his rifle and binoculars and slipped out of camp, following the same trail as that morning, as far as the rocky knob. Then he cut over the spine of the ridge and down the other side, keeping to cover and staying in thick brush as much as possible. At last he reached a point much farther down the ridge where he could see most of his farm.

He took up a position by a boulder and sat flat on the ground, bracing his elbows on his knees as he began a painstaking visual search of the area. There was nothing on the slope near him. He shifted his search to the midground, checking the buildings and sheds. Again nothing. He scanned the far ground, the tree line on the other side of the valley. There was nothing moving, except for a few small animals. The horses cropped the brown grass in the paddock, seemingly oblivious to the disturbances of the past two days.

He paid special attention to the barn. He could not forget the evidence of its being used as an observation post, or a sniper post. There was no way anyone could approach the cabin without being seen by a watcher in the barn. He kept his glasses trained on the loading platform, but could see nothing. At last he put them down and picked up the rifle hesitantly.

Francis, me boyo, he said to himself, it may be that a little recon by fire is called for. He brought the weapon to his shoulder and put the crosshairs of the two-and-a-half-power scope on the opening of the loading platform. Now where would I be sitting if I were waiting in the barn to pick someone off, he thought. The crosshairs moved to the left side of the opening. A right-handed firer would naturally take that side; it would offer him cover as he fired.

He slid the safety forward, then back again. Think about this, MacGonigal, he told himself. Are you sure he's right-handed? One of them's a lefty. Besides, what are the chances of hitting him, even if he's there? All you'll do is advertise your own position. It's like firing into the nest; it's no way to get a squirrel.

He lowered the rifle. This calls for some deep thinking, me boyo, he pondered, trying to unravel the skein of the problem, trying to put himself in his enemys' place. There were three of them. Good. That's a fact. They left in that Scout. An assumption. How do they fit together? Well, if it was one of them that tripped the claymore, he's probably hurt pretty bad, maybe dead. Another assumption. But if it's true, then maybe they were trying to get help for him. One man couldn't carry him down the path to the Scout.

Now where does that leave us? Francis, it means that they're not here. Or else it wasn't them that set off the claymore, and it wasn't them that you saw leave.

That puts me back at square one. It either was them, or it wasn't. And either they set off the trap, or they didn't. Think, MacGonigal, think.

Okay. Let's try it the other way. It wasn't them. So who was it? The wind or an animal could have triggered the claymore, but if they were there, surely they'd have been curious? So they weren't there early, in time to see the damn thing go off, unless they set it off. And if they came later, what about the Scout? When did it come? Who was in it? What did they do when it came?

He cased the binoculars. Okay, MacGonigal, you've convinced me. They aren't there. But let's play it careful, just the same. He circled through the woods until he came up on the side of the barn. He had a good hundred-and-fifty yards of open ground to cross to reach it, and he would be exposed to anyone in the cabin. He squatted in the underbrush, giving the farm one last look over.

Nothing moved. MacGonigal got his legs under him and ran for the side of the barn, his legs going like pistons. Twenty-five yards. He could feel the crosshairs of an unseen sight on his back. He redoubled his effort, running flat out. Seventy-five yards. His lungs were heaving, but a feeling akin to panic gripped him. He knew that they were there, watching, aiming. He could feel it. His boots thudded against the ground, his whole chest was on fire. He ran harder, relying on sheer will to drive his lungs and legs. The barn wall was close now, but he could feel an ache between his shoulder blades. The unseen marksman had him cold. He could feel the pressure of his finger on the trigger. In his mind's eye, he was looking through the sight with the man, watching himself run hopelessly across the open space. Another second and it would be all over. His legs were like lead, his feet sunk in sand. He willed them to drive on, but they wouldn't obey him. With a last sobbing gasp, he flung himself at the ground, rolling over and over until he reached the barn wall.

He lay there, breathing in great, ragged gasps. He would die from lack of oxygen, if not from a bullet. His heart pounded against his rib cage so loudly that he was afraid they would hear him.

At last, he got himself together and crawled around the corner of the barn, easing up to the door. He could see just the corner of the trap into the loft. He stood there, his heart still pounding, his chest still heaving, trying to sense if anyone was there. The thudding of blood in his ears made it impossible for him to tell if there was any movement in the barn. Finally he simply stepped through the door and dodged sideways against the horse stalls. He crouched there, looking up, trying to see between cracks in the loft floor. The loft was almost full of hay, though, and he gave that up as useless.

He felt an almost ungovernable urge to move, to do anything to end the suspense. He forced himself to be calm, telling himself that his opponent would be under the same pressure. He looked at his watch and made himself a promise to sit still for ten minutes. He leaned back against the side of the stall, the rifle at the ready, and waited. When he could stand it no longer, he looked at his watch again. Thirty seconds had passed.

He made himself count slowly to a hundred and looked again. A minute and a half. His back itched. Sweat trickled down from his armpits. The parka was zipped to the throat and he was stiflingly hot after his run, but he resolutely put it out of his mind. He concentrated on reciting a poem to himself, "The Baldness of Chewed-Ear Jenkins," running through the lines slowly. He recited a dozen Robert Service poems, mouthing the words in silence. He looked at his watch again. Eleven minutes had passed. He rose slowly and drew his revolver, slinging his rifle over his back, and put his hand on the ladder to the loft.

He climbed slowly, the revolver pointing toward the yawning trap door above him. As he climbed, he waited for a head to appear in that opening. One shot, that's all he would get. If he was lucky, that's all he would need. If not . . .

He reached the level of the loft floor and hesitated. Now he had changed places with whoever was in the loft. Now it was his head that would appear through the opening. He pulled his legs up another rung, so that he was doubled over, the top of his head just below floor level. With a sudden spasm, he straightened his legs and shot through the opening.

There was no one there. He investigated the loading ramp. The cigarette butts were still there, some of them with pigeon droppings on them. Nothing had been disturbed since he had been there the night before. He sat weakly on a bale of hay and let his mind and body relax. His first assessment of the situation had been right after all. They weren't there. They couldn't be. The loft was such a good sniper and observation post that they would never leave it unmanned.

Still, there was no point in taking chances. He crept up to a point where he had a good view of the cabin and the farmyard, but was still back in the shadows of the loft and invisible to an outside observer. He searched carefully and found that with the binoculars he could see through a window into the cabin. He looked carefully, alert for a flicker of movement, but saw nothing. At last he cased the glasses and went down the ladder. Taking a deep breath, he stepped out into the open. His skin crawled, but he was morally certain that there was no one watching. He walked resolutely across the open ground to the corner of the building, pausing a moment in the shelter of the massive interlocking logs.

He stepped around the corner and looked at the effect of his work. It was more impressive close up than it had been from atop the rocky knoll earlier. The little tree was blasted to splinters, merely a shivered stub sticking out of the ground. The brush was cleared for about fifty feet around the site of the blast, and larger trees bore scars of both blast and shrapnel.

The porch floor had long rips where chunks of flying metal had plowed up splinters. The wall was full of screws, nails, and nuts, many of which stuck out from the logs. The windows on the side facing the explosion were all broken, and the shattered door lay drunkenly on the front steps. In front of the window was a puddle of clotted blood. MacGonigal grinned wolfishly. I got one of the bastards, he said to himself. I got him good. He stepped up on the scarred porch and looked briefly inside.

There was some damage. The kitchen table was thrown back against the sink, apparently by the explosion of the booby trap on the door, and the window over the sink had been broken by flying fragments. The floor was scarred around the door, and near the windows fragments from the claymore had peppered the walls and floor as well. MacGonigal made a quick check of other damage. His books had not been hurt, being on the side of the room closest to the explosion, with foot-thick logs between them and the flying scrap, but the gun racks had taken a beating. He congratulated himself on moving his remaining weapons. Up on a high shelf, his beloved pipes were untouched. He took them down and shouldered the drones, but thought the better of playing. Who knew who might be listening? He locked them in their case, took them up to the loft and stored them carefully away.

He stepped back outside and minutely examined the porch and the surrounding ground. There was a lot of blood on the porch, a pool widened and smeared where someone had dragged a body away. MacGonigal sniffed at it. There was an odor of fecal material, the sign of a serious abdominal wound. Either that, he thought sardonically, or else I really scared the shit out of the bastard!

There was a jumble of footprints around the porch, too much confusion for MacGonigal to make anything of. He walked back along the path to the falls, his eyes on the ground. After a few steps he halted and squatted down to examine a splash of blood. It was pink and frothy, different in color and texture from the stuff drying on the porch. Well, said MacGonigal to himself, the lungs, too! Something tells me that this boyo won't be back to fuck with MacGonigal. I wonder how the other two are doing?

He continued to follow the trail, stopping now and then to examine splashes of blood. Down on the road, the splashes ceased, but he was able to follow footprints there. There were three sets leading up to his cabin, only two coming back. And there's the pity, he thought. I only got one of the bastards. But by the look of things, I got him pretty good.

He followed the tracks all the way to the place where they had parked their Scout. The tracks showed signs of staggering and slipping as they approached the place. The bastards are getting tired, he thought. The one that tripped the claymore can't be doing much to help them along. Maybe he's dead. He thought about that. It would be better if he were to live. He would be more of an embarrassment to Nazario that way. They'd have to get medical treatment for him, and that wouldn't be easy. Any doctor would be curious as to the origin of his wounds, and Nazario couldn't afford to attract attention.

At last MacGonigal started back. He was becoming acutely aware of his lack of sleep and the strain he had undergone in the last twenty-four hours. When he was searching his farm and tracking Nazario, his fatigue had almost disappeared, but now it came back with a vengence. He wearily made his way up the ridge and along the edge of the bluff. It took him over an hour to make it.

When he arrived in camp, Susan was sleeping peacefully in the sleeping bag. He sat down on a rock and pulled off his boots, laying them down gently to avoid waking her. He had an almost ungovernable longing for something hot, but it would take too long to fix, and he was afraid the roaring of the little camp stove would wake her. He dipped water from the spring and drank deeply, then crawled into his sleeping bag.

It was dark when MacGonigal woke. He was momentarily disoriented and stared into the darkness, not sure what had aroused him. A slight noise nearby made him turn violently. "Mac, how do you work this stove?"

He sat up in his sleeping bag. "My God, Sue, are you awake?"

"Oh, I've been up for a couple of hours. I walked up there to watch the sun go down, and then came back down to fix some supper."

He crawled out of the bag. "Find the flashlight and give me the stove. I'll fix us something."

She put both stove and light into his hand. "Well? Aren't you going to tell me what happened?"

He passed his hand over his face. "I think we killed one of them. There was a lot of blood. He was trying to look through the window when it went off. He must have caught the full blast."

She sat in silence a moment. "Only one? What about the others?"

VIII.

"I don't think we got them all. In fact, I know we didn't. The tracks showed that two of them carried down the body of the third one—I think that one is either dead or so badly hurt that we can forget about him. But the other two seemed unhurt."

She was silent a long time. He tried to make out her expression in the darkness, but failed. At last she said slowly, "So Nazario got away. He'll be back, Mac. And he'll be more determined than ever. I didn't want to say anything before, because I hoped we could put an end to all this, but now that we've struck back, he'll never give up."

"Cheer up," said MacGonigal, forcing a note he didn't feel into his voice. "Maybe it was Nazario we got. It could just as easily be him as anyone else, couldn't it?"

"No, it couldn't, Mac. He's not the sort to get himself killed. It was some flunky of his, one of his apes that we got, not him. Nazario is too careful."

MacGonigal finally got the little stove going. "Well," he said, "let the bastard try again. We're ahead of the game now. Who knows, I may just put a real crimp in their organization if they keep fucking with me."

"It won't be easy to stay ahead, Mac. You've humiliated Nazario. He'll never forgive you now."

MacGonigal's voice rose in pitch. "I've humiliated him, have I? How, by not lying down and playing dead? Well, let him pout, if he wants to. This is MacGonigal's territory, and he'll pay hell beating MacGonigal at his own game."

He shut up and turned back to what he had been doing. He drew a pot of water from the spring and put it on to boil while he dug out a packet of freeze-dried stew. Susan sat and watched while he mixed the boiling water with the unappetizing-looking contents of the package. In the dim glow from the little stove, she crouched, wrapped in her sleeping bag and parka. "Hurry up, Mac, I'm cold and hungry."

He dished out the stew and boiled more water for chocolate. They sat eating and sipping the hot, thick drink. "Right now, I wish I had a little something to put in this," he said. "It's too bad those punks smashed my last bottle of booze."

"You should have got some more."

"Too much trouble. This is a dry county, and besides, I don't drink that much, just for special occasions." He paused. "This, I think, qualifies as a special occasion. After all, it isn't every day a man finds his own home boobytrapped, sets a trap himself, and blows away one of his enemies."

They finished the stew and scrubbed the pots and plates. MacGonigal unrolled his sleeping bag and spread it out beside Susan's. He rolled up his parka for a pillow and unzipped the bag. Susan crept up to him. "Mac, you need a bath, and I'm sore all over, but . . . do these bags zip together?"

He grinned in the darkness and pulled the zipper all the way down, then mated his bag with hers. He crawled in and listened to her thrashing around in the darkness. In a moment she slid shivering in beside him. He put out his arms to hold her and realized with a shock that she was naked. "Take those damn clothes off, Mac, and be a gentleman."

He woke to the sound of an engine. It was just breaking dawn, and the niche where they were camped was still in blackness. He unwrapped Susan's arms and legs from about his body and reached one arm out of the warmth of the sleeping bags to snare his clothes. He dragged them inside the bag and held his flesh away from the cold cloth while the garments warmed up. Susan was awake. "What's that noise, Mac?"

He listened. The droning of the engine had receded, but presently it began to swell again. "It sounds like an airplane."

He jackknifed his body, pulling his corduroy trousers on. The motion pumped cold air into the sleeping bags. "Brrr! That's cold, Mac!"

He struggled into his shirt and then climbed out of the bags. Nearby, Susan's clothes lay in a pile. He gathered them up and handed them to her. "Keep them in the bag with you for a while to warm them up before you put them on."

She grabbed the clothing and disappeared inside

the two sleeping bags. He pulled on his cold, stiff boots and set about preparing breakfast. As he lit the stove, the drone of the airplane grew louder. Looking up, he saw it sweep above the crest of the ridge, bank around and come back. Its racket receded into the distance, then rose again as it made another run.

"That son of a bitch is looking for something!"

Susan's head appeared in the jumble of bedding. "Mac, do you think it's Nazario?"

"Whoever it is, he's damn interested in what's down here. Here he comes again!" The plane roared over the ridge, not fifty feet above the trees, and not two hundred above the spot where they were camped. As it went over and banked around, they could see that it was a blue and silver Cessna 170. "Hell," said MacGonigal, "that looks like Willie Jarvis's plane."

"Who's he?"

"Just a fellow that owns an airplane. Carries newspapers, flies an occasional parachute meet —hell of a lousy jump pilot, can't remember not to bank when he's making his jump run. He hires out whenever he can. Helps pay the maintenance on the plane."

"Maybe it's not Nazario then."

"I wouldn't bet on it. Who else would hire an airplane to look over my place?"

The sound of the plane was fainter now. It didn't come back, but they could tell that the pilot had changed his flight pattern and was now flying up and down Bear Creek valley. "That son of a bitch will get my horses all stirred up like that. Goddamn Jarvis knows better than that. Wait until I get my hands on him!"

The plane came around for another pass. They couldn't see it, but they could tell from the sound that it was just skimming the trees. "If the asshole isn't careful, we won't have any more worries. He'll kill himself." MacGonigal paused thoughtfully. "Be pretty rough on old Jarvis, though."

Susan looked worried. "Do you think that they saw us, Mac?"

"No, I wouldn't worry about that. They weren't even looking on this side of the ridge. They just passed over to make their turns. Besides, under this ledge, we're damn near invisible, even to an experienced observer, which they aren't. It seems like we're exposed, because we could see them so easily when they came over, but to them it's a different ball game.

"One thing sure, though. We got their attention with that claymore. They don't want to walk in here blind like they did before."

He kept one ear cocked for the plane as he gathered up their gear. "We'll stash everything out of sight, just in case, but I don't think that they've even guessed that we're not in the valley. When the plane leaves, we'll slip up on the ridgetop and check things out. Are you up to a little walking?"

"I guess so. I feel a lot better now."

He came over and pulled off her boots and checked her feet. "They look pretty good. I'll change the moleskin." He dug in his pack and produced his first-aid kit and went to work on her feet. The sound of the plane's engine droned on, sometimes growing faint, sometimes louder. He pulled her socks up and slipped the boots back on. "There, that ought to do it."

He put the first-aid kit back and dragged the two packs back behind a boulder, well off the faint trail. He listened to the sound of the plane's engine for a moment longer. "It sounds like they're going to stay up while somebody comes in by the road. I guess they figure that if we've got anything planned, they'll spot us from the air when we try it."

She looked at him. "But we don't have anything planned, do we, Mac?"

"No, not really. Just to catch them with their pants down when they make a mistake. And they've already made one, flying around like that and advertising their intentions."

"What do you mean?"

"Well, my guess is that they hope to catch us in the cabin and flush us out. If that fails—and it will —then they'll set up an ambush and try to catch us when we come back to the cabin."

"What do we do?"

"Right now?" He grinned. "Nothing. We just sit here and relax. Later on we'll go up and look things over. If they've done something dumb, we'll take advantage of them. If not, we'll sit tight. They can't stay in ambush forever. We'll watch, locate them, and wait for them to get antsy. Sooner or later, they'll get careless. We've got the advantage; we know where they are. We can watch them, and they have no idea where we are. It'll be rough on them, psychologically."

"Then what?"

"Well, the classic manuever is to catch them when they're moving out of their ambush position. It's a normal human failing to be alert and keyed up at the start, then relax and let down later. When they decide to pull out, they'll probably straggle out like a bunch of drunks the morning after. Then we'll hit them."

"How do you mean, hit them?"

He patted the Savage. "Try to get both of them close together. This baby will make short work of them, if I can catch them in the open like that. I'll have them both down before they know what's happening."

"Of course then we'll have a little problem of getting rid of the bodies, but there are places to put them. No one will ever find them."

She shuddered, remembering the two bodies in the green pickup. "You mean like the last two?"

"Even better. The difference is that somebody knew those guys. Sooner or later somebody would start asking what happened to them. So we put them where they'd be found, with a logical explanation of how they got there. With these characters, we just make them disappear."

She shuddered again. "I'll help. I know I'll have to. But don't tell me about it ahead of time. I don't want to know."

The sound of the plane's engine changed. MacGonigal stepped out from under the ledge and looked up. In a moment he saw it through the bare branches of the trees. It was climbing, describing a huge circle as it gained altitude. Susan came out to stand beside him.

"What's he doing, going home?"

"I don't know, but I'd guess he's looking for the other guy, the one that's coming in on the ground. He must be late or something."

The plane headed off to the southwest, then came back. It circled high above them, then flew off southwest again. MacGonigal grinned. "What amateurs! They might as well be trailing a banner, telling us what they're doing."

The plane remained at altitude for a while, making wide circles which narrowed as the minutes passed. Obviously, whoever was coming in on the ground was getting closer.

At last the little Cessna was almost hovering overhead. It dove and roared up the valley, then climbed out at the end of its run and made a climbing turn, to return over the valley at a height of several hundred feet. At a point that MacGonigal guessed must be over the intersection of his access road and the county road, it dove again and came flying up the valley once more, out of sight, but not out of earshot to MacGonigal and Susan. It repeated the performance again and again.

"They must be driving right in. Maybe they've got reinforcements. This seems almost like a military operation, or somebody's idea of what a military operation would be like."

They watched and listened to the plane for another half hour, while it hovered over the valley or zoomed down the access road. At last it rose to an altitude of two or three thousand feet and flew away to the northeast. "I think it's headed home now, but let's wait a little," said MacGonigal. They sat for half an hour or so, then MacGonigal picked up his rifle and binoculars, unclipped his canteen from the shoulder straps of his pack, and led the way out of the camp.

They followed the same route that he had taken the day before, moving with caution, and taking care to keep under the shelter of the trees. MacGonigal explained to Susan that if one stood against the trunk of a fair-size tree, it was almost impossible to be spotted from the air.

As they moved into position, MacGonigal pointed out the damage that the claymore had done. "He was up on the porch when it went off. There's a hell of a blood stain there. I can't really figure out why the other two weren't with him, but I guess they do have a little sense. They hung back, out of range and under cover, while the one we got went up to check things out. Must have been a hell of a shock for them!"

He uncased his binoculars and began a careful search of the farm. In a moment he stopped, staring indignantly at the barn. "That stupid goddamn bastard! Would you look at that!" He passed the glasses to Susan, almost thrusting them upon her. She took them and looked over the farm.

"What is it, Mac? I don't see anything."

"Look at the loading platform, up in the hayloft."

Obediently, she swung the binoculars in that direction, twisting the focus wheel to sharpen the image. For a moment, she saw nothing, then suddenly gave a low cry. "I see it! There's someone in there."

MacGonigal took the glasses back and refocused.

The image of the loading platform hung in front of his eyes. In the bright sunlight, a tendril of smoke danced in the opening. "The bastard is sitting there in the middle of all that hay. Damn! I hate to lose my barn, but maybe the son of a bitch will burn himself up. He deserves it, the stupid twit!"

As MacGonigal watched, a cigarette butt described a lazy arc out the loading platform and fell smoking to the ground at the base of the barn wall. MacGonigal shuddered. The son of a bitch was really trying to commit suicide! He must not realize that hay is almost as inflammable as gasoline.

As they watched the barn, the sound of an automobile impressed itself upon them. "Somebody coming," grunted MacGonigal. He couldn't see the road from where they were posted, so he rose to his feet and moved sideways to a pile of stone slabs that lay at an angle on the side of the ridge. Approaching the slabs from behind, he crawled up their steep sides until he reached a point where he could see over their tops. From there, he had a fair view of the access road and could see the dust of the approaching vehicle on the county road, although neither the vehicle itself nor the road were actually visible from his post.

He watched through the glasses as the dust plume grew larger, then hung upon itself in a curtain where the vehicle turned into his access road. In a minute it reached a point where he could see it—the same Scout that he had seen before, or one just like it. He followed the vehicle with the glasses until it disappeared from his view just below the falls. Suddenly he heard a scrabbling noise behind him. Holding to his perch with his elbows, he looked down to see Susan climbing up after him.

"See anything interesting?"

He stretched out a hand to help her up. "Keep low. Don't let your head get above those branches there, or you'll be seen from the barn," he cautioned her. She settled herself in place on the sloping rock and he handed her the glasses.

"He should be appearing at the head of the trail in a minute."

She focused the glasses and concentrated on the point where the driver of the Scout would appear. She watched patiently and suddenly gasped. "Mac, it's Nazario!"

MacGonigal already had the Savage ready, and he thrust it into firing position, sweeping the area to pick up the man in the sight. Suddenly, there he was, still obscured from the waist down by the slope of the trail. MacGonigal had a brief glimpse of a square-built man with a powerful chest, bulging jaws, high cheekbones, hooked nose, and black hair shot with gray. He had no time to take further note of what the man looked like. The range was about three-hundred- and-fifty yards, and that was a long shot for the .308. He steadied the jiggling crosshairs above the man's head and flicked the safety off. As he did so, he was conscious of the man in the barn. He would have to take a chance on that one, get him later. Right now, the thing was to get the number-one man.

He felt Susan's hand suddenly close on his bicep. "Mac, there's more of them."

He looked through the two-and-a-half-power tele-scope, and saw three more figures emerge from below, climbing up into the scope's field of view. So the bastard had brought in reinforcements! MacGonigal slipped the safety back on. Better wait. Get them all out in the open, and pick off as many as he could when they scattered after the first shot.

He tracked them through the sight, the bobbing crosshairs keeping pace with the bandy-legged, dark-complected man in the lead. The others were obviously hired help. Nazario walked down the path, while the others walked to the side of the boss and deferred to him. They were well-armed, or seemed to think that they were. They carried AR-18 Armalite rifles. MacGonigal snorted at that. The little things would spit a lot of lead, but spitting and hitting were two different things. At this range, he knew that he didn't have much to fear from the little .223 cartridge, while his own .308 ought to hold up well.

He decided to let them reach a point midway between the house and the falls before he opened up. They were approaching that point, and he kept the crosshairs steady on Nazario, leading him by about a body width to allow for his walking speed. He readied himself for the group's reaction to the shot. If they hesitated or stood their ground and returned fire, he could simply cut them down. If they ran, he would take the leading runner, causing the others to pause when that man fell, perhaps even turning them back. If they dove for cover, then he would have a duel on his hands, with the odds against him, although with the Savage, he had a great advantage, given the range.

Suddenly the group came to a halt and turned

toward him. To MacGonigal, it appeared that Nazario looked directly into the muzzle of his rifle and waved. They turned and went on. "What was all that about?" MacGonigal muttered.

"There's a man down there, Mac, at the foot of the slope. I saw him stand up and wave to Nazario . . . Look! There are two more in the cabin!"

MacGonigal swung the scope toward the cabin and picked up two men standing in the doorway. As he watched, a flash of movement at one of the windows caught his eye. There were at least five of the bastards on his place, plus Nazario himself and the three hoods he had brought with him. Nine to one—stiff odds!

Nazario and his henchmen went up to the cabin and spoke briefly with the two men standing on the porch. After a moment, the burly gangster took a short turn of the porch, obviously inspecting the damage done by the improvised claymore. He stood looking at the dark stains on the porch floor decking, then looked over toward the shattered tree where the device had been sited. One of the men from the cabin jumped off the porch and walked around the cabin, bent over, and motioned Nazario forward. He followed and bent down with the man, examining something on the ground.

"He's showing him the tripwire," said MacGonigal. In a moment the thickset figure stood erect and looked back toward the blasted tree, as if speculating. He turned and went back into the cabin, his henchmen following him. MacGonigal pushed Susan back and waited while she slid down, then followed her.

"Let's go back to where we were. We've got a better view of the farmyard and outbuildings from there."

They went back with elaborate slowness and caution, well aware that a false move might result in detection by some of the men at the farm. MacGonigal was acutely aware of the unseen man posted in the edge of the woods. For a moment, he entertained thoughts of slipping down and dealing with the man silently, but he put them aside as too risky.

They took up their original position, MacGonigal using the powerful glasses to sweep the farmyard. From there, he could see that the man in the barn had not moved. In fact he had lit another cigarette, the thin tendril of smoke drifting out of the loading platform betraying his position. All of the others were out of sight, and the farmyard looked peaceful. From time to time, however, MacGonigal could get a glimpse of a figure passing in front of one of the cabin windows.

After awhile the man in the edge of the woods, apparently cramped and bored by his long vigil, stood up and stretched. MacGonigal, absorbed with watching the cabin, started at the sound. The man was only about a hundred yards away, and could be seen plainly through the bare branches. His attention seemed to be directed entirely toward the open space in front of him, however, for he never looked behind him. MacGonigal toyed again with the idea of taking him out and rejected it again. It would be almost impossible to do it without attracting the attention of the man in the barn.

The man scratched himself, then lit a cigarette before sitting back down at the base of a big hickory tree. MacGonigal noted that he was armed like the rest with an AR-18. These people seemed to have a fascination with assault rifles, MacGonigal thought to himself. Catch them in the open, at long range, me boyo, but don't let a bunch of them get close to you in the woods. They might get lucky with those toy guns.

Nazario appeared at the door again, his three henchmen with him. They went out into the yard and the stocky gangster engaged with them in some sort of discussion, with much waving of arms and pointing. At last they split up, one man going across the yard toward the creek, a second heading up the valley, and the third walking back toward the woods, in MacGonigal's general direction. Nazario went back into the cabin.

"Looks like our friend is putting out patrols," said MacGonigal. "Let's get out of here before that goon gets too close."

He rose at a half crouch, keeping low and moving from tree to boulder, with Susan at his heels. He didn't look back, but kept moving until they were near the crest of the ridge, where he stopped behind a large rock. Below them, they could hear the gunman thrashing through the brush. MacGonigal put his lips to Susan's ear. "We'll go on up over the ridge. If this guy keeps on coming, we may just put him in the bag and let them wonder what's happened."

They moved out and soon gained the spine of the ridge. The man below them was easily located by all the noise he made. MacGonigal moved along the ridge, keeping off the skyline, aiming at intercepting the man.

He got closer, and soon they could catch glimpses of him through the trees. "Stay put," MacGonigal whispered. "I'll see if I can get close to the bastard."

He moved with great care, never snapping a twig, and moving only when the man's attention was directed to another quarter. At last he reached the bole of a big sycamore. He couldn't see his quarry anymore, but from the sounds, the man was very near, less than fifty yards away, and directly below him. He continued his blundering progress directly up the slope, heading for the tree where MacGonigal stood flattened against the trunk. Easy, me boyo, let him come to you.

By now the man was very close. MacGonigal held his rifle by the forearm and small of the stock, his fingers white against the dark walnut of the stock. He could hear the man's rasping breath as he toiled upward and the shuffling of his feet in the dry leaves. It was tempting to lean out and try to spot him, but MacGonigal remained motionless.

Then he caught sight of the man. He was big, about six-four, and beefy. He must have weighed about two-forty, and the AR-18 looked like a child's toy gun in his large hands. He moved on past MacGonigal, his attention on the crest of the ridge. MacGonigal stepped out from his hiding place and took a quick, silent step toward the man. He could see the broad back straining the checkered wool jacket the man wore, the long, styled hair curling down over his collar. MacGonigal took another step and reversed the Savage, raising it above his shoulder. He lunged forward, smashing the butt into the back of the man's head.

The man went down, but not out. He rolled as he fell, trying to bring the AR-18 to bear, but MacGonigal brought the butt of the Savage down again, this time full in the face, and felt the bones crumble. The man thrashed with the AR-18, desperately trying to get off a shot, but the safety was on, and in his confusion, he couldn't get it off. MacGonigal hit him again and again, until the man relaxed. MacGonigal brought the butt of the rifle down again.

The man's eyes were wide open, filled with dirt. The AR-18 lay where he had dropped it. MacGonigal hit him again, and once more. The man's face was a mask of blood, and his features were distorted. MacGonigal stepped back, covering him with the Savage. The man didn't move. MacGonigal reached out and touched his right eyeball with the muzzle. No reaction.

MacGonigal stood panting, feeling the sweat from his armpits run down his side. Behind him, down the slope, someone called uncertainly, "Tony? Tony? You got a problem up there?"

MacGonigal stood silent a moment. The second man's uncertainty seemed to demand action. MacGonigal could hear him floundering up the slope. He moved quickly away from the scene, joining Susan where she lay, wide-eyed behind the rock. The man below, needing all his breath for the steep climb, had stopped calling, but continued to climb. MacGonigal gripped Susan's hand, and she gave him a squeeze in return. He looked at her. She looked wild, but determined. The .22 pistol was in her fist, and he noticed that the safety was off. He gave her hand another squeeze and turned his attention to the man coming up the slope.

The man blundered left and right, at a loss as to whether to continue up the ridge, to go back for help, or to ignore what he had heard. He stood still for a minute or so, then called again. "Tony? You up here? You all right?"

MacGonigal and Susan lay motionless. Soon they could hear the man resume his climb. He came up slowly, following a little gully, not more than two feet deep, a natural path up the ridge. It was the same path the other had taken, and a few dozen more yards would bring him to where the body lay. MacGonigal waited.

The sound of the man's progress suddenly stopped. He called in a soft voice, "Tony?" When there was no answer, he went a few yards farther. "Tony?" He waited and then moved again, suddenly stopping. For a long time he made no sound, then broke into a heavy, shambling run. They could hear him crashing through the brush. He came to a sudden halt. They were so close that they could hear his sudden gasp. "Tony? Jesus Christ! Jesus Christ!"

MacGonigal, peering around the edge of the rock, could see the man standing as if rooted to the spot. He stared at the body lying a few yards in front of him. The man ran a few steps and fell to his knees, putting his ear to the dead man's chest. MacGonigal was tempted to try for him, but let it pass. Let this one go, me boyo. You'd probably have to shoot him anyway.

The man suddenly got to his feet, his eyes wild, his nostrils distended. He held the AR-18 in front of him like some kind of talisman. He looked around wildly, then turned and fled down the slope, bellowing at the top of his lungs. MacGonigal let him go a hundred yards, and grabbed Susan's wrist. "Let's get out of here while they've got their attention on him." The two of them went quickly over the ridge.

Once on the other side, they kept moving rapidly. After a few hundred yards, MacGonigal slowed down, letting Susan come up even with him. "We've got a little bit of a tactical problem here, Sue. Those guys will probably focus on this side of the valley now. If I'm right, they'll probably go over this ridge with a fine-tooth comb. We'd be better off to get our gear and get away from here."

"You don't think they'll find us? There are an awful lot of them."

"There sure are. Enough to cover the ground, if they go at it systematically. There isn't much chance that they'll find us—we can hear them coming and keep out of their way—but if they find our packs, we're in for a rough time."

"You think that they'll go that far? The camp isn't very close to the . . . the place we just left."

"Can't tell. But I'm betting that they'll cover the whole ridge. Somebody just may get the idea of walking along the foot of the bluff instead of the top. If they do that, they just might stumble on the camp."

They hurried along until they reached the overhanging ledge and the little spring. MacGonigal pulled out the packs and hoisted his onto his back. Susan lifted her rucksack and groaned. "I'm not looking forward to carrying this thing."

Concerned, MacGonigal turned to her. "If you don't think you can manage it, I can carry it for you."

"No, I can pull my weight. But I don't think I'm going to enjoy it."

He helped her on with the rucksack and buckled her waist belt, then hitched up his own pack and fastened his belt. "Where are we going, Mac?"

"I thought that we'd just keep ahead of them, move parallel to the valley, keeping on this side of the ridge. Then when we get to the head, we'll cross over and set up another camp not far from the highway. I don't think they'll suspect that we would hide so close to a road. Once we do that, I'll keep moving, go around to the other side of the valley and see if I can stir up some trouble there."

They kept moving, with an occasional stop to listen for sounds of pursuit. For a while, they could hear shouts and other sounds as Nazario's men tried to coordinate their search, but they soon left these behind. "They seem to be keeping close to the scene," said MacGonigal. "We'll go on as planned, though. By the time we get to the new campsite, they'll probably have given up the search as a bad deal."

They went on through the woods, with MacGonigal leading the way, avoiding trails and keeping to thick brush. For a long time they walked in silence, now in single file, for the thick country would not permit them to walk abreast. At last the terrain became less steep as they reached the top of the broad, plateau-like ridge that formed the watershed for Bear Pen Creek. MacGonigal turned south and wandered, inspecting possible camp sites. The ground was fairly flat and free of stones, so he found several promising sites, but rejected each one as being too exposed, especially to aerial observation. With all the leaves off the trees, it was difficult to find a place that was concealed from aircraft. At last he found a large deadfall, leaning drunkenly with its top hung in the crotch of a living tree. He dropped his pack and walked under the triangle formed by the two trees, the living one and the dead one.

."This looks like a good place. It'll give us cover from that damned airplane."

Susan was dubious. "There's no water here, Mac. Our last camp was a lot snugger than this, and there was a spring there."

"I'm deliberately avoiding streams and springs. If you want to find someone hiding in the woods, follow the streams and springs. People have to have water, and they tend to set up their camps handy to a water source. We don't want to make that mistake, not with these guys looking for us."

He opened his pack and took out a large poncho and a length of nylon cord. He strung the cord taut between the deadfall and the trunk of the living tree, parallel to the ground, about three feet high. He spread the poncho over it, pulled out the corners and staked them out with large rocks, forming a small tent. He stood back and looked at it. The deadfall and its branches almost completely covered the poncho. He looked around and found a large bush, which he cut with his pocket knife and lodged in the branches of the deadfall. Susan watched while he cut several more and a few evergreens and arranged them so that the dark-green poncho was completely covered from the air. By the time he was finished, it was undetectable from the ground as well.

He took the groundsheet and spread it inside the makeshift tent, then unrolled the sleeping bags. "We'll let them air out. We may be using them for a while, and they need to breathe." He picked up the two packs and dragged them into the improvised shelter. In a moment he came out with two canteens and a large nylon envelope. "Water sack," he said, holding up the envelope. "It holds a couple of gallons. We'll stop at a stream and fill this and our canteens before we come back here. We'll have plenty of water for cooking and drinking."

"I was hoping that we'd have some for washing, too. I'm so dirty that I can't stand myself."

"So am I, but we'll have to get used to it for a while. There's no way we can heat enough water for bathing without a fire, and that's something we can't risk. I've got a bar of soap, though, and we can sponge down at a stream. It won't be a regular bath, but it'll help."

He stuffed the water sack into one cargo pocket, clipped a canteen to his belt, and passed the other to Susan. "Now, we'll circle around and see if we can make trouble for them on the south side of the place. They won't know where the hell we are, or how many of us there are when we're finished."

He led the way south, then trended to the west. They were in the next valley to the south of Bear Pen valley, traveling high up on the developing ridgeline as it trended down from the main plateau, just under the crest. They went about a mile before MacGonigal called a halt. He found a comfortable resting place and pulled a couple of breakfast bars out of his pocket. "It's not exactly the finest cuisine, but it'll do for lunch."

They sat and munched the breakfast bars and sipped water from the canteens. "I wish I'd brought the stove and something hot to fix," he said. "It would be nice just to have a hot drink right now."

She smiled at him over the top of her canteen. "Next time we can have a picnic. Let's get this over with first."

Suddenly they heard the sound of the engine of an approaching airplane. "Do you hear what I hear?"

He cocked his head. "Yeah. Good old Jarvis must be making a mint out of this deal."

He got up and pulled back the branches of a large spreading cedar and ushered Susan under, dragging the packs in after her. They waited while the drone of the plane's engine grew louder. Craning their necks and peering up through the thick evergreen branches, they saw it pass overhead, then turn and fly along Bear Pen Creek. It flew the length of the valley, passing almost over the place where they had set up camp, then banked and came back.

"Mac! Do you think they saw our camp?"

"Not a chance. They're just making another pass at the valley." As if to prove his words, the plane flew steadily over the spot on its return pass and continued on down the valley. They lost sight of it, but by the sound, they could tell that it had completed another pass and was going around for another one.

This time it was completely out of sight for the entire pass. "They're concentrating on the other side of the valley, just as I hoped. Maybe they're searching the other valley. While they're looking in that direction, let's move."

They crept out from under the sheltering branches and headed in the general direction of the sound of the plane's engine. After a quarter of a mile of walking, during which the plane made two more passes, they saw it again. It was flying low, down the spine of the opposite ridge. They waited until it completed that pass and started another one, then climbed up the crest of the ridge. From there, they could watch the plane, but not the farm. MacGonigal let the plane go by once more, then led Susan down the ridge a little way, seeking a good observation post.

As they worked their way down, the slope of the ridge became less steep, allowing a view of the open ground in the valley below. A small outcropping of stone, with a fallen log that hung precariously blocked by two small boulders, offered a good position. Higher up the slope, a large oak leaned outward and sheltered the position from the air. They settled down behind it, took out the binoculars and watched the farmyard. There was nothing to see in the open, but with the binoculars, MacGonigal caught an occasional glimpse of figures moving through the trees on the opposite ridge. He counted three, but realized that there were probably more. He toyed idly with the idea of sniping at them, but it was an impossibly long shot for a rifle equipped with such a low power scope, seven- or eight-hundred yards. He might have got one of the searchers, with luck, but better to wait until he could be certain.

For an hour or more, the search continued. The Cessna flew again and again along the ridge, down the valley, and back up for a high look at the area. Slowly the search moved east, toward the area where they had set up their camp, and toward the end of that time, the plane was circling quite near to the camouflaged poncho shelter. MacGonigal knew, however, that the odds of the camp being found were almost nil. He enjoyed the show through the binoculars, sharing them with Susan.

At last the plane made a final pass and headed off in the direction of the airfield. MacGonigal saw several figures making their way down the ridge, heading for the cabin. They had clearly abandoned the effort to find the man who had killed their comrade, and were headed back to the shelter of the farm. One of them was coming straight down, almost as if intent on making a target of himself. MacGonigal slipped off his parka and folded it carefully, making a pad of it. He placed it carefully on the log in front of him and rested the forearm of the Savage on it. He took up a sitting position, his legs crossed, his shoulders hunched, his left hand assisting his right shoulder in supporting and guiding the butt of the rifle, and tracked the moving figure.

"Are you going to shoot, Mac?"

"If this guy offers a good target. Watch him through the glasses. I'm aiming at the one just beyond the cabin, in the blue jacket. If I miss, tell me how far and in what direction."

She looked intently through the glasses. "I see him. He's an awful long way off."

"Yeah, I make it about five hundred yards or so. But when he reaches the edge of the woods, it'll be just about three twenty-five. And it'll be a clear shot. No branches or small trees to worry about."

He kept the blue jacket in the scope. "When I shoot, tell me where I hit. Watch for the bullet to kick up dust and tell me right away, so I can adjust my aim."

"I'm watching. But if you hit him, what do we do then?"

"Just get out of here. Go back up the way we came. Keep low. I'll follow you, but I'll be a little ways behind. If you lose touch with me, go down the other side of the ridge to the stream. Turn left, upstream, and walk a hundred paces. I'll come for you."

He resumed his concentration on the man in the blue jacket. The man moved with agonizing slowness, picking his way down the slope, and MacGonigal panned the scope around, trying to spot the others. There were now five in view, moving down the ridge, but the man in blue was the closest, by a wide margin.

He turned back to his intended target. The man was nearing the edge of the trees. MacGonigal put the crosshairs on the top of his head, allowing for a foot of drop. There was a gentle breeze, so slight that it barely stirred the leaves. MacGonigal considered allowing a foot of wind drift as well, but decided against it. He held steady and let the man close the range between them.

He could see the man plainly now. He was almost out of the trees, carrying his AR-18 across his chest. MacGonigal could see that he was carrying a green nylon pouch on a web belt, extra magazines for the AR-18. Another magazine made a bulge in the pocket of his jacket. "Are you watching?"

She answered with a grunt, her tongue between her teeth as she concentrated on the man. MacGonigal steadied the crosshairs, took a shallow breath and held it, and began applying pressure on the trigger.

At the sound of the shot, the man dropped as if he had been struck by lightning. "You got him, Mac!"

MacGonigal already had thrown the lever, sending the ejected cartridge case tinkling among the rocks, and was ready for a second shot. Through the scope, he could see a huddled patch of blue cloth. He swung the scope around, looking for another target. The men on the ridge side were frozen, unsure of what had happened. MacGonigal picked out one wearing a long parka, estimated the range at about five hundred yards, held a foot over his head and slightly to the right, and squeezed the trigger.

"Where? I didn't see it! Which one did you shoot at?"

MacGonigal was back on target. The man had disappeared. No way of telling whether he had hit or missed. "Get out of here, Sue! Beat it up the hill!"

As she rose up, he fired at a third man, this time at

an estimated range of six-fifty. He saw that one hit, just to the right of the man, showering him with dirt and rocks. The man dove for the ground, his AR-18 flying down the slope. MacGonigal didn't wait for any further reaction. He jumped up and followed Susan's disappearing figure up the slope. Behind him, the sudden rattle of automatic fire broke out, but he could hear no shots passing overhead. It wasn't likely that they'd even come close; the distance was nearly twice the true effective range of any .223 weapon.

Suddenly the tempo of the firing increased, and a burst of shots rattled through the trees. Someone must be firing from the barn or the cabin. He kept running—it was automatic fire, like the rest, and not likely to score a hit. As he reached the crest, he threw himself behind a boulder and peered back around it. There were no plain targets that he could see, but there was a muzzle flash from one of the cabin windows. He brought the Savage to bear, but his chest was heaving too heavily for him to make an accurate shot. He ducked back behind the boulder and waited.

The storm of shooting died away to just an occasional shot. MacGonigal suspected that they had fired up most of their ammunition. He looked around the boulder again, and saw that one or two men were picking their way down the ridge. It was too far for a shot, but he watched them. After a few minutes, the others, emboldened by their comrades, also began to make their way down. He checked for the man in the blue jacket. He lay where he had fallen.

He looked for the man in the long parka. He wasn't in sight. That didn't prove anything, of course. He could be hiding, scared stiff by a close call, or even lightly wounded. MacGonigal turned his attention to the cabin. There was no more firing, but through the scope, he could see what might be a man's head. He raised the Savage and aimed.

At the shot, the figures picking their way down the ridge scrambled for cover, some of them spraying the air with their little assault rifles. MacGonigal threw the lever and re-aimed at the window. The shape of the head was gone. He scrutinized the other windows, but saw no sign of another target.

There was nothing moving on the other ridge, either. He lay silent for a half hour as the sun fell lower in the sky. It was growing colder, and he imagined that Susan must be having a rough time waiting for him, not knowing if he was dead or not. At last he wriggled away from his position and made his way over the crest and down the other side.

He almost tripped over her. She was concealed behind a large clump of briars, and he found himself staring into the muzzle of the carbine as he tried to pick his way around. She lowered the weapon. "I wasn't sure it was you."

He smiled. "There was a lot of shooting, right enough, but those characters couldn't hit a bull in the ass with a bass fiddle. They sprayed the whole damn hillside, and didn't even get close. I don't think they even realized that they were out of range."

"Are they chasing you?"

He laughed. "I doubt it. I let them get brave after

the first go-round, and when they got up to move, I cut down on them again. They may wait until dark to move!"

"How many of them did we get?"

"Not many. One, for sure—the guy in blue. May have scratched the second one I fired at. I shot at what I think was one in the house. Not sure that it was even a man. Could have been a curtain or something."

"But the one in blue you're sure of?"

"It wasn't a difficult shot. And that hundred-and-fifty-grain soft point will put them down if you hit them. I think he's hit solid, and if he's not dead, he's out of action permanently."

She looked up at the slowly darkening sky. "I think we better get back to camp before it gets dark."

"You're right. We'd better get moving." He unclipped his canteen and shook it. "We'd better remember to stop and get some water, too, or we're going to have a dry camp tonight."

They moved through the woods, weapons ready, but relaxed. MacGonigal thought there was little chance that Nazario's men would try their luck again that day, and his confidence communicated itself to Susan. "What do we do tomorrow, Mac?"

"Play it by ear, just like today. If they keep using the cabin for their base of operations, they'll be like sitting ducks. We'll always know where they are, and they'll have to hunt for us. And that's going to cost them," he said, hefting the Savage.

At a small stream they stopped and filled the canteens and the water sack, stretching a corner of a bandanna over the mouths to strain out leaves and bits of bark. Susan looked at MacGonigal. "I thought you brought some soap."

He grinned. "I did, but it's going to be a cold bath, and no towels. You can use my bandanna, though."

They stripped, shivering in the cold, laying their clothes aside carefully, and entered the stream, their flesh all goose pimples. They soaped and rinsed each other quickly, then fled back to their clothes, drying themselves as best they could with the skimpy red cloth. Susan crowded against MacGonigal, her flesh cold against his. He draped his parka around them both and held her close, wrapping his arms tightly around her, and they warmed each other with their body heat. At last, still cold and still damp, they parted and pulled on their clothes.

"Brr! I don't think I'll ever be warm again!"

"Me neither. And I'm still wet. My shirt and pants are damp. Let's walk fast and see if we can dry ourselves out."

They moved off at a rapid pace, so fast that Susan occasionally had to trot to keep up with MacGonigal. "Slow down a little, Mac. I don't want more blisters."

He slacked his pace and let her come up with him. "It's fun to take a bath with you, Sue, but I don't think I'll do it again until we have someplace warm to do it."

"That's what you think. If you want what I think you want, you'll take a bath before you get it."

He grinned at her lasciviously. "Come on, slowpoke. I'm in a hurry to get back. Besides, it'll be a lot warmer in our sleeping bags."

The next morning was bitterly cold. MacGonigal woke while it was still dark, and fumbled for his clothes. They had taken the damp garments into the sleeping bag with them to dry them with body heat, and now they were all wadded down at the foot of the doubled bags. He groped around, found his trousers with the flashlight in the pocket, then lay on his back, raising the top of the bag with his knees while he struggled into his clothes.

"Can't you do that without letting cold air in?"

"Afraid not, honey. Besides, it's time to get moving. If they keep following their pattern, that damn plane will be overhead by first light."

He crawled out of the bag and poured water into a pot for breakfast. While he was priming and lighting the stove, Susan dressed. "These clothes are still damp, Mac."

She unzipped her side of the bag and rolled out, reaching for her boots. "How are the feet?"

She examined them. "Okay, I guess. They're not bothering me anymore."

He held the flashlight on them. "They look all right. Think you're up to a little walking this morning?"

She groaned and pulled her boots on, thrusting her feet out to him so that he could lace them. "I suppose, if I have to. What did you have in mind?"

He concentrated on lacing the boots. "Well, yesterday your friend Nazario came in late, after the plane left. If he does the same thing again today, it would be too good a setup to ignore. We can hike back parallel to the road, cross the ridge, and be waiting for him."

"After all, he's the driving force behind all this horseshit. If we get him, I think the rest of them will pull out, especially if we get a couple of the guys with him. That ought to be fairly easy—that Scout is an enclosed vehicle, so they won't be able to react to an ambush very well."

It was too dark to see her expression, but her voice was firm. "Do you think we have a chance? If we get him, I could probably get the money without too much trouble then."

"Yeah, I think we can pull it off. That's if he comes in like he did yesterday."

The water in the little pot was boiling, and MacGonigal broke off to mix the oatmeal. "I know this is getting to be a monotonous kind of breakfast."

"I'm not complaining," she said, spooning up a mouthful. "It's good—if there aren't too many more days of it."

They finished their meal and picked up their weapons, MacGonigal checking to see that he had the water sack, spare ammunition, granola bars, and a few other things in his pockets. He took his compass and hung it around his neck so that it fell down his back. He turned away from Susan, and showed her the glowing spots on the needle and bezel. "Just keep your eye on this, and we won't get separated in the dark."

They moved out slowly, MacGonigal searching for landmarks in the darkness, threading his way through the brush and stopping frequently to make sure that Susan didn't lose sight of him. They covered perhaps a mile and a half in this manner when Susan called to him, "Wait a minute, Mac. I've got a stone in my boot."

He stopped and waited while she found a place to sit and pulled off the boot, shook it out, and pulled it back on. "Come back and help me, Mac. I can't seem to get it out."

He turned back and took the boot from her, running his hand inside the boot, feeling the smooth, slightly damp leather. "It's not in there now." He helped her on with the boot. "How does that feel?"

"It's still there. Right above the heel on the outside."

He pulled the boot off again and checked it. There was no stone that he could find, and the leather was smooth. "Maybe it's a burr or a thorn in your sock." He dug out the flashlight and looked, rubbing the spot she indicated with his finger. He pulled the sock off and looked. "It's another blister, honey. We caught it before it got big."

He paused a moment, thinking. "Damn! I didn't bring anything to put on a blister, either."

"It's all right. I can go on. It's not that bad."

He rubbed his bearded chin. "It's not all right, either. We've got a couple of miles to walk, and the same distance coming back. You'll have a hell of a blister by the time we get back."

He came to a decision. "Come on. We'll go back and doctor it."

"Oh, no, Mac," she protested. "That's ridiculous. We're facing a bunch of killers with an airplane, and you want to walk all the way back to camp just to treat a blister. The light will be here before we're done, and the plane will be up, and . . . who knows what will happen?"

"Yeah, I know." He tugged at his beard. "But I can't afford to let you go lame on me. I don't know what the hell to do."

"Look, I can stay here and wait for you. I'll be okay, really I will. And I'll be as safe here as anywhere else."

He didn't answer for a long time. "I hate leaving you in the middle of the woods like this. Shit, the bastards might just decide to comb out this valley."

"If they do that, I'll just hide from them," she reasoned. "I can hear them coming and stay out of their way."

"Yeah, but you could get lost, too. You could wind up wandering around in these woods all by yourself, with me wandering around looking for you, and neither one of us able to call or make a noise. I don't like that idea."

"We're wasting time talking about it. Suppose we do this: You take me where I can watch the farm, and I'll keep an eye on the place while you try to get Nazario."

He thought about it. "I don't like it, Sue. What happens if they come up the ridge? I'd be leaving you in a hell of a spot. After all, you're the one they want and I'm supposed to be protecting you."

"If they get too close, I can find somewhere to hide. I'll be all right, Mac. I don't need you to hold my hand. I can take care of myself."

"It's still not a good idea. Suppose you do have to hide from them? Where will I find you?"

"I can find my own way back to camp, really I can. Don't be so worried."

He was silent for a long time. "I'm not sure about this. I mean, maybe you can find the camp, and maybe you can't. You don't know this country all that well, and I deliberately made the camp hard to locate."

"Well, suppose I do this: If I have to hide, I'll go down to the stream and find a place to wait there. All you have to do is follow the stream." She paused a moment and went on, "It's the only thing that makes sense. You said yourself that I can't go with you. And if we go back to the camp, you'll miss your chance on the road. We can't move around with that airplane overhead. We could be pinned down all day, and no telling what could happen."

He thought about it. "Okay. We'll do it. I still don't like it, but I guess we don't have a choice. Think you can make it to the top of the ridge?"

"Of course I can. And I'll be careful and take care of myself, you can be sure of that."

He grunted, still not happy, and helped her to her feet. They turned and went uphill, climbing the steep slope in pitch darkness. After a half hour of stumbling, they reached the line of low bluffs that capped the ridge. MacGonigal followed the bluffs until he found an easy way up, then picked his way down the other side. About fifty feet below the bluffs, he found a deadfall held a little ways off the ground by its branches. He laid aside his rifle and broke out a few small branches, making a hollow under the mass of dead limbs for her.

"You better leave me the binoculars if I'm going to

be watching what's going on below."

Without a word, he pulled the case from around his neck and handed it to her, along with the granola bars. She took it and crawled into the hiding place he had prepared. He stood uncertainly while she made herself comfortable.

"I still don't like leaving you. Are you sure that you'll be all right?"

"Of course I'm sure. I'll stay here, quiet as a mouse, and watch them. You come back for me later. If I'm not here, I'll be somewhere along the stream. And stop worrying."

He stood a moment longer, then turned and made his way uphill, clambering over the bluffs and making his way along the other side of the crest, just below the bluff line. He went on for a mile or so, then crossed back over to the Bear Pen Creek side and began to work his way down to the access road. It was thick going, and he was extremely cautious, fearing that the road might be guarded or patrolled.

At last he reached the bottom of the valley and paralleled the creek for a quarter of a mile, then found a crossing place at the foot of a little rapids where the water was shallow enough to wade. Once on the other side, he crept forward, stopping to listen every few steps. At last, satisfied that there was no one near, he made his way out onto the road itself.

Susan huddled within the enclosing branches of the dead tree, a damp chill slowly creeping into her. It was too dark to see, and she occupied herself with thoughts of what she would do once she was free of

Nazario. There was a lot of money, more than she could ever spend. She wondered about MacGonigal as she waited for the sun to come up. Should she offer him a partnership? Would he accept it? MacGonigal was funny, she decided, a completely independent person, with his own rules, who cared nothing about the rest of the world—as long as it didn't interfere with MacGonigal.

When she first crawled into her hiding place, it was literally too dark to see her hand in front of her face. Now she realized that she could dimly make out the stark branches around her. Looking upward, she could see a faint, rosy glow in the sky. She waited, watching, as the glow increased. Almost on cue, she heard the drone of an approaching aircraft. Turning toward the sound, she soon caught the flash as the sun's rays picked up the plane. It was at two thousand feet and about three miles away, flying directly toward her. She wondered what Jarvis was like, marveling at how she could hate and fear a man she had never seen before, a man who probably didn't even know what the real reason for these flights was.

As the light increased, she tried to see what was happening in the valley, but her hiding place was too restricted. She broke a few branches. That allowed her to turn a little in her hiding place, but she was still unable to see much. The deadfall, while offering perfect concealment, was poorly sited for an observation post. Just down the slope from it grew a clump of small cedars which effectively blocked her view of everything but the paddock.

She fretted for a while, while the plane flew up and down the valley, but when it began to search the ridge on which she was hiding, she was thankful for the cover. For an hour or more, the plane went up and down the ridge, sometimes flying below the ridgetop on one side or the other.

It bothered her, however, that she was unable to see what the searchers on the ground were doing. For all she could tell, they might be closing in on the very place where she crouched. And with the constant noise of the plane's engine, she couldn't even hear them.

At last, however, the plane gave up and began searching the ridge on the far side of Bear Pen valley. She breathed a sigh of relief when it moved away, but soon began to chafe about the lack of observation into the valley. At last she decided to move. Casing the binoculars, she slung them around her neck, then, carbine in hand, she crept out of her hiding place.

At first she felt frightened, naked in the open, but she reasoned that the searchers must have given up this ridge. With their attention focused elsewhere, there was little risk in seeking a better vantage point. She made her way down to the stand of cedars, but found that as the convex ridge sloped down, the swell of the ground hid the valley floor from view. She crouched under the cedars and inspected the slope below her. There was a clump of boulders just at the edge of the swell of the ridge that seemed promising. She stepped out of the shelter of the cedars and began working her way down, favoring her sore, blistered foot.

Without warning, her feet were jerked from under her and she went sprawling and rolling down the slope. The carbine flew out of her hands and clattered away. She came to a halt against a tree trunk, the breath knocked out of her. As she struggled to fill her lungs, she saw a burly figure in a dark green jacket rise from behind a clump of huckleberry bushes. He held an AR-18 across his body.

IX.

Stunned and unable to breathe, she could barely comprehend what was happening. She was dimly aware that the man had been there all along, had heard her coming, and had lain in wait and tripped her. He came bounding down the hillside now, his big hiking boots scattering stones and forest debris. Dazedly, she remembered the .22 pistol and groped for it, concentrating on dragging it out and releasing the safety.

He was on top of her by then, and as her fingers closed around the butt, he put one cleated boot on her wrist, grinding it into the rocky soil of the ridge until she dropped the pistol. He scooped it up and put it in a pocket of his jacket, then grabbed the front of her parka and hauled her to her feet.

He drew back his hand, but the motion didn't register with her. Lights flashed inside her head. She didn't see it coming, but she realized that he had hit her, backhanding her across the face with one huge, hairy paw. She could taste blood, and her head spun, but she felt no pain after the initial blow.

"Bitch!" He struck her again. A heavy gold ring with a large stone bit into her face with each blow.

Her head rang, and she could barely hear him. "Goddamn bitch! I've got you now, you slippery cunt!" He shoved her down the slope and she fell, tumbling and rolling for fifty feet down the steep ridgeside. He was on her before she could get up. He pulled her to her feet again. "I'd kill you right here, if we didn't have orders," he snarled. "You and that goddamn boyfriend of yours did for some good people."

She was too shocked and stunned to resist him, even if resistance had been possible. He grabbed her arms, slinging the AR-18 over his shoulder as he did so, and propelled her down the slope. Her feet moved mechanically, but her legs felt like rubber. Her head swam, and she could feel nausea sweep over her. Without warning, she vomited—half-digested oatmeal and gastric juices gushed out of her mouth. He pushed her away from him and she fell, retching.

"Goddamn bitch! Cunt! Goddamn puke on a man!" He pulled a handkerchief from his pocket and scrubbed at a sour-smelling spot on his jacket. Susan, oblivious, supported herself weakly on her hands and heaved, a thin bile now running from her mouth. Her captor grabbed her by the hood of her parka and jerked her to her feet.

"Let's go, bitch. Nazario will be glad to see your little ass." He unsnapped his jacket and pulled it aside, revealing a Motorola Handi-talkie in a leather case on his belt. While Susan dry heaved, he extended its antenna and reported. She could hear a crackling reply, but was too dazed to catch the words. The man returned the radio to its case and half dragged, half carried her down the slope.

She had no choice but to go with him. He was strong, bull-like, and she had no strength left. She stumbled now and then, and he jerked her arm savagely. "Watch where you're going, bitch! Think I'm going to carry you down the damn hill?"

Her head began to clear, but as the numbness of the first shock wore off, her head began to ache and her lips and cheek felt as if they had been pulped. Her ribs and arms, which had taken most of the punishment in her fall, were a medley of pain. She tried to think, to make some kind of assessment of her problem, but the realization grew as her head cleared: There was no hope. Nazario had her, and he would kill her. But first, he would get the information about the money. What he would do after that, she didn't dare guess. She hoped that he would be angry or merciful enough to kill her quickly, but she knew that he wouldn't.

Overhead, she was aware of the plane circling. The sound of the engine changed, and she was suprised to realize that it was coming straight in, flaps down, for a landing in the paddock. She saw it hovering above the trees, drifting down, and then lost sight of it as it passed behind a stand of tall trees.

Her captor shoved her forward roughly and she staggered. "Walk, bitch! Walk under your own power." He slapped the stock of the AR-18. "Just keep moving, baby. And if you want to run, go ahead. I won't chase you. I'll just blow your legs off."

She stumbled forward, sick and dizzy. She could taste the blood and bile in her mouth and her body was sending her brain a bewildering array of pain signals. As she came out from the tree line, she saw the Cessna taxiing slowly through the paddock. It swung to a stop near the gate, the propeller still turning, and the door opened. Three men alighted and walked away. The engine revved and the plane swung around and taxied the length of the paddock. One of the three men waved to her captor, and he unclipped his radio.

"Stay here, bitch. Nazario wants the plane to get off first. Then he'll deal with you."

She stood, almost numb with shock as the plane reached the other end of the paddock, turned and came roaring back. It lifted off in half the length of the little field and went soaring overhead. She didn't even raise her head to watch it. As it passed, her captor pushed her roughly. "Let's go. There's someone who's anxious to meet you."

She walked in a daze across the space that separated them from the group, stumbling, but caught by her captor each time she came to the verge of falling. As she got closer, she saw Nazario step forward from between his bodyguards. His eyes seemed to burn holes in her, blazing out of his swarthy face. She halted a half dozen yards from him, swaying dizzily, and her captor immediately gave her a shove that sent her sprawling at his feet.

She lay there, waves of nausea sweeping over her. Nazario prodded her with the toe of his boot. "What's wrong, honey? Haven't the boys been treating you nice?"

She looked up at him, seeing his cruel hooked nose, his thin lips wet with anticipation. He reached down and grabbed her parka, pulling her to her feet. "Haven't you got anything to say to me?"

She didn't answer, and he shook her. Her head flopped back and forth. He shook her more vigorously, then struck her across the face with the flat of his hand. Her ears rang with the blow, and her vision blurred. She felt her knees buckle and she fell forward against his grip. He pushed her back, holding her erect with brute strength.

"What's wrong, you tight-assed little bitch? You don't like my company?" He shook her again, then pulled her close to him, sneering in her face. "Yeah, you little prick-teaser, you thought you were too good for me, didn't you? You thought you could get away with anything, didn't you? Well, what do you think now?"

He released her, and she fell in a heap at his feet. He turned to his henchmen. "Take her ass in the barn and tie her up."

They bent forward and grabbed her, each taking an arm, and dragged her to the barn, hustling her inside. One held her against one of the uprights while the other took a strand of binder twine and jerked her arms behind her, almost wrenching them out of the sockets. He wrapped her wrists with twine, tying them so that they cut the circulation off almost at once. When they released her, she sagged forward and began to slide to the floor. The one in front of her grabbed her by the hair and jerked her up. The other produced a second length of twine and passed it around her body, just below the armpits, and tied her in place.

Nazario came in, followed by the man who had

captured her and three others. He stood in front of her a moment, then pulled a cigar out of his pocket, bit the end off, lit it, and blew a cloud of smoke in her face. He turned to his bodyguards. "What the hell you got her tied like this for? Can't even get at her tits the way you got her tied."

Not waiting for a reply, he grabbed her hair and lifted her head against the post. He looked into her eyes and blew smoke into her face again. "Can you hear me, Miss tight-ass? You know who I am?"

She nodded weakly. He went on, "You and I got things to talk about, you know that?"

She made no reply. "You done me a pretty shitty deal. You ran off with a lot of money." He took the cigar out of his mouth and glared at her, his jaw muscles tight. "I could have put up with a lot of your shit, all your prick teasing, all your high and mighty ways, but nobody steals from Nazario." He shoved the cigar back into his mouth, his lips flecked with spittle. "You're in for a bad time, bitch."

He grabbed her parka and tried to unzip it. "God damn it! What have you got her tied this way for?"

One of his bodyguards produced a folding knife and cut the offending twine. Susan, no longer supported, sagged forward and down. Nazario seized her long hair and pulled her up with one hand, while he yanked the zipper of her parka down with the other. He grabbed her wool shirt and wrenched it open, scattering buttons over the barn floor, then thrust his hand between her breasts, wrapping his fingers around her bra and ripping it off. He flung it aside and seized one pink nipple between thumb and forefinger. "That's more like it, bitch. You and me are going to have a little fun, but first you're going to tell me what you did with the money."

He thumped her head against the post. "What do you think of this, bitch?" He thumped her again, then began to slap her—backhanded, forehanded, knocking her head from side to side. She could feel herself losing her grip on consciousness. He continued to slap her. "Let me know when you're ready to tell me something."

He released her hair and she fell and slid down the post, crumpling on the floor. "Shit! She's out of it." He kicked her lightly on the thigh. "We'll have to wait until she comes to."

He turned to the man that had captured her. "What did you do with her boyfriend?"

The man shook his head. "Didn't see him. It was just her. She came walking right past me. I heard her coming, crouched down behind some bushes and grabbed her."

Nazario struck the wall with his fist. "Assholes! That's all I've got working for me, assholes! All you had to do was wait another minute and you'd have had them both!"

The man stepped back, but said defiantly, "He wasn't there. What was I supposed to do, shit him?"

Nazario flung his cigar away in rage. "Don't smart-mouth me! You dumb sons of bitches have let that bastard run you ragged, shoot the shit out of you, and now you tell me that you didn't even see him when you grabbed the girl. The son of a bitch had to be around somewhere."

"Well, he wasn't," the man said sullenly. "If he was, he didn't do shit when I grabbed the broad.

Maybe he's pulled out."

"Pulled out? In a pig's ass, he has! That cocksucker is out there somewhere with that damn sniper rifle of his, and we're like fish in a barrel here."

His aides shuffled uncomfortably. Finally one of them spoke. "It's okay, Mr. Nazario. We've got the broad, and there's nothing he can do about that. He can rot up in those damn hills, but he can't do anything."

Nazario turned on the man savagely. "He can't do anything? Where the fuck were you yesterday? The son of a bitch starts out by blowing one of my best boys up—son of a bitch, he almost killed me! And then he clubs one man in the head, and shoots two more, and you say he can't do anything! Did you see how far that fucker was shooting? Christ, he must have been a mile away! You want to stand out in the open and let him try a shot at you?"

The man tried to calm him. "Now, Mr. Nazario, he can't do that in the dark. We'll spend the day working this bitch over, and come dark, we'll leave, and that's all there is to it. We won't have any trouble."

"Won't have any trouble! We've already had trouble. And I'll be goddamned if I'm going to leave here without getting that bastard. Nobody is going to shoot up my boys like that. We're staying around until we've got them both."

Another man joined in. "Mr. Nazario, that might not be such a good idea. I mean, like you said, the guy is dangerous . . . and we've made a lot of noise around here. We're liable to have the police or the

FBI or somebody down on our necks any time now. Maybe . . . maybe we should do with the girl and go . . . you could send somebody back later to take care of the guy."

Nazario's face turned a deep red, his neck muscles bulged. "Faggots, that's what you are! A bunch of limp-dick, chicken-livered faggots. You're scared shitless of that son of a bitch up there, and you're scared of a bunch of backwoods police."

Spittle was flying from his lips. He whirled to face a pair of his men who had withdrawn from the direct blast of his anger. "Spineless cocksuckers! We're going to get that bastard, and we're not going to leave here until we do." He whirled again to face one of his bodyguards. "How do you think we'd get out of here, anyway, dumb shit? We left the goddamn cars at the motel or at the airport. That was your smart idea!"

The man sought to defend himself. "Now, wait a minute, Mr. Nazario. You agreed that we couldn't leave the cars on the road, where somebody might find them and get suspicious, or where that boyfriend of hers might play another trick with a bomb. You agreed!"

Nazario slammed a big fist into the barn wall. "Assholes! Assholes!"

The man sought to mollify him. "Look, Mr. Nazario, we can work on her today. We don't have to step out of this barn. Tonight we can walk out. It's a long walk, but we can make it."

"A long walk," Nazario spat. "You should have thought of that before the plane took off, shithead." The man bit his words back. Nazario glared at him.

"Don't give me that look. You got something to say, spit it out!"

The man said nothing. Nazario turned and glared at the others, each in turn. "Any of you assholes got anything to say?" They remained mute. He turned back to the first man. "Okay, asshole. First we get the boyfriend, and then you walk out and get a car. Understand?"

He walked to the barn door and stood looking out at the hills. "That son of a bitch is out there somewhere right now. Probably staring right down our throats." He spun around. "Okay, any of you shitheads got any ideas how we're going to get him?"

He looked from one to the next. "Assholes," he muttered. "Nothing but assholes. Not a fucking one of you with a brain in his head."

He shook his head and pulled another cigar out of his pocket, biting the end off and spitting a fragment of tobacco in the general direction of his audience. "Okay. We got one thing going for us. We've got bait." He gestured with the cigar at Susan's crumpled form. "We've got her."

"Take that bitch out and string her up in the yard where he can see her." He paused and thrust the cigar viciously at the bodyguard he had argued with. "You take her. Anybody gets shot, I don't want it to be anybody with brains."

The man pulled out his knife again, stooped, and cut her bonds. Her arms flopped limply on the barn floor. The man stepped over her to where a hank of binder twine hung from a nail. He pulled two lengths from the tangle, then jerked Susan erect. She sagged against him, her parka and shirt open, her small pointed breasts exposed. The man looked at them. "Maybe we could have a little fun with her, first."

Nazario took a final pull on his second cigar and flung it away. "There'll be plenty of time for that. After we get the boyfriend. And after I'm finished with her." He spat on the floor. "That tight-assed bitch is going to tell me where the money is. Then she and I are going to play a few little games. Then you boys can have her."

The man hesitated. "If her boyfriend knew that we were screwing her in here, that might bring him out into the open."

Nazario looked at the man scornfully. "How's he going to know that, shithead? You think he can see through walls?" The man blinked and stammered a moment. Nazario cut him off. "No, asshole," he said sarcastically, "you got it all figured out. All you got to do is haul her out where he can see, and screw her while he watches. Why don't you do that, and maybe he'll spare me the trouble of getting rid of you." He turned to where Susan lay crumpled and nudged her with his foot. "Come on, get her out of here."

The man pulled her to her feet, his face burning with embarrassment. Susan somehow found her feet and managed to stand under her own power. The man pinioned her arms behind her and began to wrap them with binder twine. He was suddenly interrupted by a strangled, inarticulate cry. He whirled to look and released his hold on her.

"Son of a bitch! The goddamn barn is on fire!"

Susan, still only partially aware of what was going on, looked in the same direction. A thick, white smoke was pouring out of the hay. As she watched uncomprehendingly, the entire face of the stack of bales stored on the ground floor of the barn erupted in a sheet of flame. She staggered back involuntarily, lurching against one of her captors, who gave her a shove that sent her sprawling.

She lay on the ground, shaking her head, awareness coming back. She heard confused shouts and the thudding of feet as Nazario's men struggled to clear the barn. She realized that one of the men had been on guard in the loft and was now trapped there. The others sought to extinguish the flames, an impossible task, then exhorted their comrade to jump. It was a full fifteen feet, and the man was reluctant, even though the entire barn was now a sheet of flame.

Suddenly she realized that no one was watching her. She got to her feet with a great effort and staggered around the corner of the burning structure. Ahead of her was the tractor shed. Something told her that if she could gain its shelter, she would be safe. She called up her last reserves, driving her sluggish body beyond its capacity. Behind her, the tone of the shouting changed. What they were saying, she could not tell, but suddenly there was the crack of a bullet overhead. She didn't care. She staggered on.

More shots, a fusillade, ripped overhead. The ground jumped around her, spraying her ankles and legs with stones. She went on. The door to the shed was so close. If she made it, she would be all right. It was only a few more feet ahead.

As she reached the door, she saw the wood jump

and splinter as bullets slammed into it. She threw herself against it and tumbled inside. Once there, she collapsed against the tractor, feeling its cold metal against her. She slumped to the floor. More shots ripped through the shed. She was wrong. They had only to come and get her. She raised her head and looked at the partially open door.

MacGonigal examined the tracks on the road, using his faint red light and shielding it with his spread parka. There were no fresh tracks, just the signs of yesterday's traffic, the ice crystals sharp within the tread marks. He went up the road a little, and positioned himself at a sharp curve, so that he could shoot down a long straight stretch of a hundred-and-fifty yards. He made himself comfortable behind a clump of bushes and waited.

It wouldn't be difficult at all. The vehicle would present an easy target and the .308 bullets would rip through it from end to end. He rehearsed his plan; first get the driver, whoever he was. Then get Nazario, if he could recognize him. If not, lace the Scout with closely spaced shots, then reload and wait to see if any survivors emerged.

Of course, there would be the men up at the farm to think about. But MacGonigal doubted that they would be all that anxious to come pell mell to the sound of shooting. They would probably suspect a trap. He thought about it. The best escape route for him would be to remain on this side of Bear Pen Creek, and go back parallel to the access road. That would put him in a good position to ambush one of the other men, if they came down the road.

And if they didn't? He thought about it. It wasn't likely that they'd come before he'd done with his business with Nazario. In that case, all he had to do was remain quiet. They were amateurs, at least at his game, and they had proved that to his satisfaction. The sound of the shooting and the sight of the wrecked Scout would hold their attention completely. They weren't the sort to cover their flanks and rear when distracted by something. He'd have a good chance to simply let them pass him by, then either slip away or fire on them from behind.

He went over the plan again, selecting his route out, the possible ambush points along the way. He checked his ammunition; a magazine in the Savage, three extras, and two twenty-round boxes in the cargo pockets of his jeans. He leaned back against the trunk of a rough-barked pine and waited.

They were a long time coming, but he knew that they would be. He recited poems to himself, went over the intricate fingering of several pipe tunes in his mind, and kept himself mentally occupied, fighting boredom and the desire to move, to stretch.

When the sky began to lighten, he smiled to himself. If he had their pattern, the plane would be over pretty soon. They'd search for a while, maybe a couple of hours or even more, then the plane would leave, and three quarters of an hour later, more or less, Nazario and his bodyguards would come into the killing zone.

He thought briefly about Susan, but she was safe. He had made sure that she had good cover, and had left her the granola bars and what little comforts he had. In a few hours, if his luck held, he could go get her and tell her that it was all over.

Right on cue, the plane came over, droning back and forth over the valley. From his cramped position, it was difficult to watch it, but from time to time, he managed to spot it by turning his head. He was tempted to move to get a better view of it, knowing that it would be a long time before it departed and his quarry appeared, but he resisted the temptation. He sat motionless, tensing and relaxing his cramping muscles to get a little relief.

When the note of the engine changed, he didn't realize its significance right away. Suddenly it dawned on him. Shit, he thought, you've outsmarted yourself, MacGonigal. They're not coming in by road at all. Why didn't you think of that?

He rose carefully from his hiding place, stretching his aching limbs, while he pondered this change in the situation. The more he thought about it, the more he realized that the best thing to do was follow his original plan for after the ambush. He would go up the valley through the woods, coming out near the cabin. With the plane to distract them, he could probably get quite close. He might get a chance at Nazario near the cabin; the man showed little desire to thrash around in the brush with his henchmen. It would also be wise to start something in the lower part of the valley, drawing them away from where Susan was waiting.

He went up the ridge, slabbing along above the road, occasionally dropping down to where he could see the road to check for parked vehicles. He had covered a half mile or so when he heard the engine of the plane as it began its takeoff roll. He took cover and waited while it passed overhead, and watched it bank around and head away in the direction of the airfield. He remained motionless while the drone of the engine died away. Something must be up for them to send the plane back so soon. He had better get to somewhere where he could see what was going on.

He finally reached a point above the falls where he could see both the cabin and the turnaround at the end of the road. There were no vehicles there at all, except possibly for his own truck in the shed. He thought about it. They must have driven them out yesterday. Most of them must have spent the night on his farm. Nazario wouldn't have taken the chance of landing if there were no one on the ground providing security. That probably meant that they had ambushes of their own posted.

He stayed where he was, looking over the farm. He regretted that he had left the binoculars with Susan. He lay motionless, scanning the farm with care. Nothing was moving. Nazario and his bodyguards must be in the cabin. He watched the doors and windows closely, wishing again for the binoculars. With the two-and-a-half-power scope, he searched the windows and the gaping hole where the door had been, but he could make out nothing.

With his attention on the cabin, it was just by chance he saw it, a haze above the barn roof. For a moment it puzzled him, but then he realized what it was. Damn, he thought, they finally did it. They've set the barn on fire. Then he realized that this might be the chance he was waiting for. The fire might bring Nazario out into the open. He watched closely, and suddenly saw a sheet of flame appear in the loading platform. Any minute now, whoever was in there would be coming out. He readied the Savage, then lowered it. It would be a long shot, and he didn't want to alarm the people in the cabin. Let them think they could come out with safety.

He continued to watch, and saw a cluster of people emerge from the burning barn. He counted them. Six. One of them stumbled and lay huddled on the ground. Probably smoke inhalation. That made one less to worry about. The others ignored the fallen figure and seemed to be shouting to someone in the loft. Good. Their own stupidity might take care of another one.

A sudden movement attracted his attention. The fallen figure was up and moving away from the others. He looked back at the men around the barn, then looked back at the staggering figure. There was something strange about it. He put the scope on the running figure and realized with shock that it was Susan.

Before he could recover, the men standing below the loading platform had seen her. He saw weapons brought into play. It was a long shot, five hundred yards if it was an inch, but he didn't hesitate. He brought the Savage to bear and fired a quick shot, aiming about a foot above the cluster of men.

He didn't see the impact, but threw the lever and fired again with the same hold, then again, lower this time. One of the figures jumped, then he saw the third shot kick up dirt about a yard in front of the men. They scattered. In the back of his mind, he thought about Susan, but dared not look for her.

The thing to do now was provide covering fire for her, shoot as fast as he could, keep them busy until she reached safety. He fired again and once more, fumbling for a spare magazine.

As he reloaded, he saw her reach the tractor shed. He turned his attention to the men around the barn. They were running now, some toward the shed, some toward the cabin. He aimed at the one nearest the tractor shed, held the crosshairs on the top of the man's head and squeezed off a shot, bringing the scope back on target in time to see the man crumple. The others swerved and made for the cabin. He snapped off another shot, saw dirt fly behind the last one, then shifted his aim to the cabin door, waiting.

He was vaguely aware of a figure jumping down from the barn loft, but he ignored it. The last man of the group that had chased Susan was up on the porch now. MacGonigal squeezed off, then swiveled and snapped a shot at the man who had jumped from the barn. He missed, threw the lever and fired again. The man stumbled, fell, got to his feet, then sank back as MacGonigal got off another shot. He lay motionless.

He turned back and surveyed the scene. The man on the porch was down in the doorway, trying to propel himself forward with his arms. MacGonigal fired again, then cursed himself. You should have waited, me boyo. One of the bastards might have come out to help him, then you'd have had the two of them.

He looked over the scene again. There were three down, one near the shed, one halfway to the cabin, and one lying on the porch. None of them moved.

Three out of six. Not bad. But not good, either, he reminded himself. That left at least three in the cabin. He could keep them there while the light lasted, but when dark came it would be a different story.

A flurry of shots came from the cabin, sprayed indiscriminately up the ridge. Automatic fire, he thought scornfully. They'll never learn. He could see the flicker of the muzzle flash as the unseen firer hosed down the slope. When the firing stopped, he held carefully on the window while the man was changing magazines. When the shooting started again, he squeezed off a careful shot. The firing stopped.

"Stupid bastards!" Nazario thumped the wall of the cabin. "All they gotta do is watch for the bastard, and what do they do? They set fire to the fuckin' barn!"

His two cohorts crouched against the walls, warily watching the ridgeline above them, their AR-18 sat the ready. The floor around each of them was littered with empty cartridge cases.

"Goddamn son of a bitch! That bastard did for *three* good men!"

Nazario was literally frothing at the mouth, stamping up and down the cabin floor. His two surviving henchmen cringed, as much in fear of him as of the rifleman up on the high ground. Suddenly he stopped.

"That goddamn bitch got away! Who was supposed to be watchin' her?" He whirled on one of the men, pointing his finger like a weapon.

"You, you limp-dick bastard! You fuckin' let her get away!"

The accused man threw up one arm, as if to protect himself. "Not me, Mr. Nazario! It was . . . It was . . ."

He never finished. Nazario lunged at him, striking him full in the face. The man went down, curling himself into a tight ball on the floor.

"Goddamn son of a bitch! Goddamn limp-dick bastard!" Nazario kicked the man hard as he lay there. He whirled and faced the other man, who cringed and backed away. He turned back and kicked the man lying on the floor.

"Son of a bitch! Stupid cocksucker! You and that other motherfucker that set the barn on fire!" He kicked him again.

He stopped, and with a visible effort, pulled himself together. His face was still mottled, suffused with blood, and his breath came in great panting sobs, but he had himself under control. "OK. That fucker is out there with that sniper rifle. Here's what we'll do."

He nudged the prone man with his foot, forcing him to a sitting position. The man's nose was broken, and blood streamed down his shirtfront. He held his side as if his ribs were broken.

"That bitch can't go far. She's right out there somewhere. That bastard will have to come and get her. All we got to do is wait for him."

He paused, looking around the cabin. "You take the front windows," he said, gesturing to the man who crouched by the door. "And you take the back.

I'm goin' upstairs and watch out the windows up there."

He turned and began climbing the steps to the loft while the other two watched him. At the top he turned back, looking down at them. "When that motherfucker shows up, blow his shit away."

He paused a moment. "You limp dicks better not miss, either!"

MacGonigal waited, watching, sizing up the situation. Uncomfortably, he realized that his initial assessment had been right. They could wait comfortably behind the thick log walls until night came. There was no way he could reach Susan, no way she could get out unseen. From the way she had run, he was sure that she wouldn't be in any shape to get away in the darkness. They'd wait until dark, then go out in safety and get her.

He thought hard. There had to be some way, something that he could do, but there didn't seem to be any solution. They had him. He might get away, almost certainly would, but they would have Sue. He could try to intercept them in the darkness, get them as they were trying to get away with her, but it would be risky. Too risky, he decided. He would be helpless as long as they had her.

Maybe he could work his way down when the light got bad, catch them coming out of the cabin. He thought about it. It wouldn't work. By the time it was dark enough for him to move in, it would be dark enough for them. And in the dark, at close range, they would have all the advantages. The only time spray fire was an advantage was at short range, when it was too dark to see a target.

Don't give up, MacGonigal, he counseled himself. There has to be a way. You've got all day to think about it. But with a sinking feeling, he realized that he was wrong. There wasn't any solution. They had all the cards. All they had to do was wait.

Inside the tractor shed, Susan waited, leaning hopelessly against one of the big rear wheels, for them to come and get her. The firing had stopped, and they must be closing in, surrounding the shed to make sure of her. She waited a long time, a strange lassitude possessing her.

Still they didn't come. At last she roused and crept to the door. Through the crack, she could see a man lying motionless, a pool of blood spreading around him. A fierce feeling of satisfaction surged through her. So they had shot one of their own people! Then she realized that it didn't make any difference, there were still plenty of them left, enough to do whatever they wanted. She sat back on the dirt floor and waited, but no one came.

At last she began to wonder, running through the confused events of her escape in her mind, trying to sort things out. She remembered the frantic run to the shed, the rattle of fire. She thought. It seemed that she remembered hearing something else, a heavier, booming shot now and then, amidst the high rattle of the assault rifles. Her heart leaped. It must be Mac! He's out there somewhere!

She sank down on the floor, tears running uncontrollably from her eyes. Mac was out there and he would come and get her.

She lay there a long time, then picked herself up, moving stiffly. She gathered her torn shirt about her and zipped the parka up, shuddering. They had come so close, but now Mac was here. Mac would come for her.

She wandered around the shed, noticing the light streaming through the cracks in the rough wall. She put her eye to one of the cracks and looked out. The cabin was only a short distance away, and she could see a figure through one of the cabin windows. That's where they were. Mac had them trapped in the cabin. They couldn't get out, not past Mac and his rifle. She went around the walls, looking out. She saw a man lying between the barn and the cabin, and another one lying on the porch, half in and half out of the door. She felt a sudden surge. Mac had got three of them! He'd get them all, and then it would be over!

She wandered around in the shed, and then she suddenly remembered: They had stashed guns in all the outbuildings! She climbed up on the workbench and felt in the eaves. A hard solid object. She took it down. Mac's bagpipe case. She put it aside and searched again. This time she was successful: a long, heavy bolt-action rifle, with a plastic box full of ammunition.

She crept back to the crack and looked toward the cabin. From time to time, she could see someone pass in front of the window. She raised the cumbersome weapon and aimed. The sights wavered, wandering all around. She couldn't hold it steady. She lowered the rifle. She couldn't do it. She'd miss. She looked at the ugly weapon. She didn't even know how to reload it. She didn't even know if it was loaded.

She put it on the bench and examined it, finally figuring out the bolt mechanism. She pulled it back, ejecting a cartridge into the dirt. She picked it up and tried to reinsert it into the weapon, but failed. She could see the fresh brass of the ammunition in the magazine. Experimentally, she pushed the bolt forward, feeding a cartridge halfway into the chamber. That would have to do. She pushed the bolt home and locked it. If she couldn't hit them at this range, at least she could wait with the rifle ready. If they came for her after dark, she would be ready for one of them.

The day passed slowly, and she heard no more sound of firing. From time to time she peeked through cracks in the walls of the shed, trying to fathom what was going on inside the cabin, but she saw little, no more than an occasional form passing a window. At first it didn't bother her. She remembered MacGonigal's talk about putting their opponents under psychological stress, and she thought that he was probably waiting silently up on the ridge side for his enemies to grow restless and careless.

But as the afternoon wore on, she became less certain of herself. What if MacGonigal had been wounded? As she thought about it, it seemed to her that there had been a terrible amount of shooting. Surely, some of it might have taken effect, even if it was only sprayed in his general direction. She also began to realize what MacGonigal already knew, that when night came, the advantages would be reversed. They would come for her, and

MacGonigal, assuming he were still alive, could do little but get himself killed trying to save her.

She sat on a stool at the back of the shed, nursing the heavy rifle on her lap. She would try for them when they came, but she realized what a futile gesture it would be. She might hit the first man through the big double doors, and she might not. She wouldn't get a second shot—the bolt was too stiff, she was too unpracticed.

For an hour or more, she watched the ridge side, steeped in gloom. Nothing moved up there, no sign that MacGonigal was alive or dead. Suddenly something crystalized in her mind. If someone was going to break the deadlock, it would have to be her. She stood up, no clear plan in mind, other than the determination to do something to bring a halt to this game of watching and waiting to die.

She put the rifle aside without a second thought. It wasn't the weapon for her. But there had to be something, some weapon, some idea. She looked around the shed. There were several cans of gasoline on a low rack against one wall. She picked one of them up. Empty. She tried another. Also empty. The fourth one was half-full, and the last one was full. She looked at them speculatively, then went into the room that served as MacGonigal's shop. A plan had formed in her mind.

She emerged with a coil of wire. Picking up one of the empty cans, she wired it to the front of the tractor, strapping it firmly in place in front of the radiator. That done, she looked around the back of the shed. There were the sacks of fertilizer, the same nitrogen fertilizer that MacGonigal had used to make the claymore. One of the bags was half full. She dragged it to the front of the tractor and began scooping handfuls into the empty jerry can. After a few handfuls, she got the half-full can and slopped a little gasoline inside, stirring the gooey contents with a stick.

She kept it up, scooping the fertilizer in, and mixing in the gasoline until the can was nearly full. Then the thought struck her, what would she do for a detonator? She went back into the shop and poked around. There were MacGonigal's reloading tools, bolted to an old chest. She pulled out the drawers. Some smokeless powder, bullets, caps, a dozen substances and gadgets that she couldn't identify. In the second drawer, she found the black powder, three cans of FFG, one of FFFG. She took out two cans and brought them back to the front of the shed.

The problem was solved now, if she could figure out how to set off the powder. She found some sacking and cut it into strips, rolling the strips and soaking them in gasoline. They would do for a fuse—or maybe not. She unscrewed the top of one of the cans of black powder and poured a little out, smearing the black grains on the gasoline-saturated cloth.

She made two fuses that way, gasoline-soaked strips of cloth, with the last foot or so smeared with black powder. She took a center punch and drove it through the caps of the powder cans and inserted her makeshift fuses. Then she put the cans of powder inside the jerry can full of explosive slurry, led the fuses back over the hood of the tractor, and tied the ends to the steering wheel.

She stood back and looked at her creation. She took a deep breath and climbed up into the driver's seat. For a moment, she just sat there. Then she pulled out the choke and pressed the starter. The Farmall sprang to life immediately. She sat a moment longer, then she put it in gear, advanced the throttle and let the clutch out.

"What's that fuckin' noise?"

Nazario stood at the head of the loft steps. His two cohorts looked up at him, but made no reply.

"Don't you bastards hear it? Somebody just started an engine. That fucker's up to something!"

The tractor burst through the doors of the shed and went roaring across the lawn. She struggled with the wheel, turning it and aiming for the front of the cabin. The tractor seemed so slow! But there was no reaction from the cabin. She got the vehicle lined up and pointed at the front porch, the steering wheel twisting violently when the front wheels encountered the steps. She held the wheel with all her strength, fighting it, forcing the vehicle up the steps. The big driving wheels kept pushing, and the front end began to rise, up and up, until she was afraid that it would turn itself over backwards.

She shoved the throttle forward again, until it was up against the steps, and the tractor drove on, engine bellowing. It gave a last lunge, the hood rising alarmingly, then falling with a bone-rattling crash onto the steps. She saw the door in front of her, and for the first time became aware of the bullets crack-

ling around her. The air was filled with sound, the
roar of the tractor, the rattle of the assault rifles,
inarticulate shouts from the men in the cabin.

The nose of the tractor entered the shattered
door, the narrow furrow-following front wheels allowing it to pass. She tore the butane lighter from
under the band of her wristwatch where she had
secured it, and held it to the knot of the fuse where it
was tied to the steering column. The gasoline flashed
in her face, and she threw herself backwards, falling
off the tractor and thudding to the floor of the porch.
Stunned, she managed to scramble to her feet and
run blindly. She had no notion of where she was
going or why, but something drove her legs. Then a
wave of heat washed over her, and she knew nothing
else.

MacGonigal saw the doors of the tractor shed
burst open and the tractor come flying out. For a
moment, he stared at it in amazement, then threw
his rifle to his shoulder. He had no idea what Sue had
in mind, but he would give her covering fire.

He worked the lever of the Savage, firing methodically at the windows of the cabin, trying to just clip
the lower sill, then moving on to the next. He was
aware of the tractor turning, heading for the cabin,
but he had no time to wonder why. He fired the last
round in his magazine, reloaded, and brought the
weapon to bear again, only to find the scope filled
with the tractor, its hood pointed up, the big rear
wheels throwing dirt backwards as it sought the
traction to continue its mad course. He fired at the

windows on either side of the door, first one, then the other, then back again. The hood of the tractor came down, then Susan was out of the seat and running back toward him, a tiny figure in the scope, long legs flashing, long brown hair streaming behind her.

"Holy shit!"

The shout electrified the men in the cabin. The man at the window fired an entire magazine full-automatic, spraying the trees and sky in his surprise. Nazario pulled him roughly aside and looked out the window. The tractor was so close that it almost filled his field of vision. He fired a long burst, most of which went over the tractor. He threw the AR-18 down and drew his snub-nosed .38.

"Shoot, you assholes! Shoot!"

His two men began firing at the tractor, which had reached the porch steps by now. As it lunged upward, rising higher and higher with its engine blaring, they shrank back in fear, their weapons forgotten. Nazario stepped into the shattered doorway and fired his .38 directly into the front of the vehicle.

It was rearing up over him now, like some prehistoric monster, and he stood there, holding the .38 in both hands and clicking away, unaware that he had fired the last round in the cylinder. He could see flames running down the hood of the vehicle now.

"The motherfucker's trying to burn us out!"

His two men scrambled back, while he continued to squeeze the trigger on his now-impotent revolver. He saw a flash of long hair and slim legs.

"It's that bitch . . ." The rest of his thought was lost in a tremendous agonizing ball of flame.

The explosion caught MacGonigal completely by surprise, startling him. The cabin blew apart in a huge ball of flame, followed by a second ball—a huge double explosion. He saw Susan go down, blown forward by the shockwave. He had a dim recollection of the shockwave propagating itself up the ridge, a vast, invisible bubble, its rapidly moving surface marked by the rippling and shredding of the brush.

For a long moment, he simply looked down on the scene. The cabin, or what was left of it, was blazing furiously. Bits and pieces of flaming debris were still falling. The whole valley was full of smoke and flame, the barn smouldering and the cabin burning fiercely. He stood, heedless of any danger from below. No one could have survived the blast.

He went down the slope in long, loping strides, leaping from rock to rock, risking his neck at each jump. He reached the edge of the trees and saw Susan lying there, a small, still figure in faded jeans and dark green parka.

The heat from the burning cabin was intense. He grabbed her and dragged her into the tree line, then lifted her up and bore her away. A hundred yards he carried her, or perhaps more, the sound of her breathing and heartbeat against his chest reassuring him that she still lived. At last he put her down and looked at her, running his hands over her to check for broken bones, opening her clothing to look for concealed wounds.

She was scorched, but she had no burns. Her face was swollen and bruised, and her hands, arms and stomach, which had taken the force of her fall when she was captured, exhibited bruises and abrasions. MacGonigal saw that her shirt was open, the buttons gone and one of her nipples bruised, and for a moment a dark cloud descended over him: The bastards who did that were dead, beyond his reach now. He regretted it deeply.

At last, satisfied that she had no serious injuries, he carried her to the tack room and made a bed for her of feed sacks, covering her with horse blankets. He left her and went out and surveyed the ruins of his farm. There were two bodies lying in the yard. He dragged them up to the cabin, shielding his face against the heat with a water-soaked bit of sacking, and rolled them over the burning logs.

That done, he went back to the tack room and looked in on Susan. She was sleeping soundly, breathing regularly. He kissed her bruised face tenderly and then he left her, hiking up the valley to strike their camp and bring back their gear. With the cabin gone, they would need it.

She was still asleep when he got back, lying as he had left her. He made a fire in the little potbellied stove, then made a more comfortable bed for her with the sleeping bags, then pulled back the saddleblankets and stripped her, pulling the clothes off of her limp, unprotesting body.

Naked, she was a mass of bruises and abrasions. He took out his first-aid kit and went gently to work, cleaning her injuries, painting them with antiseptic, taping and bandaging. At last he finished. He slipped her into the down bag, pulled the hood around her head, kissed her and went out.

It was almost dusk. He stood there a long time, looking at the smouldering remains of his farm. At last he went over to the shed where she had been hidden during the battle, and which she had burst out of to put an end to it all. The shed was empty and forlorn, the tractor gone, now a mass of twisted metal in the remains of the cabin. A few tools and things lay scattered on the dirt floor. He picked them up and put them on the bench. The Mauser rifle lay on the bench where she had left it, loaded and cocked, the safety off. He picked it up and drew the bolt back, ejecting the round in the chamber, then shoved it forward, depressing the top cartridge in the magazine to let the bolt pass over it and close on an empty chamber. He held the trigger back as he turned the bolt handle down, allowing the firing pin to go gently forward.

Lying next to the rifle was the black case containing his pipes. He took out the key and unlocked it, folding back the protecting towel and taking out bag, drones, chanter and blowpipe. He fitted the instrument together and blew up the bag, striking in the drones and tuning them. Then he walked outside and began to play, very slowly. The ancient Irish lament, "Oft in the Stilly Night", floated across the valley.

As the last note drifted over the valley, he lifted his left arm, releasing pressure on the bag and stopping the music abruptly. He tucked the pipes under his arm and walked back to the tack room through the gloom.

It was dark in there, with a faint illumination

escaping from the fire door of the little stove. He put the pipes aside and groped for a lantern. As he did so, he heard a sleepy voice say, "Is that you, Mac? I thought I heard the pipes."

He stared toward her, his face softening in the darkness. "Yes, it's me, little one. Everything's all right now. Go back to sleep."

He abandoned his search for the lantern and stripped off his clothes and slid into the double bag beside her, tenderly holding her to him. She put her head against his chest and fell asleep.

He woke early, while it was still too dark to see. The fire had gone out in the stove, and he forced himself out of the sleeping bag and into his cold garments and went to the wood pile. As he was building the fire, he heard Susan stir. "Is it morning already?"

"Just about. You lie there for a while. I'll warm the place up for you."

She stretched and groaned. "I don't think I can get up, Mac."

"I don't wonder. You're bruised all over. Nothing serious, though. Stay in bed, and I'll fix you something to eat."

"Mmm. I could use some breakfast. I need a bath, too."

"I sponged you off last night. You were out of it and don't remember. But I'll get some water from the creek and heat it for a bath. How's that?"

"That sounds good." She lay there for a minute, then said, "Mac . . . what about Nazario? Is he . . . ?"

"Dead? Yeah, honey, he's dead. You did for him. I ought to paddle your butt for what you did, though. You damn near got yourself killed."

She was silent a minute. "What about your cabin, all your things?"

"All gone. There was a hell of a fire after the explosion. None of them got out, but I saved a few things, my pipes, the gear we had with us. The rest is just ashes now."

Her voice was tinged with concern. "What will you do? Your house and everything gone, just burned up like that."

"I'll have to rebuild it. I built it in the first place, so I suppose I can do it again."

"I'll pay you for it, Mac. It's all my fault anyway. I'll share the money with you, give you half of it."

He grunted as he worked at the stove. "Forget it. I told you I don't want your money."

"I can't forget it. If it hadn't been for me, none of this would have happened."

He cracked an egg from the henhouse into an aluminum frying pan. She could hear it sizzle and sputter, and the odor made her mouth water. "Mac," she said, "I can't just leave you like this. I know that you don't have any way of replacing everything you lost. I want to pay you back."

He said nothing, but continued to work at the stove. After awhile, he brought her her breakfast. She was too sore to sit up comfortably, and he had to feed her, forkful by forkful.

After she finished, he went out to the stream and came back with two buckets of water. He put them on the stove to heat and crouched beside her. Idly, he put one hand out and stroked her hair. "I love you, Sue."

"I love you, too, Mac. That's why I want to share the money with you."

"You can't. It's a curse. You'd never be sure if it was yourself or the money I was after. And I wouldn't be either."

He got up several times to test the temperature of the water, returning silently to her side each time. At last he lifted the buckets from the stove and put them on the floor beside her. He unzipped the bag, pulling it back to expose her nakedness in the slowly growing light. With a cloth, he began to gently soap her body, rinsing the soap as he went. When he was finished, he patted her dry with a piece of blanket and pulled the down bag over her. "Lie there and get some rest. I'll go out and clean things up a little."

For two days they stayed in the tack room together, MacGonigal nursing her until she was able to get up and walk stiffly around. On the third day he left her and took the truck into town, buying a few staples that would last without refrigeration, an ice chest, a few tools and other things. He came back and began work, felling and peeling trees as he had when he first came to the valley.

Susan watched him work, fixed meals, and slowly mended in spirit and body. At first she was reluctant to walk around the ruins of the cabin, but on the fourth day, she forced herself to go over and peer in. There was nothing recognizable, just ashes, stone from the fireplace, twisted and rusting bits of metal.

The woodstove seemed intact, although the stove-pipe was gone.

MacGonigal came over, his shirt stained with sweat, his hairy forearms full of sawdust. "I think I can salvage that stove. I'll borrow a bulldozer and clean away the rest of the mess—and destroy all the evidence of what happened here at the same time. In a couple of months, you won't know anything happened."

She looked at him. "Mac, I'm going to pay you back for all this, every bit of it."

"Okay, that's fair. I'll send you a bill one of these days. Now, let's drop the subject."

They worked together, with him felling and stripping the trees, and she hauling them to the cabin site with the little bulldozer he had borrowed. By the end of the second week, the foundation was laid, and MacGonigal had enough logs to begin laying in the walls. They were at work hoisting logs into position when they heard a vehicle on the approach road. Susan stopped work and stared at MacGonigal. "Somebody's coming, Mac!"

MacGonigal nodded, picked up the Savage that leaned against a nearby tree, and walked to the falls, where he could look down on the road. In a few minutes he saw it, a police vehicle, its color and dome light conspicuous. He felt Susan's hand on his arm as she saw the car. He put his hand over hers and watched the vehicle approach.

As the car pulled into the turn around at the foot of the falls, he gave her hand a reassuring squeeze and started down. The door opened and Harvey Siler manuevered his bulk out. "Howdy, Harvey,"

MacGonigal called from halfway up the trail.

The sheriff, his belly oozing over his Sam Browne belt, watched as MacGonigal came down the trail. "This just a visit, or more business?"

The sheriff pushed back his hat. "Business, bad business. I got some questions for you."

"As if I didn't have enough troubles. You know that my cabin burned down?"

The sheriff pushed his hat back. "Yeah, I heard that. That's a shame. How'd it happen?"

MacGonigal grimaced. "My own fault. I was doing some work with the tractor around the cabin. Stopped right by the front porch to fuel it, and spilled gas on the exhaust. Didn't save much, and the wind blew sparks into the hay barn and I lost it, too."

"That's really tough, Mac." The sheriff's face didn't show the sympathy his words implied. "You got insurance?"

MacGonigal made a face. "Not a damn cent. That's why I'm working so hard. I've got to rebuild it all myself, and I've got to get it up before hard winter sets in. Right now, I'm living in the tack room."

The sheriff hooked his thumbs in his belt. "Well, I won't take any more of your time than I have to, but if you don't give me some straight answers, you're liable to have a different roof over your head, come winter."

MacGonigal looked at him. "This have anything to do with George Harris?"

The sheriff's eyes narrowed. "How'd you know?"

"Well, since you've only been out here one time, and that was about George Harris, you might say that it was just a wild guess."

"You don't have to get sarcastic. You could be in a lot of trouble. You been withholding evidence, boy."

MacGonigal's eyes widened. "Me? What evidence?"

The sheriff glared at him. "Don't play games with me, Mac. I want to know about those guys that have been up here. How come you didn't tell me about them?"

MacGonigal was ready for him. "You mean they didn't check in with you? Damn it, I told 'em just like you said, that if they wanted to talk to me, they'd have to get your okay first. I even told them that I'd have to have your orders in writing before I gave them anything." He paused. "That was right, wasn't it, Harvey? That was what you said for me to do."

The sheriff glared at him. "What in the hell are you talking about?"

"The state police. Didn't they check with you? They came up here two or three times. Had an airplane flying around, too. I told them that I was one of your deputies, and to talk to you. The last time, they landed right in the paddock, scared hell out of my horses. I told them to get the hell off the place, unless they had something from you in writing."

The sheriff exploded. "State police, shit! Those were the sons of bitches we been looking for! They're the ones that killed your friend Harris. And Henry Carberry."

MacGonigal feigned surprise. "Henry Carberry? He's dead?"

The sheriff looked at him with his little, pig-like eyes. "Yeah. We found him dead not far from his hunting cabin. Matter of fact, the reason we went up there looking for him was because of you having Lloyd MacCorkle call Henry's wife and tell her that the cabin had been broken into."

MacGonigal affected a shocked look. "How do you know it was the same people? Did they . . . ?"

"No, they didn't torture him, if that's what you mean. They hit him in the face a couple of times, and shot him behind the ear, just like Harris."

He paused, rocking back on his heels. "Which brings me to why I'm here. Those 'state police' of yours hired Jarvis's plane, and they were checked into a motel. A couple of days ago, the motel owner called us. They left, without paying their bills, and strangely enough, they left their cars. You know anything about that?"

MacGonigal's eyes opened wide. "I don't know a thing about it, Sheriff. Matter of fact, the only vehicle I ever saw them use, except for the airplane, was a Scout."

The sheriff's eyes narrowed. "Yeah. When we got to checking, we found that one car was missing. The Scout. Guess where we found it."

"Not on my property?"

The sheriff looked at him as if he were retarded. "No! At the airfield. Jarvis said that he flew them around here a couple of times, and the last time he landed, they stayed here."

MacGonigal scratched his forearms, digging saw-dust out with his fingernails. "Well, that's true, like I told you. They did come around. I told them that they had to check with you, because I was a deputy. Then they flew back in, and I told them again, and made sure that they understood. They left, and I haven't seen them since."

"How'd they leave?"

"Drove out, I guess. I didn't follow them, but I heard the engine."

"How come you didn't let me know about all this right away?"

MacGonigal scratched a little. "Well, the first time, I just told them to go see you. I figured they would. The second time was the day that my cabin burned, and I had my hands full." He paused. "And to tell the truth, I didn't think it was all that important."

The sheriff's face turned a beet red. "You didn't think it was important! You didn't think it was important! A gang of organized murderers comes into this county, and you stand there and talk to them, and you have the gall to face me and tell me that you didn't think it was important! Hell fire, boy, there was a gun in that Scout that matched the one that killed Harris and Carberry!"

MacGonigal backed away. "Look, Sheriff, I didn't know any of that stuff. I did what you told me. If you'd told me to report stuff like the state police questioning me, I would have."

Puffing with exertion from his outburst, the sheriff wedged himself back into his car. "Well, you just bet your ass you better tell me everything that happens from now on, MacGonigal! You just bet your ass!"

He slammed the door and started the car, taking off in a cloud of dust, even as MacGonigal reassured him, "I will, Sheriff, you can count on me."

He climbed back up the trail to find Susan waiting for him at the top. "What did he want, Mac?"

"He wanted to ask about Nazario. They left their cars, and they traced them here. They found the gun that killed Carberry and Harris in one of the vehicles, and they found Jarvis, and he told them about flying around here and landing with Nazario and his hoods."

"What did you tell him?"

"Told them that they represented themselves as state police, and that I didn't tell them anything, and that they left."

They were walking as they talked, and they had arrived at the tack room. Susan opened the door. "Why don't you put things away, and I'll fix something to eat. I think we've done enough for now."

He went back and tidied up the work site, then returned to the tack room. It was a fairly decent place, although small. They had moved the saddles and gear to the tractor shed to make room for a makeshift bed and a rough table. It was cozy, with the little potbellied stove glowing in one corner. MacGonigal sat on the edge of the bed and pulled off his boots, extending his feet toward the fire.

"Mac, what are we going to do now?"

He looked up at her. "First of all, we've got to get you out of here. I think I'm pretty well covered, but they'll check every stranger in the county. Also, the boys who were looking for you—if we didn't get them all—aren't on the scene, and you can lose their trail now."

He stood and faced the stove, warming his hands. "I'll take you into Little Rock and put you on a plane. You go ahead and carry out the rest of your plan."

"But what about you? I mean . . . I owe you something for all this . . ."

He didn't turn. "Drop me a line when you get everything worked out, and I'll send you a bill."

"I thought we meant more to each other than that."

He still didn't turn. "We do. But the money is a problem. You go ahead with your plans. Any time you want to come back and visit, you're welcome. And if you get in trouble, let me know. I'll take care of it."

"You'll take care of it. You sound so damn confident."

"Yeah. When you play with MacGonigal, you play it MacGonigal's way."

"That's where you're wrong, Mac. That's where you're dead wrong."

Something in her voice made him turn. She stood behind him, feet apart. As he watched, she crossed her arms, grabbed the bottom edge of her sweater and stripped it off over her head, exposing her high, pointed breasts. With one hand, she pulled open her jeans, letting them fall to the floor and stepping daintily out of them. Her long brown hair hung in a cloud around her, enhancing her nakedness. MacGonigal caught his breath, unable to move. She dropped the sweater and crossed the floor to him, her hips swaying cat-like. She began to unbutton his jeans.

"Tonight we play it Susan's way."